Esmeralda licked her lips. She wanted Elliot Brand panting for her, desperate for her....

She wanted to make him forget logic and common sense and his love for his home and the Brand family name, all for the sake of one brief moment in her arms.

But she was the one who kept seeing illicit images in her mind. She was the one who kept feeling as if her soul had been touched by hellfire, and forgetting that it was all just make-believe. An act. A means to reclaiming what was hers.

Dios. She wanted him as much as he wanted her. More, perhaps.

She was in trouble. Her entire plan was in jeopardy. For her body had no common sense, and it was not listening to her brain. Instead, it was yearning to mate with the man who was her sworn enemy....

Dear Reader,

Happy holidays! In honor of the season, we've got six very special gifts for you. Who can resist *The Outlaw Bride,* the newest from Maggie Shayne's bestselling miniseries THE TEXAS BRAND? Forget everything you think you know about time and how we move through it, because you're about to get a look at the power of the human heart to alter even the hardest realities. And you'll get an interesting look at the origins of the Texas Brands, too.

ROYALLY WED, our exciting cross-line continuity miniseries, continues with Suzanne Brockmann's *Undercover Princess.* In her search to find her long-lost brother, the crown prince, Princess Katherine Wyndham has to try life as a commoner. Funny thing is, she quite likes being a nanny to two adorable kids—not to mention the time she spends in their handsome father's arms. In her FAMILIES ARE FOREVER title, *Code Name: Santa,* Kayla Daniels finds the perfect way to bring a secret agent in from the cold—just in time for the holidays. *It Had To Be You* is the newest from Beverly Bird, a suspenseful tale of a meant-to-be love. Sara Orwig takes us WAY OUT WEST to meet a *Galahad in Blue Jeans.* Now there's a title that says it all! Finally, look for Barbara Ankrum's *I'll Remember You,* our TRY TO REMEMBER title.

Enjoy them all—and don't forget to come back again next month, because we plan to start off a very happy new year right here in Silhouette Intimate Moments, where the best and most exciting romances are always to be found.

Enjoy!

Leslie Wainger

Leslie J. Wainger
Executive Senior Editor

Please address questions and book requests to:
Silhouette Reader Service
U.S.: 3010 Walden Ave., P.O. Box 1325, Buffalo, NY 14269
Canadian: P.O. Box 609, Fort Erie, Ont. L2A 5X3

MAGGIE SHAYNE

THE OUTLAW BRIDE

INTIMATE™ MOMENTS®

Published by Silhouette Books

America's Publisher of Contemporary Romance

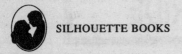

SILHOUETTE BOOKS

ISBN 0-373-07967-2

THE OUTLAW BRIDE

Visit us at www.romance.net

Printed in U.S.A.

Books by Maggie Shayne

MAGGIE SHAYNE,

a national bestselling author whom *Romantic Times Magazine* calls "brilliantly inventive," has written more than fifteen novels for Silhouette. Her Silhouette single-title release *Born in Twilight* (3/97) was based on her popular vampire series for Shadows, WINGS IN THE NIGHT.

Maggie has won numerous awards, including a *Romantic Times Magazine* Career Achievement Award. A three-time finalist for the Romance Writers of America's prestigious RITA Award, Maggie also writes mainstream contemporary fantasy.

In her spare time Maggie enjoys collecting gemstones, reading tarot cards, hanging out on the Genie computer network and spending time outdoors. She lives in a rural town in central New York with her husband, Rick, five beautiful daughters and a bulldog named Wrinkles.

Chapter 1

Esmeralda Maria Conchita Montoya glared at the smug banker across his desk. "This is not right," she said, all too aware of the odds against her. She was a woman, she was a Mexican, and her accent was as touched by her heritage as was the color of her skin. And this banker was a Brand. Allen Brand, whose entire outlaw family was now squatting on Esmeralda's land. "My father was tricked. The ranch rightfully belongs to me."

The banker, handsome and dressed in clothing so new it practically gleamed, checked his pocket watch as if he were bored. He irritated her, looking so suave and elegant and well-bred, not a hair out of place, when she knew perfectly well he was little more than scum.

All the Brands were scum.

"It's all perfectly legal, little lady," he drawled. "Right there in front of you in black and white." He glanced down at the stack of papers he'd placed in front of her, tapped them with a forefinger for emphasis, then lifted his brows and his gaze as one. "You *can* read, can't you?"

"*Sí.* I can read. It is all very clear, in black and white, as you say. Your bank made a loan to my father. You gave him three years to pay. There are still six months left."

"My bank made a loan to your father, and that ranch was his collateral. You do know what collateral is?" She only narrowed her eyes on him. He went on. "And it does say, on page two of this agreement, that I have the right to demand the full amount should your father be unable to meet his quarterly obligations to this bank."

"You gave him your word that would not happen. He told me so himself."

The man shrugged, leaning back in his leather chair, arms folded behind his head. "Maybe he lied."

Esmeralda rose from her chair as if she'd been shot out of it. Palms flat on the gleaming surface of the desk, she leaned towards him. "My father never lied in his life."

Allen Brand's brows rose again. He sat straighter in his chair, and she had the satisfaction of seeing the slightest hint of alarm flash in his eyes. He straightened his bolo tie, cleared his throat. "Nonetheless, I'm only bound by what is written in that contract, and there is no promise not to foreclose in there. Only my right to do so, should he be late in meeting his obligation. He *did* miss his last payment, after all."

"Because his cattle were rustled on the way to market—by your two outlaw brothers and their gang of cutthroats!"

Again the banker shrugged. "That's no fault of mine."

She pounded a fist on his desk so hard that the ornate kerosene lamp that sat there seemed to jump. "Do you think I am stupid, Señor Brand? Eh? You put them up to it. It gave you the excuse you needed to steal my father's land from him!"

Brand's gaze dipped to the lower left drawer. She'd noticed it move in that direction several times before, and was sharp enough to realize he likely kept a gun in there. If he reached for it, she would slit his throat before he could thumb the hammer back.

"I did not *steal* anything." His well-manicured, callus-free hand inched closer to that drawer. Esmeralda's own hand—smaller, but quicker, she thought—moved lightly over her skirts, and underneath them she felt the hardness of the blade she wore strapped to her thigh.

"I took possession by legal means, and if your father were here, he would tell you so," Allen Brand went on. "But since he saw fit to go into hiding somewhere, sending his little girl to tend to his affairs—"

"My father is dead." She stated it flatly, stepping away from the desk and turning her back on the man, refusing to let him see her pain. But she was not stupid enough to lose sight of him, even then, lest she feel the burn of a coward's bullet in her back just as her father had. Instead, she paced to the window, as if to look outside. In the thick glass, she kept his reflection in plain sight. She almost hoped he *would* go for the gun. Her fingers itched to close around the hilt of her blade as she drove it into his gut.

But that would be wrong. With a free hand, she caressed the pendant she wore, and thought of her father and all the things he had taught her. Long ago, when she'd been a young girl, she'd told him she was in love for the first time with a boy she'd known all her life. Eldon Brand. This banker's youngest brother.

Luis Montoya had just nodded thoughtfully, silent for a long moment, and then he said, "This you must remember, little one. There is nothing more important than family." She could almost hear his voice again now. "For a woman to love a man, she must love his family, too. And they must love her. For a woman marries not just the man, but his family, as well."

She remembered nodding slowly. "*Sí,* this I know. You have told me this before."

"He comes from a bad family, little one," her father told her seriously. "Once, there was a chance the Brand children would grow up well. But when their parents died, that chance died with them. They did not stick together, but scattered, and most of them— all of them, I fear—went bad. No family." He shook his head slowly, sadly.

Imagine her beloved father feeling sorry for the bastards who had killed him. Imagine *her* having ever been attracted to one of them. She shook off the memory, tried to focus on the present. She'd been away from home for a long time, but nothing looked so very different.

The dusty streets of Quinn were busy. Women in long skirts and bonnets carried baskets or tugged children to and fro. Buggies and buckboards passed slowly, raising dust clouds in their wake. A man sat in a chair outside the saloon across the way, his feet propped up on the boardwalk's rail.

"I...didn't know your father had died," the banker said, and for once she thought there might be the ring of truth in his words. Again she fingered the pendant she wore: a small quartz crystal, cut into the shape of a skull by unknown hands, centuries ago. It had been in her family for many, many generations. Some claimed it had magical powers—that it was supposed to restore balance to mankind, to restore its holder to her proper place in the scheme of things. It had been given to her by her father, just before he died.

"Surely your brothers Waylon and Blake told you that one of their filthy gang shot my father when he tried to stop them from stealing his cattle, no?" She turned slowly to study his face.

"I'd heard he was wounded."

She nodded. "*Sí*. Wounded. He sent for me. Pedro, Father's most trusted hand, took the fastest horse from our stables and came for me in Mexico. Pedro told me what you and your family had done, and he brought me back home, where I should have been all along. I held my father's hand as he lay dying of blood poisoning, Señor Brand."

Allen Brand braced one hand on the back of his chair, his head lowering slightly. "I'm sorry for your loss, Esmeralda."

"Are you?"

"Of course I am. For heaven's sakes, I've known you since we were both knee-high to a yearling calf. But surely you can see this is over now. Your father is gone, and any claim he may have thought he had to the ranch is gone with him. You'd best forget about all of this and go back home to Mexico."

She shook her head. "You have known me so long, and yet you know me so little. I was only visiting my aunt in Mexico. My *home* is on my father's ranch, where I was born and raised, Allen Brand. He may be gone, but rest assured I am here. And I am staying here until I avenge my father's murder and reclaim what is rightfully mine."

He locked eyes with her. She did not flinch, and it was he who looked away first. "You've been away a long time, Esmeralda. Years. Your father sent you south for your own good, you know."

"*Sí.* I had no mother to help him raise me. He wanted me to have the finer things, to learn to be a lady, to learn manners and wear dresses."

Allen nodded slowly. "And it looks as if those lessons took. You've grown into a beautiful young woman."

"He also sent me away so that I would be beyond the reach of men like you and your brothers," she told him. "Do not be fooled by these frilly skirts, Allen Brand. I have not changed so much from the girl who could outrun you, outride you, and outfight you."

He sighed, lifting a brow and tilting his head. "Maybe you haven't changed all that much, Esmeralda, but things around here have. You don't even know what you're up against."

"Oh, I know exactly what I'm up against. A liar and a thief. The only difference between you and your outlaw brothers is that you wear a fancy suit, and a quill pen is your weapon. If you refuse to give the land back to me now, I will go to the sheriff and ask him to place Waylon and Blake Brand under arrest for the murder of my father."

Allen Brand smiled very slowly. "The sheriff's office is right where it always was," he said, nodding toward the window that faced the street. "You go right ahead and file those charges."

"Do you think I will not do it?"

"I don't care what you do. I've tried to be kind to you, Esmeralda, for old times' sake, but you won't listen to a thing I tell you. So do what you will. Now, if you don't mind, I have a business to run." He strode across the office, opened the door. "Run along, like a good girl."

"You will be sorry for this, Allen Brand!" She stomped out and slammed the door behind her, marching through the bank and cussing in Spanish all the way. She'd worn her best dress, bought new boots, even captured her wild, unruly mass of black curls beneath a fancy French bonnet. She had thought that if she'd looked like a lady, the way her aunt had taught her, she might be treated with a scrap of respect, perhaps even taken seriously. Instead, she'd been treated like a minor nuisance. But what did she expect from a thieving Brand? They were all alike. They didn't care about the black-velvet piping that lined the edges of her cropped jacket, or the white blouse with its frilly collar underneath.

She stepped from the boardwalk down into the rutted edge of the street, only to jump back again as she was nearly run down by a careening wagon. "Gol'dern Mexican whore! Watch where you're goin'!" the driver shouted, shaking his fist at her.

She shook her own fist and shrieked back at him in her native tongue. Only to go silent when she felt eyes on her. Every person in town had stopped what they were doing to turn and stare at her vulgar dis-

play. And their expressions said what they thought of
her. She'd barely been back in town two full days,
and already most of the residents knew of her mission. To take her land back from the Brands. Why
they all were against her from that moment on, was
beyond her. She eyed them all, spat on the ground,
picked up her skirts and petticoats, and stomped
across the street. There she mounted the boardwalk
again and strode right up to the sheriff's office. But
the moment she flung the door open, she understood
the banker's arrogance.

For yet another Brand sat at *this* desk. His scuffed
boots were propped up on the dull, worn wood, and
there was a silver star pinned to his chest. The giant,
hulking, snake-eyed firstborn of them all, Garrison
Brand.

"Well now, if it isn't that Mexican spitfire I hear
has come to town for revenge." His boots clomped
to the floor, and he sat straighter in his chair. "No
luck at the bank, I take it, Esmeralda? So what brings
you to my office?"

Her throat suddenly dry, she rasped, "Y-your...
office?"

"That's right." He tapped his badge and rose to
his full height. Then he walked around the desk to
stand close to her, look down at her. He made her
feel like an ant on the floor, and he knew it. "We
Brands have done all right for ourselves, Esmeralda.
We *own* Quinn, Texas. So you may as well scoot your
bronze hide back to the other side of the Rio Grande,
honey. You got no business here."

She backed away a single step, but kept her eyes
on his, nodding slowly. "*Sí*, I understand it now. One
brother is the swindling banker, and the other is the

sheriff. Two are outlaws, free to run wild without any fear of the law. What are the youngest two Brands doing, Garrison? Do they serve as judge and jury of this town, eh?''

Garrison smiled slowly. He would have been a handsome man, if not for the evil in his eyes. "Why did you come here, Esmeralda?"

"Oh, I think you know why. I come here to charge your brothers with murder. My father's murder."

He lifted a brow. "Ol' Montoya died, did he? About time, I'd say."

"I do not care what you think! My father is dead, my land is stolen, and your brothers belong in jail. If you think you can frighten me into giving up, you are wrong, Garrison Brand."

"If you don't give up, little lady, the only person landing behind bars is gonna be you. An' if you think one person in this town will take your part against a Brand—*any Brand*—you're dead wrong."

She clenched her teeth, drew a breath through her nose, and felt her nostrils flare as she blew it out again. "Quinn is not the only town in Texas with a lawman. Believe me, Garrison Brand, I will find one—an honest one—and see you all in prison for what you've done."

Garrison lowered his head, shook it slowly. "Get out of my town, Esmeralda. By sundown."

"And if I don't?"

He glared at her, but said nothing. Esmeralda turned and walked away.

She went back to the boarding house where she'd rented a room last night—for, only hours after she and Pedro had buried her father, an army of thugs in the employ of Allen Brand had arrived with guns drawn to order her off the property. Pedro had apologized, but then he'd fled in fear. She had been given no choice but to comply.

It galled her that her father lay buried on the land those Brands now claimed as their own. She hadn't told them where he rested, though, for fear they would desecrate his grave out of sheer meanness.

At the boarding house, Esmeralda found her satchel sitting on the front step, her belongings packed inside. Frowning, she pounded on the door.

Mrs. Tremont opened it, saw her and scowled. ''I'm sorry, Miss Montoya, but I cannot tolerate your kind here. This is a decent establishment. Had I known you were runnin' about town casting aspersions on its finest residents, I'd never have let you through the door.''

Esmeralda eyed the woman without blinking. ''Tell me the truth, Señorita Tremont. Do not stand here and lie to my face.''

The older woman blinked, averting her eyes.

''You fear them. Everyone in Quinn fears them. Yet you let them continue to run roughshod over you, over the law, over the entire town.''

''Hush!'' The woman glanced up and down the street nervously. Her voice lower, she said, ''Allen Brand holds the mortgage on this place, young lady. If I cross him, I could lose everything.''

''I see.''

The older woman looked ashamed. ''I wish I could help you. It's a shame what happened to your father, but it wasn't my fault. Why should I risk everything I have for...'' Her voice trailed off.

''For a Mexican?'' Esmeralda asked. ''My father used to say the hottest places in hell are reserved for those who, in times of trouble, do nothing. You are a coward, Mrs. Tremont. Quinn has become a town of cowards.''

''How *dare* you!''

''Kindly return my money. I paid you for a full week in advance.''

The woman sniffed. ''Really? Do you think the sheriff would believe you?'' She slammed the door in Esmeralda's face.

Her father also used to say one could catch more flies with honey than with vinegar. Perhaps she should try to remember that phrase.

Clutching her satchel, Esmeralda battled tears of outrage. To hell with them all. She would go to El Paso. She still had a gold eagle in her pouch. She would find a judge there, or a lawyer, or perhaps even a U.S. Marshal. And then she would come back, and she would bring the Brands to ruin. Every last one of them.

Slogging tiredly along the boardwalk, she knew it would be a full hour before the next stage came through, and she had yet to eat today. She started to go into the town's only eatery, but the owner closed the door before she could even step through, and she heard the bolt being slid home. So the Brands had made the rounds, it seemed. They'd warned the entire town not to dare associate with her. A small chill raced up her spine. The sooner she could shake the dust of Quinn from her pinching, button-up boots, the better. She had not intended to put herself completely at the mercy of a band of outlaws, but that was precisely what she had done. She was not safe here. No wonder her father had refused to let her come back home, even when she'd begged. No wonder.

She kept walking, no longer as confident. As she passed the bat-wing doors of the saloon, the raucous laughter from inside billowed out. Someone called "Mexican whore!" as she passed, and she went cold inside, quickening her steps.

Then the doors slammed open, and boot heels slapped the boardwalk behind her. She whirled in time to see the youngest of the Brands, Eldon, tall and lanky, hat tipped at a cocky angle, bearing down on her. "Goin' somewhere, Esmeralda?"

She said nothing, just backed away. He used to be so different. Funny, but always mean. Always. He was as handsome as ever. Dark eyes like velvet, a strong jaw, hair the color of russet. Yes, she saw through it all now. She saw the evil inside.

He smiled and kept coming. "Oh, come on now. You can't come to town, run all over spreading lies about my family, and then leave without even saying hello. Can you?"

"Leave me alone, Eldon. Your family has won. I am leaving."

"Oh, I don't think I should let you go just yet. Not until you've learned to respect your betters, at least." He lunged forward. She backed away, but he caught her all the same. Dropping her satchel, Esmeralda pounded his chest, but Eldon Brand was strong, and in no time at all he had her slung over his broad shoulder and was striding away with her toward his waiting horse. Her bonnet fell from her head, and her hair spilled free.

"Let me go!" She beat his back with her fists, infuriated to hear drunken laughter coming from the saloon. "Help me! Help me, someone!"

Jenny Brand stood in the bat-wing doors, shaking

her head. She wore a glittering, scandalously low-cut dress of brightest red, and had painted her face. "When you finish, little brother, don't forget you still owe me for that bottle!" she called.

"Yeah, yeah." He slapped Esmeralda's rump hard. "Don't worry, Jen. This won't take long."

"See she don't give you the clap," Jenny called, and her patrons in the saloon roared with renewed laughter as Eldon slung Esmeralda over his saddle, mounted his horse and kicked it into a full gallop.

He didn't take her far. Just beyond the edge of town, riding into a cluster of boulders and tumbleweed. He drew the mount to a halt, turned, and shoved her off. She landed on her back on the sun-baked ground. Hair in her eyes, she pushed herself up, hands behind her, and when he dismounted and came closer, she spat at him.

He only smiled. "I like a little fight in my women," he said. "So you just give me a good struggle, Esmeralda. I'll enjoy it all the more."

"Stay away from me, Eldon Brand!"

He kept coming forward, unfastening his belt as he did. "I'll know it's all make-believe, though. You want me. You've always wanted me."

"Keep your hands off me!"

Esmeralda had taken all she was going to from this family. Her hand slid beneath her skirts to the blade she kept there. It was inside her garter, cool against her thigh.

Eldon straddled her, dropped to his knees, and reached up to part her cropped jacket and grip the neck of her white, frilly blouse. He tore it open, popping its buttons. Her hand closed around the hilt of her blade. ''Don't make me hurt you, Eldon. Stop this now.''

He grinned at her and gripped the front of the chemise she wore underneath. She pulled the blade, drove it upward and into his chest. For a moment he just froze there, staring down at her with wide, surprised eyes. Blood bubbled from his chest when she yanked the knife out. Then from his mouth when he tried to say something. He fell sideways even as his eyes glazed over.

She jumped to her feet and stood there, staring down at him. Dead. He was dead. ''*Dios,* what have I done!'' She backed away, the knife gleaming scarlet in her hand. She stared down at it, at the blood on her hands, on her once white blouse and chemise, and she began to tremble.

''Hold it right there!'' a voice shouted. ''Dammit, what the hell have you done to my brother!''

She couldn't turn, couldn't move. Shock seemed to have paralyzed her. She was still standing there when Waylon Brand, the famous outlaw, slid off his horse and raced toward his fallen brother, while Blake, the quiet giant, walked up behind her and pressed his gun barrel to her spine.

''Eldon?'' Waylon rolled his brother over, shook him. ''Eldon, come on!'' But Esmeralda knew it was no use. She'd knifed the man right through his black heart.

''He…he hurt me. He was going to…to rape me. I had no choice—''

''Shut up, whore!'' Blake's pistol barrel drove into the small of her back. ''I oughtta shoot you right here.'' He looked past her. ''Waylon?''

"Dead," Waylon said softly, his head hanging low. "She killed him, Blake. She killed our baby brother."

Blake swore loud and long. Waylon's eyes looked damp. He lifted his head, looked her right in the eye. "Get a rope," he told Blake.

There was a long moment of strained silence then, as she stood there between them. Waylon, whipcord-lean, with a legendary temper and looks as dark as her own. And Blake, as big as Garrison, but blond rather than brown-haired. Quiet, for the most part, but a Brand through and through, and just mean enough to prove it.

"No." It was Blake who spoke.

Waylon's gaze snapped to his brother's then. "Why the hell not? She killed Eldon in cold blood. I say we string her up here and now."

Blake shook his head. "The whole family deserves to see her hang. Hell, the whole town. Be good for 'em. A nice reminder of what happens when someone dares to mess with the Brands. Besides, it's the way Garrison would want it."

Esmeralda's blood ran cold. She wasn't frozen anymore. In fact, she was suddenly struggling without even thinking about it. Fighting for her life while the hulking Blake held her firmly and almost effortlessly. They were going to hang her! Kill her! Take her life!

Waylon got to his feet and backhanded her. She went still, first with shock and pain, and then, slowly, she slipped into darkness.

The next time she opened her eyes, she was in a jail cell, facing a barred window, beyond which men scurried to construct what would obviously be a gallows. And it wasn't going to take long, either, at the rate they were going.

"Don't you worry, Esmeralda." The sheriff's voice drifted lazily into her cell. "We're gonna hang you with a brand-new rope. And that's way better than you deserve."

Lowering her head, Esmeralda automatically closed her hand around the cool, glass-like stone she wore around her neck. In his final moments, her father had asked her to get it from the small wooden box he kept under his bed, and he'd pushed it into her hands, saying it would protect her and set her on the right path.

She closed her eyes and held it tight. "Father, if this crystal skull of yours truly has any magic in it, I need it now. I need it as I have never needed it before."

Chapter 2

Quinn, Texas, 1999

You'd have thought all hell was breaking loose the way everyone was acting around here, Elliot thought. Wes had called him at the Texas Brand this morning, sounding all wrought up and asking for a hand. Naturally Elliot was happy to oblige his brother, and he picked his sister Jessi up on the way for good measure. But really, things weren't nearly as bad as Wes had made them sound on the phone. Then again, Wes *did* tend to overreact to things.

Taylor, Wes's wife, looked like hell. And that was saying something, because Taylor was a knockout on her worst day. Still, she was sacked out on the sofa in the living room when Elliot and Jessi arrived at their brother's Sky Dancer Ranch. Taylor's face was sporting a greenish tinge, and her hair was a mess, and two minutes after Elliot and Jessi walked in, Taylor got up and ran for the nearest bathroom with a hand to her mouth.

"Dang, Wes, what'd you do to her?" Jessi asked, only half kidding. She looked a little worried.

Wes, as dark as Taylor was—they were both half Comanche—shook his head. "Damned if I know. She's been like this since sunup. And I've got two mares about to foal out in the stables, and a fence down in the north pasture, and—"

"Take a breath, big brother," Elliot said. He sauntered easily into the kitchen, began making a pot of coffee, and kept on talking. "We're here, we'll handle it," he said, raising his voice so they could hear him in the next room. "You know you're gonna give yourself an ulcer with this attitude?" He flicked the button on the coffeemaker and went back to the living room just as Taylor came back. She walked like a zombie, head hanging down, feet dragging. Wes eased her back onto the sofa and tugged a blanket over her.

"Stomach bug, Tay?" Elliot asked.

"I don't know," she muttered. "But I do know I can't lie around here all day."

"Sure you can. The world is gonna go on just fine if you take a day off." Elliot grinned. "Now, Jessi's gonna check on those mares, and I'm gonna fix the fence that's down, and Wes is gonna call in some reinforcements. Chelsea will come over to play nurse-maid to our ailing sis." He shrugged, looking at Wes. "See? Simple. No need for panic."

"Nothing ever rattles you, does it?" Wes asked.

Elliot made his palm flat and moved it in front of

him. "Steady as a rock. I don't believe in getting rattled."

"I'll run out and check on those mares now," Jessi said. But she had a speculative look in her eyes when they lingered on Taylor. "Maybe you should see a doctor."

"No time," Taylor said, lifting her head weakly. "I have to go to the university today."

"The hell you do!" Wes tried to ease her back onto her pillow.

"No, Wes, I have to. It's important I get this find under lock and key as soon as…oh, God…" Clutching her belly, she lay down again.

"Hey, Taylor, will you relax?" Elliot got to his feet. "You need something taken to the university, just give it to me. I can run it over there for you."

She opened one eye. "Really?"

"Sure. I assume you don't need to be an acclaimed archaeology professor to deliver relics, just to dig them up, right?"

Taylor licked her lips. "It's a very, very rare find, Elliot. I think it might be Mayan. It's important it gets there safely. I need it under lock and key as soon as possible. All right?"

"Hey, you know you can depend on me."

She looked doubtful. "No side trips. None of this casual Tom Sawyer attitude, either, Elliot. You need to take this seriously. Straight to the university. I know you think nothing is all that important in life, but this is. Okay?"

He held up his fingers in a Boy Scout salute. "Yes, ma'am. On one condition. You let Wes take you to see Doc while I'm gone. Just in case. All right?"

She rolled her eyes. "Jessi's a vet. That's gonna have to be close enough for now."

Elliot shook his head and sent his brother a look that said he ought to make his wife see reason. Wes gave him a bare nod of acknowledgment, then vanished for a second. He returned with a small cardboard box, taped shut and marked "Property of Texas State University, Archaeological Department." He handed it to Elliot.

Elliot took it, and when he saw the serious looks on Wes and Taylor's faces, he pretended to trip, sending the box flying into the air as he stumbled. They both lunged for him, shouting, hands outstretched, as he snatched the box out of midair and sent them a wink. "Just kidding."

Taylor collapsed back on her pillows with an indulgent half smile and a shake of her head. Wes swore at him. Jessi punched him in the shoulder. "Go on, and then get back here and help me with those foals."

"I won't be an hour," he promised, and headed back into the kitchen. He stopped only long enough to fill a borrowed cup with the freshly brewed coffee, and then he went straight out to his pickup, set the box on the seat beside him and started off on his mission of dire importance.

He grinned, shaking his head. To Wes, everything was of dire importance. To Elliot, nothing was. He just went with the flow, rolled with the current. Life was so easy if you just let it be. He never got emotional or upset or exchanged a loud word with anyone. Not ever.

He had just driven through the town of Quinn and was on the barely blacktopped road leading out of it when his curiosity began niggling at him. Taylor had seemed as concerned with the safety of whatever trinket was in that box as Wes had. Must be something pretty special. Mayan, she'd said. That would make it old. Really old.

He looked at the box. He probably shouldn't open it up to take a peek. But then again, if he put it right back in, no one would ever know the difference, right?

He looked at the box again. Mayan. It must be something.

What the hell, he thought. It certainly wouldn't hurt to take a peek. Aside from being calm and a bit of a practical joker, Elliot was also known for his curious nature. He kept one eye on the road, set his coffee cup on the floor, and reached over to pick at the tape on the box with his free hand.

It took a moment to get it loose, but he did. And then he automatically glanced behind him, as if he feared being caught. Grinning at his own silliness, he saw nothing but the town of Quinn at his back as he drove slowly away from it. He dug into the box, feeling past all the paper packing...and finding at last what felt like a small stone.

He pulled it out and looked at it. "Whoa, this is pretty neat." A small crystal skull, just the right size to fit in the palm of his hand, stared back at him from empty eye sockets. "Hey, fella. You look worse than Taylor does." Grinning at his own joke, a common occurrence with Elliot, he turned the thing over in his hand, checking out the back. There were words etched into the quartz there. Foreign. Not Spanish, but something else. He read them aloud, trying his best to pronounce them phonetically. And as he did, it seemed the skull-shaped hunk of quartz crystal in his hand started to get hot.

He shouldn't have looked away from the road when he did, because a small deer leaped in front of him, and he saw it too late to brake in time. He jerked the wheel, skidded sideways and wound up on intimate terms with a big old oak tree. There was a hard impact, and his head snapped forward, cracking against the steering wheel. Damn.

He drew a deep breath, lifted his head, and saw that his windshield was cracked, the nose of his truck crumpled, and the deer was bounding merrily away as if it hadn't just royally screwed up Elliot's day. Man, Wes was going to be upset with him. Messing up a simple errand so thoroughly.

His head hurt, and his hand sort of burned. The stone he'd been holding must have flown out of his grasp, and he didn't see it on the floor anywhere. Damn. Taylor and Wes were going to shoot him if he lost that thing. The windows were down. Maybe it had flown out. It was probably lying on the grass somewhere in plain sight.

No problem. Nothing to get upset over. Accidents happen. He would find the danged rock, and his insurance would pay for the damage to his truck. No big deal.

He got out of the truck and turned back the way he'd come, figuring once he located that hunk of quartz, he would have to walk the short distance back to Quinn and use a phone. But the town he saw up ahead was not Quinn.

It was duller and...and older...and...

Holy cow, a horse and buggy were bouncing over the main road! And there was another one. Was something going on in town that he didn't know about? They were sure raising a helluva dust cloud behind them.

But wait a minute. The streets were paved. So where was all that dust coming from? What the hell?

He rubbed the sore spot on his head, gave it a shake, and turned back toward his pickup, almost as if to ground himself. Never mind horses and buggies and dirt where blacktop should be. He needed to find that rock.

But his pickup wasn't there. The tree was. But it was unscarred. The ground, too, was unmarred by tire tracks or skid marks or even so much as a bent blade of grass. The pickup had vanished.

Elliot searched for his legendary calm as he felt disorientation hit him between the eyes so fast it made him dizzy.

"Okay, so maybe I banged my head just a little harder than I thought." He touched the spot, and his fingers came away with traces of blood. Closing his eyes, he gave his head another shake, opened them again. No truck. And that odd horse-and-buggy town was still in the distance...

...looking like some cheap movie set.

Hey, maybe that was it.

Right, El. They're making a movie right in your own town and you never heard a thing about it. That's likely.

He dismissed the voice of reason, gave his head another stern shake. "What else could it be? Doesn't matter. It's no big deal, and all this has some simple explanation.''

Even the vanishing pickup truck? I don't think so.

"It does. I'm gonna walk back to town, even if it is looking mighty strange to me, and when I get there, this is all gonna make perfect sense. I'll probably have a good laugh over it.'' He smiled. ''Yeah, it's gonna be a tale to tell all the baby Brands when they get a little bigger. Sure as shootin'. And once I hear it and finish laughing, I'll use a phone and get some help. Simple. No problem.'' He licked his lips.

Right. So where did your pickup go?

"I'll think about that later.'' He forced himself to walk toward town and refused to listen to the questions in his head, questions like, even if it *was* some kind of movie set or reenactment, how had they set it all up in the time it took him to drive the length of a football field and hit a tree? His head hurt more with every step, and his hand still burned a little. When he looked at his palm he saw the shape of that stupid rock of Taylor's, tattooed into his flesh like a brand.

But things only got stranger. As he got closer to the town, it looked more and more like a movie set from an old western, only there were no cameras in sight. No director. Just plank-board sidewalks and buildings from a bygone century, with hitching rails in front, horses tied to many of them. And right in the center of all of it, there was a great big ol' gallows standing in the middle of the road. A whole crowd of people dressed in old-west getup were gathered around it. Women in bonnets and long skirts, and men in Levi's and scuffed boots and dirty hats. Come to think of it, the men's clothes looked typical of any period in Texas history, including today. Except for the gun belts. They all wore gun belts.

And they were all looking up at the gallows. Standing near the back of the crowd, Elliot looked up, too. Then he blinked and looked again, because the most incredible woman he had ever seen stood proudly up there, chin high, long, jet-black curls blowing in the dusty wind. Her eyes met Elliot's and widened in blatant horror. Then Elliot's gentle, sweet-natured big brother Garrett lowered a rope around her neck and pulled it tight.

Elliot nudged the nearest person, a man in dusty clothes with a long, drooping mustache. "What's going on here, anyway?"

Without glancing his way, the man said, "A hangin', boy. What's it look like?"

"Right. Come on, really. I'm serious."

"So's that noose, son. Don't go frettin' none. She may be purty, but she's just a murderin' Mexican—" He'd turned toward Elliot as he spoke, and then just stopped talking. His mouth gaped, and he blinked. "You...you're alive!"

Elliot didn't know what the hell to think. The guy was backing away from him, pointing at him and gaping like a fish starved for air. Elliot shrugged and started making his way through the crowd, toward the gallows. Garrett would explain all this. But with every step he took, more of the actors, or whoever they were, gasped and pointed at him. One woman screamed, and another one fainted. The crowd around him parted like the danged Red Sea, and he found

himself with a clear view of Garrett up on those gallows.

"Hey, big brother, what the heck are you doin' to
that lady?"

Garrett glanced down, then did a double take. "El?
Jesus, El? What...how...?" Then he did two things
that made Elliot realize this man was not his brother.
He grinned broadly, showing off badly stained teeth
with empty spaces in between, and he yanked the rope
off the woman then shoved her toward the plank
steps. Hard. Garrett wouldn't so much as frown at a
woman, and this—this—*imposter*—was manhandling
one. Shoot.

"Eldon!" a feminine voice from behind him said.
"Waylon said you were dead! Said that trollop had
knifed you but good!" Elliot turned slightly to see
Jessi...only...*not* Jessi. She was dressed like the ma-
dam of some old-west whorehouse, and her face had
ten years' more wear on it than Jessi's ever would.

Okay, his mind was processing the information
fast. First, these people who looked like his family
were *not* his family, and second, they were going to
realize that he was not who they thought he was—
this Eldon character—any minute now. He waved
weakly at the Jessi clone turning his back on her just
as the Garrett double reached the bottom of the steps
and shoved the woman, whose hands were bound behind her, at Elliot.

"Guess we don't need no hangin' after all," the
bully said with a gap-toothed grin. "Hot damn, I'm
glad to see you, little brother."

Elliot caught the woman, his hands on her shoulders. She straightened and stared up at him. And there

was pure, unadulterated hatred in her huge black eyes…and fear, too, though she was trying to hide that. A bruise marred her dirt-streaked face, and blood was drying on her dress.

"Won't Waylon and Blake be surprised when they go back for Eldon's body only to find he's done got up and left!" the one who looked like Jessi shouted. She came up behind him and slapped his shoulder. "You don't know how lucky you are, Esmeralda Montoya. Nobody messes with a Brand in this town and lives to tell the tale." Then she laughed. "Too bad you didn't take five minutes longer gettin' here, little brother. The bitch would've been danglin' by then. Shoot, maybe we ought to hang her anyway, just for sport."

Instinctively, Elliot pulled the woman—Esmeralda—tighter to him, his arms going around her shoulders. She pulled back, but he held her fast, and she stopped struggling. She probably knew she was surrounded by people who would just as soon see her dead, unless this was all some sick joke. But the look in her eyes just now had hit Elliot hard. It told him in some unspoken way that this was no joke. He would work it all out later. Right now, all he wanted to do was get out of here, and it looked as if he'd best take this woman with him.

He wished to God his pickup would materialize. Doubting it would, he chose the next best conveyance. A horse stood about ten feet to the left. He tried not to let his fear show as he eased the woman in that direction, though she kept planting her feet and resisting every few steps.

"So, El, what happened out there? Shoot, we

thought you were dead!'' the big guy with the badge pinned to his shirt said.

"Guess I fooled you, huh?" Elliot managed. "Listen, uh, I need to, um…" He was easing to the left as he spoke. But the Garrett twin was frowning, now, squinting at him.

"Hey…hey, wait a minute. You ain't my bro-''

Elliot had no time to think. He just snatched the gun from the nearest guy's holster and leveled it. "Stay right there. Don't move."

The guy's brows went up, and his eyes widened. "Who the hell are you?"

Elliot was still edging toward that horse, holding the girl in one arm with everything he had and keeping the weighty six-shooter pointed. "Get your hands up," he ordered. "And don't worry about who I am. Now back off, all of you."

As he looked around, the crowd did what he said. The saloon woman said, "What's goin' on, Garrison?" and the sheriff said, "Danged if I know, Jenny."

Elliot didn't know, either. Right now, all he knew was that he was beside the horse, and the woman in his arms was still looking at him as if she would like to gut him. "It's me or them," he told her. "And even if I were this fellow everyone seems to think I am—a man I'm assuming you weren't real fond of— you'd still stand a better chance with one bastard than with a pile of 'em, don't you think?"

Her black eyes narrowed. Dark lashes and dark brows and bronze skin on a fine, small face. Damn, but she was a pure beauty. He turned her around, anchored an arm around her waist, and hefted her right off her feet and onto the back of the horse. The chestnut mare danced a little, snorted. She was small, but looked fast. Good. Elliot climbed on behind the woman, gathered up the reins and dug in his heels.

They were off like a shot, galloping at full-tilt, and the second they were, men started scurrying like rabbits, pulling guns, shouting and racing for their own horses.

"Shoot," Elliot muttered, and for once in his life, he was rattled.

Chapter 3

"You have to stop!" the woman said. It was the first time she'd spoken, and Elliot found he liked her voice, if not its tone. It was deep and rich, and laced with a thick accent that fit her looks. Dark, exotic and intense. It was exactly how he'd expected her to sound. While he was cocking his head, looking down at her and wondering about her, she spoke again, louder this time. "This animal cannot take much more! You have to stop."

"Yeah. You're right about that." The horse was damp with sweat, hotter than hell and blowing hard. He looked around, spotted a stream nearby, and guided the tired animal into the water. The mare tugged at the reins, trying to lower her head for a drink, but Elliot held her firm, made her go a few more yards, until they were behind a stand of trees, before he eased up and let her drink.

He drew a breath, watching while the mare drank,

making sure she didn't overdo it. He used the time to untie the woman's hands. "So...Esmeralda, is it? You want to tell me just what the hell I walked into back there?"

She turned halfway around to glare up at him. "You can fool your own brothers, Eldon Brand, but not me. Never me. You think just by taking a well-needed bath and scraping the whiskers from your face you can convince me you are someone else? Eh?"

Elliot licked his lips. "My name is Elliot. Not Eldon."

She studied him for a long moment, tilted her head to one side. "You are a Brand, that is plain enough."

"Yeah, I'm a Brand. Elliot Brand, but I don't know you, and I never met those bastards in town before in my life."

"You look like Eldon," she said. "Only... cleaner."

"Well, I'm *not* Eldon."

He tugged the reins when he judged the mare had drunk enough, and she lifted her head. Elliot hated to, but he nudged her into a brisk walk, following the stream for a ways, and finally emerging into a copse of trees. There he dismounted. Then he turned to grip the woman around the waist and help her down. She stiffened at his touch, but she let him help her. She was so wary, though—her eyes on his hands, and her body poised as if ready to react to the slightest move on his part. She pulled away from him the minute her feet touched the ground.

"Look, it's pretty clear you don't believe me. But I'm telling you, lady, I don't have a clue what's going on here. I don't know where the hell I am, or how I got here, or—"

"You are in Quinn, Texas, Señor Brand. And what is going on is an execution. I murdered you—or your twin—and I was about to hang for it."

Elliot nodded slowly. Quinn, Texas. Hell, he'd had a knot in his gut, fearing she would tell him just that. "They…um…don't hang people where I come from."

"No?"

"What…um…what's the date, Esmeralda?" He didn't look her in the eye when he asked the question.

Her voice was softer. "Eleven October, eighteen hundred eighty-one. What difference can that possibly make?"

He blew a sigh. "A lot. Oh, hell." This was all some delusion. He was probably lying hunched over his pickup's steering wheel right now, with a massive concussion or worse, and all of this was a coma-induced dream. Shoot, he hoped he would come out of it okay. Hoped he didn't die. Wished to hell his brothers would show up and get him out of this mess, the way they always did. Come on, Garrett. Shake me or slap me until I wake up, he thought.

Someone shook him. Not Garrett. The lady. "Hey? What is the matter with you?"

He looked at her. "Damned if I know. So why don't you tell me about this Eldon? Why'd you kill him?"

Again that narrow-eyed look. "Are you pretending…or are you really a different man?"

Elliot shrugged. "Okay, let's try this, then. *How* did you kill him?"

She lowered her eyes. "He tried to rape me. I drove my knife into his heart, all the way to the hilt."

Bloodthirsty little thing, wasn't she? He fought off

a full-body shudder. "And you know for a fact you stabbed him, right? I mean, that's his blood on your blouse there?" He nodded at the all-but-shredded little half jacket and the bloodstained white cloth underneath.

"*Sí*. He bled like a pig."

Only, when she said it, it sounded like "peeg." Damn near made Elliot grin. He liked the way she talked. Blood lust aside, of course. "Well, then, we can get this out of the way pretty easily." Elliot reached up to his own shirt, untucked it. The woman took a step away from him as he began undoing the buttons, and he realized what she thought. So he gave up the unbuttoning and ripped it open instead. Better to get to the point as soon as possible. Hell, she might just knife him again, otherwise. "There," he said. "Look at my chest. You see any stab wounds? Any blood?"

She stood stock still, staring at his bare skin, blinking in shock. Slowly, she stepped closer and, lifting her hand, pressed her palm to his chest. Elliot felt a ripple run through him—a delicious little shiver instigated by that touch, and he thought maybe it wasn't a real good idea to have her hands on his bare chest. Not a good idea at all. She was the kind of trouble he didn't need. Even if she *was* just part of some delusion.

Finally she lifted her head, met his eyes. Hers were wide and dark and frightened. "You are not Eldon Brand," she said slowly. Her hand was still resting right over his heart, warm and soft and small.

"No. I'm not. I'm Elliot. You can trust me, okay?"

Her brows slammed down into a frown, and her

hand fell to her side. "*Trust you?* You are still a Brand, *señor.*"

"You say that like it's a bad thing."

She glared at him and, reaching to her throat, fingered the chain she wore. As she did, the pendant at its end came out from beneath her blouse, and Elliot saw it, caught his breath and blinked in shock. It was the crystal skull! "Where...where did you get that?"

She lifted her brows, then looked down. "This? It has been handed down through my family for generations. My father gave it to me just before he died. Murdered by more of your stinking family," she added with a scowl.

Hoofbeats sounded in the distance. Their pursuers were coming. Hell. "What *is* that thing, Esmeralda? What does it...what does it mean, what does it do?"

"Do?" She lowered her eyes, averting her gaze. "What makes you think it can do anything, *señor?* I don't know what you mean."

"You're a really lousy liar." He heard a shout, then splashing. He gripped Esmeralda's shoulders. "Listen, I was perfectly okay an hour ago. I was running an errand, and the date was October eleventh, *nineteen*-ninety-nine."

She sucked in a breath, looking up at him fast. "You are loco!" she whispered, taking a step away from him.

"I'm not loco, dammit, I'm here, and I got here when I held that very stone you're wearing in my hands and read what was written on the back!"

Shaking her head, she took another step backwards.

"Look, dammit!" Elliot held up his palm.

She looked, then came closer and looked again.

"Dios," she whispered, seeing the burned shape of the skull in his palm. "What can this mean?"

"I don't know. Let's get out of here, find a better place to hole up, and try to figure it out." He reached for her hand. She looked at it, shaking her head slowly.

"I cannot go with you. You are a Brand. Your family stole my father's land and his cattle, and then his life. I would sooner take my chances on my own than to trust a Brand. Any Brand."

Elliot opened his mouth to argue, just before he saw the riders crashing through the trees, guns raised. He grabbed Esmeralda, flinging her to the ground and landing on top of her, just as the first shots were fired. Then he swore as he realized he was trapped. Stuck right here. There were men on all sides, all of them getting off their horses now. They formed a wide circle around them, and began closing in.

"Toss your gun out, fellow. You don't wanna die for trash like her!" someone yelled. Sounded like Adam, but he would never call any woman trash. The Brand boys hadn't been raised that way.

"You want her, you're gonna have to go through me," he shouted back.

She turned her head, staring up at him as if shocked. Then she looked out at the others, moving ever closer around them. "That is Allen Brand, the banker," she whispered, pointing. "And his brothers, Waylon and Blake, the outlaws. Garrison, the sheriff. They will kill you. They will kill us both."

Elliot was good and riled, a state he didn't remember ever being in before, as he looked down at her terror-stricken eyes. "They'll try," he told her.

"We have no chance!" she pleaded.

"We have one." He nodded down at her. "The pendant."

She shook her head slowly, her hand closing around the skull and lifting it. "It is only carved stone."

"It got me here," Elliot told her. "I'm sure of it. Maybe it can get us out." He looked up, saw the men coming closer. Men who looked startlingly like Garrett, and Adam, Wes and Ben. Only mean, cruel and murderous.

Esmeralda grabbed his hand, pressed it over hers, where she gripped the skull, and said a prayer in Spanish. Then she began reading the words on the back of the skull. But even as she did, the men came closer.

"Toss the gun down, pard, and hand over the lady."

"Get the hell away from us or I'll shoot!" Elliot said, aiming his stolen six-gun.

There was a blinding flash of light in his eyes, a huge pain shooting through his head, dizziness…

…and then clarity again. He lay on top of Esmeralda, who was cringing beneath him, hands to her eyes, shaking all over. He lifted his head and saw the circle of men still closer, all peering at him. Lifting the gun, he said, "I mean it! Back off or I'll blow you to kingdom come!"

They stopped. They looked at each other, then at him, their faces utterly puzzled. "Uh, Elliot? Hey? You okay? It's us, all right? Take it easy," Garrison, the evil sheriff, said, his star winking in the sunlight.

Elliot frowned, looking down quickly to make sure the hammer of his gun was pulled back. But there was no gun in his hand. He was pointing a finger at the men around him. And…and his pickup was right behind him, its nose crumpled against that big old oak tree. And the men surrounding him were…his brothers.

Oh God, thank God, it was all just a dream, and he was…he was…he was…

Lying on top of a trembling, frightened woman…a woman from another time. And she, in turn, was staring at his brothers, hatred and terror in her eyes as they all surged forward at once.

Esmeralda blinked the dizziness from her eyes and scrambled out from beneath the stranger's protective body. Facing the others, she backed up slowly. "Stay away!" she shrieked. "Stay away from me!" She backed up until her back pressed against something cool and hard. Jumping, she looked behind her. The thing was so foreign, so strange to her, that she only frowned, staring at it. And then another such beast roared past, made a squealing sound, and slid to a stop. Esmeralda screamed at the top of her lungs and dove facedown onto the ground, covering her head with her arms.

"What the hell?" someone said.

"Damn, he must have run her over or something!" another shouted.

"Wait…wait, guys." That voice was the one she knew. Elliot, the stranger who'd saved her from the gallows. The man who looked like the most evil of men but wasn't him. Couldn't be him, for he had saved her life, risking his own to do it.

Yet, did that matter? He was a Brand. Bad blood. Bad family, her father would say.

"Just stay where you are, okay?" Elliot said.

Then he came to her, knelt beside her, and his hands closed on her shoulders. "Esmeralda, it's all right." He leaned closer, his voice dropping to a whisper. "It was the crystal. It worked. We...we're in my time now. We're safe."

Blinking in shock, she dared to lift her head and look around. Those evil men were all standing there staring at her in confusion, and a woman had jumped from the noisy iron beast and joined them now. Jenny Brand, the saloon matron and whore. Only...younger.

"Esmeralda, do you understand me?" Elliot asked.

She shook her head. "How can you say we are safe," she whispered harshly, "when they still surround us?"

"That isn't them. These are my brothers. My *real* brothers. Look closer. No guns. And...they're all clean. No whiskers. Look at Garrett, he has all his teeth and everything...."

Blinking slowly, she took a second look, just as the big one, the sheriff who had only an hour ago tried to hang her, tipped his head to one side and said, "Elliot? Did I just hear you tell that girl that I have all my teeth?"

"Oh, hell, what's going on here, anyway?" the female cried. She came forward, prying Elliot away, and staring down at Esmeralda with concern in her brown eyes. How strange she was, with her red hair cropped so short. "Are you hurt, hon?" she asked. "Come on, let me take a look at you."

With her hands—gentle hands, Esmeralda noted—she helped her get to her feet. Then her eyes widened as they raked over Esmeralda's bloodstained blouse. "Landsakes, she's bleeding! Garrett, you'd best get an ambulance!"

"No," Esmeralda said. "I am fine. It is not my blood."

Elliot came back to her then. "She's right, it's not."

The girl frowned. "Not her blood? Well, then, whose blood is it?"

"No one's…probably the deer that caused all this," Elliot said. "I must have hit it."

"I don't see any deer, Elliot," the sheriff said, looking around.

"Doesn't matter. Probably ran off. The point is, she's okay. We both are."

The woman put her hands on her hips. "Oh, *sure* you're okay, Elliot! Except for that bump on your head, and the bruise on the lady's face, anyway." She shook her head. "What happened out here? Elliot, you were gone for hours. When you didn't come back, we got worried and headed out to look for you."

Esmeralda watched him, wondering what he would say. He only shook his head. "A deer ran out in front of me, I jerked the wheel to avoid it, and um… Esmeralda was…just there."

"But you're both okay?"

Elliot nodded. Esmeralda, hesitantly, nodded as well.

"Well, I still think you're both shaken up. Poor thing, nearly getting run down by my lunatic brother." Jessi stroked Esmeralda's hair and shook her head. "Let's get you back to the house, clean you up and…and…" She was eyeing Esmeralda's dress again now. "My goodness, that's quite an…unusual outfit."

"Is it?" Esmeralda didn't think so. The woman

was dressed much like the men…who had to be her brothers. The resemblance was too strong to be missed. But she didn't look like the same Jenny Brand Esmeralda had known. She had kind eyes, a soft, smooth-skinned face.

"She was on her way to a…a costume party," Elliot said quickly. "Right, Esmeralda?"

Esmeralda looked at him, saying nothing.

"Listen," Elliot went on. "She's pretty shaken up. Jessi, let me take your pickup and drive her back to the ranch, okay? You can pile in with the boys."

Jessi eyed her brother, then slanted a perceptive gaze at Esmeralda. "Well, shoot, I guess. Just don't wreck it like you did yours, Elliot, or I'll kick your tail all the way to the Texas Brand. And then I'll make you buy me a new one." She put her hands on her hips, grinning at her brother expectantly. When he said nothing, her smile died, and she frowned. "What, no comeback? Nothing about how it would take ten clunkers like mine to live up to a new one?"

Elliot tugged his gaze from Esmeralda's to glance at his sister. "What?"

"Nothing," she said, looking from one of them to the other again and again, a frown knitting her brow. "Never mind. I'll see you at the ranch."

Elliot nodded, taking Esmeralda's hand and guiding her toward the odd metal carriage that waited at the roadside, while his family looked on curiously. When they were out of earshot, he leaned close. "We can't tell them what really happened. Where you… really come from."

"Why not?" she asked, staring up at him. He had the bluest eyes…kind eyes. And his face lacked the harshness of Eldon's, she saw that now.

"Well, because they'd never believe it, for one thing. Look, all we have to do is act normal until we have a chance to…to figure out what we're going to do next. Okay?"

Looking around her, she glimpsed the town in the distance. It was different. The road was hard…and black. Like stone. And there were ropelike things strung from towering poles, stretching endlessly in either direction. Carriages without horses moved this way and that. "I am not so certain I know what normal is, Elliot Brand. This…this is not my world."

"I know just how you feel."

She met his eyes and knew he did. He'd been in her very position only a short while ago. How it could be true, she could not imagine. But there was no doubt it was. "I am afraid," she said.

"I know. Tell you the truth, so'm I." He reached up to open a door. "Come on, get in. We'll figure it out as we go, all right?"

She eyed the machine. Its seats looked soft, but it was foreign to her. "Is it safe?" As she asked the question, she eyed the other one, its front crushed against the large tree.

"I promise, you'll be safe," Elliot said. "We'll go very slowly. It'll be just fine."

She looked at him, doubting his words, but not his intent. "All right." She climbed in. But as soon as Elliot made the machine begin to move, she thought she was going to be sick.

"Are you sure Elliot was okay?" Garrett asked. He was driving his pickup, which, thankfully, had a back seat, because Wes, Adam, Ben and Jessi were all crammed in with him.

"Sure," Jessi said. "Just a little bump on his head was all." She frowned through the windshield at her old clunker of a pickup, just ahead. "Gotta wonder, though."

"Yeah. Gotta wonder." Garrett looked down at his speedometer. The needle hovered between twenty and twenty-five miles per hour. Sighing, he settled back in his seat and resolved to endure the slow, slow trip back to the Texas Brand.

Elliot watched her. She clutched her stomach for most of the trip, staring out the window with wide, frightened eyes. Gasping and pointing every now and then at such mundane things as the neon Budweiser sign in the window of La Cucharacha and a tractor putting along slightly slower than they were.

As Elliot looked on, she spotted a couple of teen-agers with big hair and short skirts and too much makeup, and she muttered in Spanish, crossing herself as she did.

Scared. Poor thing was scared witless.

"Look, it has to be that pendant of yours," he told her. "And if it is, it can get you back where you came from just as easily as it got you here."

She turned to stare at him. "And if it does, what will I return to, Elliot Brand? Your murdering brothers and their gallows?"

"Those were not my brothers." His lips thinned as he thought it over. "Must have been...my ancestors."

She sniffed indignantly, but she wasn't fooling him a bit. She was more scared than she was mad. No matter how she might try to hide it.

"I cannot stay here, and I cannot go back. The

legends told in my family about the pendant were lies!''

"Legends?'' Elliot eyed her, but kept track of his speed, too. He was determined to go slow. Not upset her. "What legends?''

She waved a hand with an expressive snap of her wrist. "Foolish tales. They don't matter.''

"They might. Tell me.'' They were leaving the town behind them now and heading away from it, toward the ranch. A five-minute trip that was going to take them at least twenty minutes.

She sighed, looking away from him to the rolling fields beyond the roadside. "It was said the skull had powers. That much must have been true, I suppose. But my family believed it was created by some ancient mystical race, and that its task was to set our world right when things went wrong. To restore human beings to their proper place and time.'' She shook her head. "All it has done for me is take me away from all I know and love.''

"Didn't seem to me like there was much to love about it.''

Her head swung around, eyes and nostrils flaring at once. "There was my land. My father's land. My home. I went there to take it back from those who stole it away. And now thanks to this stupid…'' She reached to her throat, but stopped speaking when her palm flattened to her chest. Looking down fast, she sucked in a breath. "*Dios!* It is gone! The pendant is gone!''

Elliot swore, barely resisting the urge to slam his foot on the brake pedal. Then he calmed himself, gave his head a shake and wondered why it was suddenly such an effort to keep his legendary cool. "All right, it's all right. It probably fell off back there in all the excitement.'' And his brother was going to skin him alive if he didn't find it, he added silently. Shoot. ''We'll go back and look for it. But later, okay?''

''Why later? We should go now, before someone else finds it and takes it for their own, no?''

''No one's gonna find it. Look, it's gonna look mighty odd to the family if we go rushing back there now. And I still think it's best we don't tell them any of this.'' She eyed him, doubt about his wisdom blatantly plain in her face. ''They'd think we were both insane,'' he told her. ''They'd probably drag us off to some headshrinker somewhere for treatment.''

''Headshrinker?'' For just a second she looked terrified.

''That's just an expression. I meant a doctor for crazy people. A psychiatrist. You understand?''

''No. I understand none of this.''

''Look, just follow my lead. Play along with me on this. Here, we're almost home.'' He nodded ahead at the sprawling ranch that was just coming into view.

Esmeralda looked, and then she went very still. ''This…is *your* home?''

He allowed a small smile. ''Yep. Finest ranch in the great state of Texas. We call it the Texas Brand.''

He waited for her reply. Waited, fully expecting her to make some comment about the beauty of his home, the way most people did the first time they set eyes on it. Instead, he only heard a low hissing sound, like a snake about to strike, and when he looked at her, he saw utter fury in her eyes.

''You are right, Señor Brand. It *is* the finest ranch in all of Texas. But it is not yours.''

''Huh?''

"This is my land! Your thieving family stole it from my father. I came to this town to take it back, only to face your murdering brothers and their tricks. I nearly died to get this land back from you, and I tell you now, Elliot Brand, I do not care what time this is. It is still my land. And I will have it back. On my father's memory, I vow it!"

As she spoke, the pickup rolled underneath the arches of the Texas Brand, and Elliot stopped it in the driveway, right in front of the house. He just sat there, staring at her.

She was breathing hard, her face flushed from her recent rush of emotions. They seemed to surge and wane in her like waves on the ocean. She sure wasn't level, or steady as a rock, the way he was.

"I don't know what to say to you," he said at last, speaking slowly, softly. "Esmeralda, this ranch has been in my family for over a hundred years."

The anger left her face, and her lips parted. "A...a hundred years? Is that how far I have come?"

He nodded. "Almost a hundred and twenty."

Her eyes closed, but he'd seen the moisture gathering in them before, and he saw it again now, squeezing through to glisten on her dark lashes. "My aunt Maria...my little cousins... Oh. Oh, all gone. All of them gone..." Her voice was a tortured whisper now. With trembling hands she fumbled with the door, got it opened and half climbed, half fell out of the truck. Then she stood on the ground, looking around, at the house, the stable, the barn. The horses in one pasture and cattle in another, more distant one. Elliot got out and walked around the pickup to stand beside her.

"I know it's a lot to deal with, all at once. Just

take it easy. Take your time. Try not to…Esmeralda?''

She didn't seem to be hearing him at all, and then he heard the sound that was so familiar he hadn't even noticed it at first. It was the mosquito-like hum of a very small airplane. And as the craft passed overhead, he saw it, saw Esmeralda's neck arch as she tipped her head back. Only…she kept right on going.

He caught her before she hit the ground. Passed out cold, she was limp as he gathered her up into his arms and carried her toward the house.

Chapter 4

Elliot did his best to ignore the questions of a half dozen concerned Brands as he carried Esmeralda straight through the parlor and up the stairs to his bedroom, but ignoring his well-meaning siblings had never been what Elliot would call easy. Still, they did back off and remained at the foot of the stairs while he carried the lady up.

She was small. Tough to tell that with the layers of torn, dirty skirts and God only knew what underneath, but she was light in his arms. He took her into his bedroom, lowered her onto the neatly made bed, and then sat down on its edge to pat her face a few times.

Lord, but she was a pretty thing. Especially when her blazing black eyes with their boiling emotions were closed. Just soft paintbrush lashes resting on her cheeks now. No scowling, doubting, wary expression. Soft coppery skin, full lips.

He caught himself licking his, and stopped it. "Wake up, Esmeralda. Come on, you fainted, but it's okay now. Wake up." He patted her cheek again.

Her lashes fluttered twice, and then her eyes opened, and so did her mouth. She took one look at him and cut loose with an earsplitting shriek. Elliot clapped his hand over her mouth, but not fast enough. The thundering of booted feet told him that much. Then the door burst open and Garrett stood there looking mean as a bear with a toothache. "What the hell are you doin' to her, Elliot?"

"Elliot?" the woman echoed, and then she relaxed again, nodding. "Oh, *sí,* Elliot. I forgot."

"That's okay," Elliot said. "You're entitled, after all this." He looked at his brother, who was frowning and studying Esmeralda as if he were wondering about her mental state. "She's just a little disoriented, is all," Elliot told him. "Just give us a minute, okay?"

Even as Garrett nodded, his wife, diminutive Chelsea, was shoving past him and coming into the room. "No, we're not giving you a minute," she said. For a little thing, she sure had taken over as ramrod of this spread. "The boys filled me in—or rather, they told me as much as you told them, which is not the whole story. Is it, Elliot?"

Elliot did his best to look puzzled. "Gee, Chelse, I don't know what you mean."

She narrowed her eyes on him, but her face softened when she turned to the woman in the bed. "You poor thing. Are you sure you weren't hurt in the accident?"

"I am fine."

Tilting her head to one side, Chelsea said, "Well,

you don't *look* fine. You look like you just had the scare of your life.'' Leaning over the bed, crowding between where Elliot sat and Esmeralda lay, Chelsea cupped the girl's chin, turning her face to one side. ''And what about this bruise, hmm?'' And as she asked, she sent Elliot a scowl.

''Oh, Elliot did not do this. It was another man. He—''

She stopped when Chelsea went white, and her eyes widened. ''A man did that to you?'' she asked, her voice dangerously soft. Elliot knew damned good and well about Chelsea's hot buttons; men who beat up on women were the hottest. And for good reason. Now his sister-in-law was good and riled. ''Who was he?'' she asked. ''Tell me his name, and I'll have Garrett find him and lock him up.''

Esmeralda's eyes sought Elliot's. He gave her a very slight shake of his head, side to side. ''I don't…know his name. But…it will not happen again. Of this I am certain.''

Chelsea shook her head. ''Unless you killed the son of a bitch, I don't know how you can be.''

Esmeralda's eyes widened, shot to Elliot's. He put a finger to his lips.

''Anyway, it's over. And I understand if you're not ready to talk about it yet. But whatever happened to you, you're safe here.''

''Safe.'' Esmeralda repeated the word as if trying it out for the first time.

Elliot thought Chelsea was getting choked up at this point. She no doubt thought she had a runaway battered woman on her hands. And, in a way, she did. She just had no idea how far Esmeralda had actually run.

"Oh, I know that's tough to believe," Chelsea went on. "It was for me, too. There was a time when I thought no place was safe, and that no man could be trusted. But believe me, no one will lay a finger on you here. You can trust me on that. Whoever hurt you would have to get through a solid wall of overprotective Brand men to do it. And if…if you need a place to stay for a while…well, you couldn't have picked a better one."

Esmeralda tilted her head, studying Chelsea closely, oddly, as if she'd never seen her like before. "I…thank you."

"And if you decide you want to talk," Chelsea went on, "you just come to me, okay? I'm good at listening."

She was, too, Elliot thought. A full-blown psychologist now, with her degree in hand. Chelsea counseled battered women, helped them heal. She was damn good at what she did. Though he would be willing to bet that if she heard Esmeralda's story, she would find herself at a loss.

"For now, though, I'll bet you'd like a bath and a change of clothes, wouldn't you? Make you feel like a new woman."

Looking down at her tattered, stained clothes, Esmeralda nodded. "*Sí.* That would be wonderful."

"I'll get it running, then." Chelsea got up, patting Esmeralda's hand, and headed for the bathroom.

But as soon as she opened the door Esmeralda was sitting up, peering inside at the tub and fixtures, and when Chelsea snapped on the light, Esmeralda clapped a hand over her mouth to prevent a squeak of surprise. The look on her face, though, as she stared wide-eyed at the light coming from the bathroom, was obvious. She looked ready to spring at any second from the bed and either run for the hills or rush in for a closer look—as if that hand over her mouth were all that was holding her down.

"Chelsea?" Elliot was on his feet, taking Chelsea's arm and tugging her from the room as fast as possible. "Why don't you go find some clothes and let me run that bath, huh? I can, uh…I can take care of…you know, the water."

Chelsea turned in the doorway, frowning at him. "What is wrong with you, anyway? You're acting so…" Then she slid her gaze past him to the woman who was already creeping out of bed, peering into the bathroom like Alice getting her first glimpse of Wonderland. "Oooooh," Chelsea said. "Oh, so it's like *that*, is it?"

"Like what?" But Chelsea was already turning to stroll away, her step almost bouncy. "Chelsea? Hey, I don't know what you're thinking, but if it's what I *think* you're thinking then…ah, hell." She was beyond hearing him, anyway. Women! They all had one-track minds.

With a frustrated sigh, Elliot went back into the bedroom to see to his charge. His responsibility now, he supposed. Hell, she didn't have anyone else to guide her through life in the twentieth century.

Esmeralda had located the wall switch, and was flipping it on and off and on again, her eyes on the light fixture in the bathroom ceiling.

"It's an electric light," Elliot explained. "Every home has it nowadays. And running water, too. Hot and cold. I guess this is all new to you, huh?"

She nodded, turning her attention now to the

gleaming bathroom, and the bathtub and the toilet. She pointed at the latter. "What's this?"

"It is like an outhouse. Look." Elliot lifted the lid, and as she watched, he flushed it so she could see the water swirl and go down.

A long sigh came floating from her. Then she turned. "And this is a bathtub?"

"Yeah. You just flip this lever here, and that keeps the water in. Then you turn it on, like this." He cranked the nobs. "Hot, cold. Feel."

Esmeralda put her hands under the water, feeling it grow warmer and cooler, and nodding excitedly. She didn't look angry or suspicious or scared now. She looked like an excited child, and her eyes sparkled. She even smiled, and when he looked up and saw the transformation of her face when she did, he almost fell into the tub.

Shaking himself, he went on. "So you just adjust it to the temperature you want and let it fill. When you're done, flip the lever, and the water goes down the drain."

"Amazing," she whispered. "This...world of yours...is so different." Meeting his eyes, she seemed to be searching them.

"Look, I know it's all got to be very confusing to you. But...well, I'm gonna help you adjust to everything. Explain it to you as we go along. The thing is, you're going to be seeing a lot of things you've never seen before. But you'll have to try not to act surprised by them...at least, not in front of the others."

She lifted her brows. "I will try...but it will not be easy."

"No, I know it won't." He drew a breath, wanting to put her at ease, at least a little bit, but he wasn't sure how. "Look, what Chelsea said goes for me, too. You're welcome to stay here just as long as you want. I mean, until we figure out what to do."

Uh-oh. That look was back. Her eyes flashed, and she tossed her head. "Oh, *sí,* that is so *very generous* of you, *señor.* Allowing me to stay on my own land for as long as I wish. What more could I ask for?"

"Hell, are we back to that again?"

She narrowed her eyes on him. Then averted them. "No."

"No?"

Her back was to him now as she leaned over the tub, moving her hands beneath the flow of the water, playing with the knobs. Elliot touched her shoulders, closed his hands over them and turned her gently to face him again. "What do you mean, no? You mean you're just letting it go, just like that?"

She shrugged.

Elliot shook his head. "I don't know you very well, Esmeralda, but I know better than to believe that. What are you up to?"

"I can be up to nothing, Elliot Brand. Because I know nothing. Not whether I will stay in this time or find a way back to my own. Not how to live or what the laws of this place might be. I have no plan. I have no means of making one. So for now, *sí,* I will let this matter go. And I will learn. I will learn all I need to know, and then I will decide what I must do."

Elliot sighed in relief so great his shoulders almost sagged with it. He'd been half-scared she was going to go shouting her claims to the Texas Brand to anyone with eardrums, and that wouldn't have been good. How the hell would he have explained that?

"Thank goodness," he said. And he offered her a

smile. "That's the best thing to do, Esmeralda. Honest, it is."

She nodded, turning away and shutting off the water flow.

"You sure are a fast learner," he said.

"Oh, *sí,* very fast. It would be a wise thing for you to remember, Elliot Brand." She straightened, lifted her hands and peeled off the short jacket. Then she began unbuttoning her bloodstained blouse. Her eyes were on his, dark, challenging, calculating.

Elliot felt his face go beet-red, and quickly turned his back. "I'll, uh…I'll just leave you to your bath, then," he blurted, and then he left that room as if the devil were after him.

He met Chelsea on the way out. She had a stack of clothes in her arms and a speculative gleam in her eyes. "Go on, I'll take care of her from here," she said. "I think your brothers would like a word with you downstairs."

Oh, hell, he was going to get the third degree for sure. Well, nothing to do but buck up and face it. He didn't need to take anything he didn't want to. And he wouldn't.

When he arrived in the parlor, the boys were waiting. Adam, Wes, Ben and Garrett all sat perched like vultures waiting to pick his bones apart. Little Bubba sat on Garrett's knee, turning the pages of a Dr. Seuss book as if he were actually reading it.

Wes went first. "Where's Taylor's find, El? I didn't see it in the pickup. Just the empty box."

Licking his lips, Elliot lowered his head. "I don't know."

"You…don't know?"

He lifted his head to meet his brother's eyes.

"That's right, I don't know. I took it out of the box to see what all the fuss was about, and it must have flown out of my hand when I hit the tree. I looked, Wes, but I couldn't find it."

Wes jumped to his feet, started to swear, then glanced to where his nephew sat on Garrett's knee and bit his lip.

"I'll go back and look some more," Elliot said. "It's probably lying in plain sight and I was just too shaken up to notice it."

"Taylor said that thing was important, El. You have to find it."

"And I will."

"Fine." Wes lowered his head and took his seat again.

"Now," Garrett said, "about the woman."

Elliot's head came up. "What about her?"

"Chelsea seems to think she's in some kind of trouble."

Adam pursed his lips, nodding. "And she seems to think you're about to join her there."

"Yeah, well, Chelsea's way off base on this, believe me."

Adam looked at Garrett. Garrett lifted his brows. "She's...awfully pretty," he said.

"So?"

"So...be careful, Elliot. She's obviously...involved. Maybe even married. I don't want you making yourself a target for whatever lunatic put that bruise on her face."

"Yeah, a lot you know, big brother. She's not involved, and she's not married, and the lunatic is long, long gone. Trust me on that."

"Yeah?" Garrett absently stroked Bubba's hair. "And how do you know all that?"

"I just do."

There was a collective sigh. Adam said, "Look, you're man enough to make your own decisions. We just don't want you walking into a mess of trouble."

"Hey, that's your department. I don't *do* trouble. You—all four of you—do a fine job of that without my help. I found this woman, and she needed help, and I gave it to her. We're Brands, that's what we do—what any of you would have done. So get off my back already."

They looked at one another. Ben, always quiet, got to his feet. "I've got a wife to get home to. I hate leaving her alone for a second with the baby already two days overdue. Elliot…if you need me…"

"You all act like I've caught some dread disease! I'm fine. For crying out loud, what's with you guys?"

Ben shrugged, slapped Elliot's shoulder as he passed and headed out the door. "I should go, too," Wes said. "Taylor was feeling better earlier, but who knows when this bug she has will come back."

"Yeah, me, too," Adam said. "Kirsten's been dealing with the contractors all day. She's probably ready to skin me by now." He chewed his lip. "Elliot, I'll come by in the morning, and we can get that pickup towed in."

"No need. You've got to get your dude ranch ready to open. I'll just call that new guy in town. What's his name—you know, just opened up a body shop on the River Road. He has a tow truck."

Adam shrugged. "Okay."

Ellliot glanced at Wes. "Tell Taylor I'm real sorry

about that skull thingie, but I'll get it back for her. And that's a promise.''

Wes's scowl softened a bit. "Yeah, well, accidents happen.'' He shook his head. "Besides, you've got enough to deal with right now. I suppose I can lay off you…for the moment, at least.''

"Shoot, I don't have anything to deal with besides a banged-up truck and too many brothers with active imaginations. No doubt sparked by one matchmaking sister-in-law. And speaking of females, where is Jessi, anyway?''

"Took her truck and headed home,'' Garrett said. "She couldn't wait to tell Lash that her brother had brought home a stray. And she didn't seem all that happy about it, either, Elliot.''

The others filed out, and Elliot was watching the door close behind them when he heard footsteps on the stairs. He turned, and then he just stood there like an idiot, staring.

Esmeralda was coming down the stairs, wearing a snug-fitting pair of jeans and a pretty white button-down blouse with flowers embroidered on the shoulders. Her hair was gleaming, curling, still damp but not real wet. Shoot, Chelsea must have demonstrated the wonders of the blow-dryer. But damn, the woman looked good. She looked sweet and soft and good. Dark and exotic and…just good.

Garrett nudged him with an elbow, and Elliot realized he hadn't even noticed his brother getting up or setting Bubba down. "Well, you're just in time. I've got dinner warming in the oven,'' Garrett said.

But Elliot was still staring, and now Esmeralda was staring back. Her eyes on his like laser beams. It made him feel odd inside. His stomach sort of roiled and lurched, and his hands itched.

"This…is all right, no?" Esmeralda asked, and she finally looked away from him, down at the clothes she wore.

Elliot found his voice. "Looks just fine," he said.

"You look lovely," Garrett added. "I hope you're hungry."

"Oh, *sí*, I am." She came across the room to where Elliot stood, and he managed to get his feet unstuck from the floor, turn and guide her into the kitchen. It was a big kitchen, really half kitchen, half dining room. Garrett had the table already set. Elliot pulled out a chair for her, and Esmeralda sat down. But she wasn't looking at the food Garrett began piling in front of them, or the plates. She was checking out the range and the fridge, and eyeing the microwave, with the green numbers of its digital clock glowing the time at her. Man, she must feel the way he would feel if he got beamed up to the starship Enterprise.

When everyone was seated, Garrett said, "So, Esmeralda…tell us about yourself. Where are you from?"

"Quinn," she said. Then she looked up quickly and added, "But I've been away for a long while. In Mexico, with my aunt."

"I see. I don't think I know your family. What's your last name?"

"Montoya," she said. "But, um…I no longer have any family living in Quinn. I haven't for…for a long time now."

"Where are your family living now, Esmeralda?" Chelsea asked.

Esmeralda looked down quickly, and Elliot thought

her eyes dampened a bit. "They are not living at all. I mean, they have all died. I have no family anymore."

"I'm so sorry." Chelsea's voice was sincere. She had that look in her eyes, though. The one she seemed to have picked up from Jessi. The one that said she wanted to keep this newcomer, take her in like a stray pet.

"It has been a very long time," Esmeralda said. "But it doesn't feel as if it has been more than a day."

"No, of course not. Grief is like that."

"*Sí.* I guess it is." Esmeralda began eating, signaling an end to that part of the conversation. Elliot couldn't do more than watch her. She ate with gusto, tasting each dish and then diving into it as if she were starved. He'd never seen a woman put away so much food in a single sitting.

Eventually she paused long enough to glance his way, which was not hard, since he was sitting right next to her. "Are you not hungry?"

Elliot looked at his food, the fried chicken leg on his plate. "No, I...don't seem to be."

Esmeralda shrugged and took his chicken.

"You hear that, Garrett?" Chelsea asked. "Your brother isn't hungry. I didn't think I'd ever hear those words from his lips."

Garrett just smiled and went back to eating. Bubba was eyeing everyone with interest, watching the goings-on with a keen eye, too keen for a four-year-old. The kid would start school in the fall, and Elliot fully expected his genius nephew to skip the first few grades.

When everyone was quiet, Bubba looked up at Elliot and tugged on his sleeve to get his attention, his face very serious.

"What is it, Bubba?"

"Is she your new girlfriend?" Bubba asked, dead-pan.

Elliot wanted to crawl under the table. "That's Esmeralda. And she's a friend."

"Es…mer…"

"You can call me Essie, little one. It is what my papa used to call me," Esmeralda said.

Bubba grinned. "Essie!" he said, triumph in his voice.

"That's very good," she told him, and Bubba beamed.

Her voice grew so much softer, sweeter, when she spoke to the child. And it was genuine. Nothing hiding beneath the surface.

Elliot got up when the meal was finished and started clearing the plates. Bubba gripped Esmeralda's hand and was tugging her back into the parlor, jabbering something about the Star Rangers, and she was smiling down at him. Chelsea said, "All right, but just a half hour, young man, and then it's time for bed."

As Bubba led Essie out of the kitchen, into the living room, Chelsea shook her head. "I swear, if I let him, he'd watch that TV twenty-four hours a day."

"Yeah," Elliot said, "he loves his…television… oh, crap!" He dropped the plates back onto the table and raced for the living room.

Too late. Bubba was thumbing the remote and the scenes were changing on the TV screen one after the other. Esmeralda was standing in the middle of the parlor, with her back to Elliot, facing the television screen. Her knees seemed to weaken a bit, and she reached out for something to grab onto, but nothing was there. At least, not until Elliot lurched forward. "It's all right," he whispered, as her hand closed around his forearm in a death grip. "Damn, I should have warned you about this. It's nothing to be afraid of."

She turned and searched his face, then glanced back at the TV screen as Bubba paused in his channel surfing to watch something being blown up. Big explosion, fire, fake bodies and parts thereof flying hither and yon. Esmeralda shrieked, and the next thing Elliot knew, her face was buried against his chest and she was trembling all over.

"Bubba, flip it to *Star Rangers,* would you? You know you're not supposed to be watching that kind of garbage," Elliot said, and his voice sounded hoarse to his own ears. Shrugging, Bubba obliged, and finally the cartoon characters filled the screen.

Elliot's arms were around Esmeralda now, his hands on her back, moving in soothing circles as she curled closer to him. "It's okay, I promise. It's not real, that thing. It's just make-believe. Pretend."

She was still shaking. Damn. He held her tighter. "It…it frightens me, that box," she muttered, her lips moving on his shirt as she spoke.

"I know. I know. But it can't hurt you. It's not real, Esmeralda."

Sniffling, she lifted her head. "Not real?"

"No. Did you ever see a play? Actors on a stage, pretending?"

Blinking, she said, "I have never seen one, but I have heard of such things."

"That's all this is. Actors pretending. People watch the stories. But none of it's real."

She took a quick glance at the Star Rangers. They were being chased by some giant hairy monster with dripping fangs. She shook her head hard. "I do not like it."

"No, I'm not too fond of it myself. You don't have to watch. Come on, we can just go—"

"No, wait." Her eyes were still glued to the screen, as the Star Rangers, cornered by the angry creature, looked doomed. "I...I will just see this...*uno momento*." Peeling herself away from Elliot, she moved closer to the TV, and as he watched her, wondering why he felt so cold and his arms felt so empty all of a sudden, she moved still closer, gaze still fixed on the screen. Then she sat down on the floor beside Bubba, as mesmerized as he was.

Bubba leaned toward her. "Don't worry. They'll get away. The Star Rangers *always* get away."

"*Sí*, but how? They are trapped," she whispered back.

Just then one of the Rangers performed some physically - impossible - unless - you - happened - to - be-a-cartoon leap, landing on the monster's head and snapping a blindfold around its bulging eyes. Unable to see, the monster swung its claws uselessly, hitting only air, while the other Rangers cast a net over its head and wrapped it up, nice and neat and immobile.

"Oh! How clever they are!" Esmeralda said, clapping her hands. "Now they will kill the beast, no?"

"Nah. Star Rangers never kill anybody."

"No?" Esmeralda asked. "Why not?"

"'Cause it's a kids' program," Bubba answered,

nodding sagely. "And grown-ups don't like kids watching stuff like that."

Esmeralda shook her head and shrugged helplessly. "Then what will they do with that beast?"

"Watch." Bubba pointed, and they both fell silent. Shortly, a helicopter hovered on the screen and dropped a cable, which the Rangers hooked to the net. Then the copter took off, carrying the monster away.

"He can live out his days safely on Monster Island," one Ranger said. "And he won't be able to hurt anyone there."

Very politically correct, those Star Rangers, Elliot thought.

The theme song came up, and Bubba sang along. Esmeralda began bobbing her head in time. And when it ended, Elliot realized Chelsea and Garrett were standing right behind him and had probably witnessed the whole thing.

"Time for bed," Chelsea said.

"But—"

"No buts, Bubba. Bedtime is bedtime, you know that," Garrett added.

Bubba sighed, but got up and went to his parents, collecting a hug and a kiss from each of them. "I think Essie was scared of the TV at first, Mamma," Bubba told her, his voice too old for him. "But then she kinda liked it."

Chelsea shot Garrett a frown, but tousled her child's hair lovingly. "Well, who could not like the Star Rangers?"

"Can Essie tuck me in?" Bubba asked. "Please?"

"Sure, if she's not too tired." Chelsea looked at Esmeralda, who was getting to her feet.

"Oh, *sí*, I would love to tuck you in, little one."

She came forward and took Bubba's hand, and he led her up the stairs, singing the *Star Rangers* song all the way. Halfway up, Esmeralda joined in.

Elliot intended to follow. But Chelsea's voice stopped him. "Odd, wasn't it, her reaction to the television?"

Elliot stopped, but didn't turn. "Oh, it was just the violence, I think. Some people are, um…more sensitive than others, you know."

"So sensitive they cry out, hide their eyes and shake all over?" Chelsea asked. Elliot just shrugged. "You were pretty sensitive yourself, holding her like you did."

"Well…I mean, I was just…"

"Best get on up there, El," Garrett interrupted, saving his hide, Elliot thought. "Bubba will have her telling him stories till dawn, if you don't watch it."

With a quick nod, Elliot raced up the stairs.

Chapter 5

Children were still the same. At least that much hadn't changed. Esmeralda tucked the child in, as he excitedly told her all about himself and his home, the horse his daddy had given him a year ago, and how he would go to the stables to feed and groom it with help from his uncles. She sat there and let him talk until he'd talked himself out, and finally his eyes began to droop tiredly, but still he talked.

And still she stayed.

What had happened to her? How had she ended up in this foreign world, this strange place where seemingly kind people wore the faces of murderers from a time long past? They'd been good to her, these Brands. So far. They welcomed her among them, or seemed to. They apparently worried for her safety, had even offered their protection. She had no sooner arrived here than they had closed ranks around her.

Like a family of her own. Were they truly what they seemed? Could they be?

Esmeralda found it difficult to believe. They were descended from the cruelest men she had ever known. Blood will tell, her father used to say. And their blood was Brand blood. Bad blood. The Brands were an evil breed, and that, at least, was not in question. She'd suffered enough to be certain of it. It was difficult to see this bunch the way they were trying to make her see them—as decent, caring folk.

Yet…it was equally difficult to see them as evil. Especially with this little one in their midst, so obviously happy and well-loved. She stroked the boy's hair, smiling and nodding as he talked on and on. He barely drew a breath between tales, so replying was unnecessary.

She supposed there was a slight chance that these newfangled Brands truly were different from their forebears. No matter, though. Even if they were as kind as they seemed, it didn't change the facts. They were living on her land. This sprawling place they called the Texas Brand—it belonged to her. Somehow, some way, she must get it back. She owed it to her father, and her mother, who were buried in this ground. She could do it here, now, in this time…or she could try to find a way to return to her own world and accomplish the deed there. But either way, her goal remained the same.

And she sensed that it would be far easier to battle these twentieth-century Brands than to try to fight their low-life ancestors—men who would kill her as soon as look at her. Far easier.

Before she began, she would have to learn. She

must be able to exist in this world before she could do battle in it. And she would.

"I think he's asleep," a deep voice said softly.

She turned her head to see Elliot Brand standing in the doorway, watching her. She'd been absently stroking the small child's silken hair, lost in thought, but comforted somehow by the act. "*Sí*, he talked himself out, I suppose." She got to her feet, reached for the lamp beside the bed, then paused with her hand in midair.

"I'll get it." Elliot came in, leaning past her to touch a button on the lamp's base. "You just turn this. See?"

She nodded, and he turned the tiny knob, plunging the room into darkness, except for a small glow near the floor beside the bed. It gave a minuscule amount of light...enough to see by, though. "That's his night-light," Elliot said, following her curious gaze. "So if he needs to get up he doesn't get hurt fumbling around in the dark."

"And so he will not be afraid," she added.

She saw the dark silhouette of Elliot's head, backlit by the child's night light, move in a nodding motion. "Come on." He took her elbow, cupping his palm around it, and led her toward the door, then through it into the hallway. And again she felt something warm where he touched her. A pulsing feeling of intense awareness. It could not be attraction. For how could she feel attraction for a man who looked so much like the one who'd attacked her? Ah, but she could. And she knew it. Perhaps all too well. For a time she'd believed herself in love with this man's evil ancestor. Eldon...darkly handsome, whipcord lean, strong and powerful.

But despite his outer beauty, the man inside had been as ugly as the devil himself. Heartless and cruel. Because of her weakness toward him, she'd suffered far more than she should have from his cruelty. Even when she'd long since realized he was no good, even when she'd told herself that her youthful longings had been misguided and foolish, she'd still felt something stir inside her when Eldon Brand had come around.

It had broken her heart to drive a blade through his.

This man, this Elliot, could be his twin, so the feelings he stirred to life in the pit of her belly made some kind of twisted sense, she supposed. But she must fight them, must not let her heart soften toward this man as it had toward the other one. She had no wish to suffer that way again.

Only she could grant him the power to touch her. To hurt her.

"You…um…can use the guest room," Elliot was saying. "It used to be my sister's room…Jessi, you remember?"

"Sí."

He kept speaking, his hand still on her elbow, as he led her down the hall. "She still uses it when she stays over, but mostly it's for visitors now." He stopped outside a door. "It's, um…right next to my room. So if you need anything…" He shrugged, not finishing.

She did need something; his help. She needed him to teach her the ways of this century, for there was no one else who knew the truth about her or would even believe her if she told them. She needed him. Therefore, she had to be kind to him—even while keeping her heart cold and removed. Safe. She had to use this man.

Esmeralda realized she'd made a grave mistake in telling him her feelings about the Texas Brand—that it was rightfully hers and that she intended to take it back. She should have thought before she'd said those things to him, but as usual, the words had spewed from her lips, driven by a gust of emotion. She would have to careful with him. If he turned on her, she would be lost and alone in a world she knew nothing about.

Reaching past her, Elliot opened the bedroom door. "Chelsea left some more clothes in there for you. A nightgown and such."

"I...thank you. She is very kind."

"Yeah, she is."

She didn't go into the bedroom, just stood outside the door, waiting. No doubt he would make a lewd suggestion soon. She had never met a man who didn't. Especially one in such a position of control over her. He all but held her life in his hands. Surely he would expect compensation. And while many white men would mind their manners around women of their own kind, few had any compunction when it came to a Mexican. She would give him what he demanded. She would see he was well-pleasured. And he would, perhaps, be less likely to turn her out in the morning.

"Well," Elliot said. "Good night, then."

She frowned at him, tilting her head to one side. "You mean...you aren't coming in?"

He got an odd smile for a moment, lowering his head, shaking it. "I think my brother and his wife already have their imaginations working overtime. I don't want to give them any more ideas."

She was completely confused. "I thought...you would expect..."

He looked up slowly, searching her face, slowly understanding her meaning. She had to look away, but he was suddenly gripping her shoulders. Not hard, just enough so she couldn't turn from him completely. "Expect what, Esmeralda?"

She shrugged. "Compensation," she said. "For your trouble."

"You mean...you mean sex, don't you? You thought I was going to try to..."

She shrugged. "When a white man does a favor for a Mexican woman, he usually expects to be... repaid."

"No," he said sternly. "Not around here. Not in this time. Esmeralda, things have changed. You understand? You don't just sleep with someone because they did you a favor. For God's sake, is that the way your life was back then?"

She lowered her head quickly, swallowing hard. "Only when I lived in Texas. It is why my father sent me back to Mexico. But as soon as I returned, it was the same. The men...your people...knew they could get away with it. I was nothing to them but a Mexican whore, to be used as they pleased." Lifting her head, meeting his eyes, she saw the horror in them. "And now you think the same of me, eh?"

"No!" His voice came out loud, but he hushed it and hurried on. "No, Esmeralda, I don't think that at all. My God, you poor thing."

She widened her eyes. "Do not let yourself believe it mattered to me, Elliot Brand. No man ever touched my soul. No man ever could." It was a lie, of course. One man had.

He tilted his head to one side. "That tough, are you?"

"*Sí.*" She said it with a firm nod. "I am strong. My skin is like rawhide."

He shook his head slowly.

"You don't believe me? You think I curled up on the floor and wept over it?"

"No. I think it bothered you so little that you knifed the last son of a bitch who tried it."

She looked away, gave a careless shrug. "He needed killing."

"They all did." Elliot's hand came to her chin, tipped it up so he could stare straight into her eyes. "It's not like that anymore. It doesn't matter if you're male or female, Mexican or Chinese, Esmeralda, if any man puts his hands on you against your will today, he'll go to prison for it." His lips thinned. "If he lives long enough to stand trial."

She lifted her brows and tried to tell herself this was not real. *He* was not real. He couldn't be.

"We treat women with respect nowadays. Especially in Texas. Especially in this family. You understand?"

She nodded slowly. "*Sí.*"

He stared at her, as if trying to determine whether she really did understand what he was telling her. "And you don't owe me anything," he added.

She only shrugged. She did, actually. She owed him for saving her life, for letting her stay here. But she supposed he owed her more. Her home. Her ranch. Her heritage.

"So you can sleep soundly. No one's going to be paying you any visits in the middle of the night."

She nodded, searching her mind for words. But all

that came out was, "I will never sleep, all the same.
There is too much...too much to think about. So
much to learn."

He sighed. "Must be pretty overwhelming." Then
he seemed to think for a moment. "Tell you what,"
he said at length. "If you're still awake after everyone
else is asleep, I'll take you downstairs and show you
how things work. Explain everything in this house
that's new or strange to you. Okay?"

She smiled in spite of herself. "I would like that
very much."

Elliot nodded. "Agreed, then. Try to get some rest
in the meantime. I'll come back for you in a couple
of hours."

"All right." Nodding, she stepped into the bedroom that was to be hers, found the switch on the
wall and turned on the lights.

"You're getting to be a pro already," Elliot muttered, then he turned and went to his own room.

Elliot sat in the dark. Esmeralda reminded him of
Wes, the way Wes used to be, before he found Taylor
and his heritage and his calling. A bundle of anger,
all wrapped up tight inside, and building, always
building. Things had happened to her. Bad things.
Unfair things. But she acted like they were nothing.
Said she was tough. So tough she would have taken
him to bed tonight if he'd demanded it. He could
imagine what that would have been like. Her lying as
still as a stone, staring unblinkingly at the ceiling,
feeling nothing. What man would want a woman if
he had to have her like that?

But Esmeralda wasn't tough at all. Elliot could see
right through her. She was hurting. Elliot knew that

kind of pain. He'd seen it before. In Ben, and in Adam. In Wes. And he knew, just as he'd known with each of his brothers, that if Esmeralda didn't let that pain out, it was going to eat her up inside. Destroy her soul. Leave nothing behind but an empty shell. Add to that the confusion of being yanked out of her world, away from everything she knew and understood, and plunked down at the end of the twentieth century…Elliot figured it would be a miracle if she avoided some kind of explosion or breakdown or whatever happened when a person as volatile as Esmeralda was pushed beyond her endurance.

Maybe he could help her avoid that. Maybe… Hell, if anyone could, it ought to be him. Cool, calm Elliot Brand, the guy who went through life utterly unruffled. He was her opposite. If she was fire, he was water. Cool, soothing, calm water.

He sat alone in his room for a couple of hours, trying to figure out how he could get through to her. But he couldn't seem to find that cool, calm guy he knew himself to be. Something inside him was all off-kilter. He felt jittery, nervous…as if he was walking on unstable ground, as bits of it were crumbling away from beneath his boots.

Two hours later, Elliot crept to Esmeralda's bedroom, and for some reason his heart was pounding and his hands shaking as he reached for the doorknob. He paused, licked his lips, took a breath. What the hell was he so wrought up about? It wasn't like him. Totally unfamiliar territory to him, in fact, and he decided he didn't like it. He reached for calm, found something vaguely like it, and figured it would have to do. He turned the doorknob, thinking there was no sense knocking first. If she was asleep, it would be mean of him to wake her. He opened the door slowly, peered inside.

Hell.

She was lying on the bed, turned onto one side, facing him. The blankets came up as far as her hips, and ended there, in a wrinkled bundle of blue and white. His gaze slid slowly upward from there, and he didn't know if he intended that or not. It just sort of happened. She wore a pretty white nightgown, with pearl buttons up the front, and a thin edging of lace at the V-neck. No sleeves to speak of. Her hair spread out beneath her, cushioning her cheek on the pillow, covering her shoulder in a teasing, peek-a-boo game. And her dark eyes, when he finally got around to focusing on them, were wide open and staring straight into his. For just a second he forgot that he was cool and calm and unflappable. For just a moment he felt a rush of confused excitement. Something that made his skin prickle and his spine tingle and his stomach churn.

Then he bit his lip, gave himself a mental shake. "You...um...ready?"

"*Sí.*" She flung the covers back and got to her feet all in one graceful motion. Her legs were bare from just below the knees, where the nightgown ended, down. Her bare feet were tiny. And sexy.

Sexy? Since when were *feet* sexy? Elliot didn't even think feet were *capable* of being sexy. What the hell was wrong with him?

She came forward, toward the doorway where he stood. And he muttered something really intelligent like, "Don't you, um...want a robe or something?"

She frowned at him, gave her head a shake. "It is very warm here, Elliot. No, I am fine as I am."

The word "fine," he thought, was an understatement. But he wasn't going to argue. There was nothing wrong with the nightgown, unless you counted the fact that he could see her shape silhouetted underneath it every time she walked past any source of light. But nothing real. Just shadows. Tempting, curvy shadows that made him wish he could see more. Then made him wish he would stop thinking such uncharacteristic thoughts.

He guided her down the stairs into the darkened parlor. The only light was that of a thin crescent moon coming through the wide windows, so he took her hand so she wouldn't trip in the darkness. She let him hold it without objection. Even turned hers and linked her fingers through his. Soft and small, her hand. Warm, strong in spite of its size.

He swallowed hard and took her into the kitchen, and only then did he turn on a light. She blinked in the sudden brightness, shook her head. "I will never get used to that."

"Yeah, you will," Elliot said. "You want to sit down? I can make you a cup of tea or something...."

"No, no. I am too eager to learn. There is so much..." Already she was walking to the refrigerator, opening the door. "This is...like an icebox, no?"

"Yes, it's called a refrigerator. Keeps food cold." He joined her there as she repeated the word slowly. Closing the door, he opened the smaller one on top. "This part's the freezer. Keeps things even colder."

"Ahh." She examined the small freezer, closed the door, and then eyed the apparatus on the outside of the door. Lifting a hand, she touched it before Elliot could tell her not to, and small ice chunks clattered out to land at her feet. She jumped backward with a small squeak of alarm. The motion put her back flat against Elliot's chest, and his hands closed on her bare, smooth shoulders automatically. He closed his eyes and tried not to groan out loud.

"It's okay, it's okay," he said, to himself as much as to her. "No harm done." Releasing his hold on her with no small twinge of regret, he bent to scoop up the ice, then dumped it into the sink. "That's just an ice maker. For…like on a hot day, when you want a really cold drink." She frowned at him, so he got a glass from the cupboard and demonstrated, first filling it with ice, then with tap water. "See? Instant ice water."

She was still frowning. "It seems…wasteful. Why would anyone need their water so cold?"

Elliot shrugged. "Well, I don't know. It's just…the way it's done. Nowadays, I mean."

"Hmmph."

He didn't think she much approved of his wasteful society. He supposed wasting ice for such trivial things as cold drinks must seem to her like the height of foolishness. Ice must have been a precious commodity where she came from. But she was already moving on, examining the range, the oven, the microwave, as Elliot followed her and tried his best to explain how each item worked. They spent an hour in the kitchen, as she tried things out, practiced with the microwave, learned to read a digital clock.

By the time they moved to the parlor it was past 1:00 a.m., and he wondered why he wasn't bleary-eyed by now. But he couldn't remember a time when he'd been more wide awake. It was her, he realized. Her curiosity, her innocence, her energy. The way she got so excited over the smallest things. It was contagious, and volatile, and maybe a little bit addictive.

And probably why he'd been losing his grip on calm and balance and sanity from the first moment he'd set eyes on her.

In the parlor, she approached the television set with wide, wary eyes.

"This is the most amazing of all," she said, eyeing the dark, silent box.

"Yeah. It is. You want to know what's even more amazing?" She looked at him, dark brows raised. "How it works. Come here, I want to show you something."

He took her arm and led her through the house to the front door, and through it onto the porch. The breeze was chilly, and it blew her nightgown around her legs. He was still in his jeans. "Are you cold? I can get you a jacket if—"

"I am fine. Show me this wonder."

He nodded, but for just a moment his eyes were caught and held by hers. The way the stars were reflected in their ebony depths mesmerized him. And he almost swayed closer to her, before he caught himself and pulled back. He cleared his throat. "This is gonna be a little hard to follow."

"I do not imagine I will understand it, even when you explain it to me."

He smiled at her. "Sure you will. You're smart."

She dipped her head. "I do not feel so smart in this strange world of yours, Elliot. I feel the greatest of fools."

He was quick to shake his head. "Don't. You're not, Esmeralda."

She didn't smile, but he saw a flicker of gratitude in her eyes.

"Okay, well, here goes. You saw the airplane earlier. The craft that flew through the sky, over our heads? You remember?"

She nodded, her eyes widening with the memory.

"It's a mode of travel people use every day. Airplanes carry people all over the world in just hours."

"*Dios!* This is true? You…you have ridden in one of these…airplanes, Elliot?"

He nodded. "Yes, many times. But there is more. See, airplanes only fly from place to place on Earth. Man has invented spaceships…flown all the way to the moon. Even walked on it."

Her eyes narrowed on his face. Then, with a knowing smirk, she shook her head hard. "No, Elliot, don't tease me. You say you do not think me stupid. Don't test my intelligence by spinning such tales and trying to make me believe."

"It's true, Esmeralda."

She stared at him for a very long moment. Then, slowly, she sank down onto the uppermost step of the porch, tipping her head back and staring in wonder at the moon. "It cannot be…. Elliot?" Her voice dropped to a whisper. "What did they find there?"

He smiled. "Not much. The moon is pretty barren. No life. Just rocks and craters and dust."

"Oooh, but to see it…"

"I'll find you some pictures. But we're getting off the subject. I told you all this so I could explain how the television works."

"*Sí, sí.* But what can spaceships and men on the moon have to do with the little box that holds tiny people inside of it?"

He smiled widely, utterly enchanted by her. "We take pictures of people with a machine called a camera." She nodded. "Nowadays, some cameras take moving pictures. The pictures are sent out with special signals, to satellites we've put in outer space. The satellites are like…like big objects that constantly orbit the earth." He made a circular motion with his finger to demonstrate. "The signals hit the satellites, and then those same signals are sent back down to…to these things, all over the world." He got up, stepped off the porch and pointed at the dish mounted on the roof. "That's a satellite dish. It is hooked to the television. It catches the signals sent from the satellite in space and sends them to the television."

She eyed the thing, but shook her head. "It is all so…so confusing."

"I know. You probably didn't need to know all of that. All you really need to understand is that the images on the television aren't real. They're stories acted out by actors, just like I told you. Sometimes they get pretty violent, even frightening. But it's all make-believe."

"You are sure it's not real?" she asked, wide eyes staring into his in a way that seemed almost… trusting.

"No. It's not real. It's just a new way of telling stories."

She blinked, seeming to understand that concept, at least.

"Come on, I'll show you how to change the channels and run the VCR."

She looked at his outstretched hand, then shook her head. "No…I…I don't want to learn any more just now."

He tilted his head to one side. "Okay. All right, that's fine." She didn't move. Just stayed where she was, standing barefoot on the cool grass, with the breeze chilling her body and having the expected results—which were clearly visible through the thin nightgown she wore. "Uh…so what do you want to do?"

Lowering her head—to hide her eyes, he thought—she said, "I want my pendant back. I want…I want to go home."

Hell, was she crying? He touched her bare shoulder, slid his palm over it. "It's going to be all right, Esmeralda. If you want to go back there, I promise I'll find a way to get you there. But…but you have to know what will be waiting."

"How can I know? Nothing is real, nothing is as it seems, and I… Elliot…if I could travel forward in time, why can I not go backward as well? Why can I not go back to…to a time before my father was murdered? I could protect him, and he might…" Her voice seemed to choke itself off, and she turned her head again.

"Why do you do that?" he asked her.

"Do what?"

"Hide your tears? As if you're ashamed of them. You shouldn't be, you know. I cried when my parents died. I still do, sometimes. Hell, Esmeralda, you have to cry, or go crazy. I know you're hurting. So there's no need to try to hide it from me."

She looked up at him, very slowly. He saw the wetness gleaming in her eyes, the tracks of tears on her cheeks. "To show a man your weakness is to give him a weapon to use against you," she told him.

"Now, come on. You don't really think I'm the kind of man who'd do that, do you?"

Sniffing softly, she shook her head. "No. I don't. And that frightens me, Elliot. For I could easily be wrong about you."

"Only if you think I'd do anything to hurt you," he said. The next thing he knew, he was pulling her closer, and her head was resting on his chest, and her shoulders were trembling, and he was holding her.

Damn, she felt good in his arms. Soft and small, and in a second she seemed to relax against him, and that felt even better.

He wanted to kiss her.

The realization hit him right between the eyes with the force of a wrecking ball, and it almost sent him reeling. What a stupid, harebrained notion! He must be an idiot to even think of such a thing...especially given her history with men, and her tendency to blow molehills into mountains and mountains into entire planets!

Yet he kept thinking about it. About what her lips would taste like, how they would move against his, how they would feel.

To hell with the consequences, he decided with a totally uncharacteristic lack of logic. He was going to do it.

Chapter 6

She must remain unmoved by him!

Esmeralda heard the words echoing in her mind even as her body began to soften, melted, it seemed, by Elliot Brand's warm embrace. His chest felt good, solid and strong beneath her head. His arms were tight and warm around her. His voice was kind and sincere...if a bit uncertain.

Yet she could not afford to soften toward him. He was her enemy, she must remember that. Just as Eldon had been. And as for his sweet embrace and soft words—those were likely as false as were her own. And even if they were genuine, that would change the moment he realized that her intent was to reclaim her home. There was no doubt in her mind of that. While she must act the part of grateful guest, she could not let that pretense become real. She *must* not!

Stiffening slightly, she pulled away from him. "I...think it is enough for tonight, Elliot." She knew that he realized she was no longer talking about the lessons.

He nodded, looking confused and maybe as alarmed by that warm awareness between them as she was. "Okay. Look, I know I said we'd creep out and search for your pendant, but the family knows it's missing now, so there's no need."

"You told them?" She knitted her brow.

"Well, they don't know it's yours. You see Taylor…Wes's wife, she found it. Wanted to take it to a university near here, so they could try to figure out how old it was, who made it and so on. It's…it's what she does."

Narrowing her eyes, Esmeralda said, "I see. But it *is* mine, Elliot. In my family for generations, just as this…" She bit her lip to stop herself from finishing, the sentence. *Just as this ranch is mine,* she'd been about to say, and she thought Elliot knew it. She saw that brief flash of understanding—and perhaps alarm—in his eyes. "It is mine."

"I know."

He said no more. So she did. "When we find the pendant—"

"*If* we find it," Elliot interrupted.

"*Sí.* If we find it, I will claim it as my own."

He nodded slowly. "It means a lot to you, this pendant?"

She made her eyes widen in surprise. "It has sent me forward in time, Elliot Brand. It has mystical powers, and it is rightfully mine. But even if it were but an ordinary amulet, it would mean a great deal to me. As would anything my father gave to me before he was murdered."

He nodded, his eyes soft and sympathetic, his hand

running gently over her hair, as if he would soothe her somehow. "Okay. Okay, if we find the amulet, it's yours. I'll just have to tell Wes we didn't have any luck. Though I'll tell you, Esmeralda, it pains me to lie to my brother."

She blinked, because his words surprised her more than once. First, that he would concede ownership of her pendant to her so easily, and then that he—or *any* Brand—would find deceit offensive. "We could," she said softly, "tell him the truth."

Elliot looked at her, really hard. "I don't know. I want to. My instincts are telling me to do just that, just spill it all. Keeping secrets from my family isn't something I'm accustomed to, and I sure as hell don't like it. But something else is telling me to keep my mouth shut. How could I expect them to believe any of this, after all? I'm not even sure I believe it myself. Part of me still thinks this is all some dream I'm having—that I'm lying in a hospital bed somewhere with a head injury from that crash, and the rest of this is all just in my mind."

Tilting her head slowly, she tried to follow his words. "You think I am just a part of some dream you are having, Elliot Brand?"

He shrugged. "I *did* hit my head. Maybe you are."

"I am no dream," she said, slightly offended that he might think so, though she didn't know why she should be. "And if you think I am, you are a fool."

"Hell, it's no more far-fetched than anything else that's happened today."

"No?" She put her hands on her hips, lifted her chin. "I've known a lot of men, Elliot Brand. I know the way they think, and I know the way they dream. And I know that if this were all a part of some dream of yours, you would not be spending all of your time teaching me about space planes and air ships and *sat-o-lite* plates. Would you, Elliot?''

He only blinked down at her, looking shocked and embarrassed. But she knew she'd hit her target well, for his cheeks darkened so that the blush was visible even by the light of the waxing crescent moon. He wanted her. She had seen it in his eyes, felt it in his every touch, from the moment she'd met him.

Smiling a little sheepishly, averting his eyes, he stuffed his hands into his pockets. ''I suppose you have a point there.''

She was surprised he admitted it. Sighing, she turned and, lifting the hem of the white nightgown, started up the porch steps. ''Thank you for the lessons,'' she said, her back to him. ''Good night, Elliot Brand.''

''Good night,'' he said, very softly. But he didn't follow her inside.

Damn her for putting the suggestion into his head.

Elliot rolled over and punched the pillow. He tried to tell himself he might have been doomed to dream about her all night even if she *hadn't* brought it up, but her assumption certainly hadn't helped any.

Every time he closed his eyes, every time he even started to drift off, she was there…in his room, standing beside the bed, staring down at him with those dark, exotic eyes full of mystery. She would unbutton that innocent-looking white nightgown, one button at a time, starting at the neck and moving downward. Every time she got a little farther before he would wake up in bed, coated in sweat, shivering, shaking and gasping for breath—and wishing to God he could stay asleep long enough to see what happened next.

She slept later than was her custom in the morning, likely due to the mental and physical exhaustion of yesterday's happenings…and, of course, her late night being tutored by Elliot.

He, she was surprised to learn, had risen early and left the house before she even came down the stairs. It angered her just a bit to think he had slept so well that he had been able to rise by dawn, while she had tossed and turned all night, battling odd dreams that made no sense—dreams in which he swept her into his arms and kissed her. Ridiculous! She used to dream about Eldon that way. And look what he had done to her!

Even more ridiculous was the small niggling of guilt that had begun to pester her. The ranch was rightfully hers. She had nothing to feel guilty about. She hadn't even *done* anything to reclaim it—yet.

At any rate, by the time she woke and dressed, she seemed to be the only person left in the house besides the sheriff's wife, who was humming and stacking dishes into one of the many machines Elliot had introduced her to last night. The dish-washing-machine.

Secretly, Esmeralda thought people had become incredibly lazy, if they no longer felt they could so much as wash a dish without help, but she wouldn't say so.

"Esmeralda," Chelsea Brand said with a smile when she saw her in the doorway. "You must be starved. I kept a plate hot for you. Come, sit down. You want coffee?" She was pouring it before Esmeralda could even finish nodding, and as she took her seat, Chelsea set first the steaming mug and then a heaping plate down in front of her. "How did you sleep, hon?"

"Er...fine. Thank you."

Chelsea pulled out a chair beside Esmeralda's and sat down with her own cup of coffee. "You... um...look better this morning."

"*Sí*, I feel a good deal better."

"So...have you decided what you are going to do?"

Esmeralda glanced up at the woman, frowning. "Do?"

"About this guy...the one who hit you. You don't have to go back to him, you know. I mean..." She bit her lip. "I'm sorry. It's none of my business. But you can stay with us for as long as you need to."

Esmeralda understood at last. "Ahh. No, I...I will not see him again. However...ah...there is a matter you might perhaps help me with."

"Anything. You name it."

Esmeralda nodded. "Elliot...he tells me you help a lot of women deal with certain troubles."

"Yes, I do. No woman needs to let a man brutalize her, Esmeralda. Not in this day and age. It's unacceptable, and yet some women continue to stay with abusive men. You, though..." She shook her head slowly. "You don't seem the type to take it."

Esmeralda smiled. "You are right about that. I am not."

"Good for you." Chelsea smiled back.

Esmeralda had her figured out by then. The woman was a crusader, defending the rights of other women, protecting them, helping them, on a mission, it seemed. Her cause was a good one, Esmeralda thought. Yet, she also thought something else.

"Not so good for me, I am afraid."

"No? Do you want to talk about it?"

Esmeralda nodded. "But I must have your promise this discussion will go no further. I—"

"Say no more. I promise, this is just between us."

The guilt prickled a bit more insistently. Esmeralda shook it away. "*Gracias*. This is my problem, Chelsea. I had a home, property, but it is now in the possession of…of this man."

Chelsea frowned. "Whose name is on the deed?"

"His. Although…only because he tricked my father. Now my father is dead, and the land that should have been mine, my home, is owned by a swindler."

Chelsea sighed heavily, shaking her head. "I see. Well, you could always take him to court and fight for it that way. But it would be expensive and could take years. It would be so much easier if you were married to the man."

Esmeralda's head came up. "Why?"

Chelsea just blinked at her. "Well, because of community property laws. If you were married, you'd be entitled to half of what he owns when you divorced him. Some judges might give you more, considering what you've been through."

A huge fluttering sensation filled Esmeralda's chest, and she felt her eyes widen.

"Esmeralda?" Chelsea said. "Oh, God, you aren't…are you? Married, I mean?"

Esmeralda blinked down her excitement. "No. No, I am not married."

Chelsea sighed so hard she nearly sagged in relief. "Thank goodness!"

When Esmeralda tilted her head, searching Chelsea's face, Chelsea blushed a little and looked away. "I mean…well, I just thought…" She shrugged. "I'm relieved for Elliot's sake."

"Why?"

Smiling slightly, Chelsea said, "Oh, come on. I've seen the way he looks at you, Esmeralda. How protective he is of you. How…how scattered and distracted he's been since he brought you home. Not himself at all."

"Isn't he?"

"No. He isn't. He's always so calm, so darned unflappable. You came along and shook things up for him…and to be honest, I think you're exactly what he needed. You've knocked him for a loop, you know."

Esmeralda shook her head, bewildered by Chelsea's words. "No. I…I didn't know that at all. I never meant to…"

"Oh, Esmeralda, I know you didn't." Lowering her eyes, Chelsea paused, then said, "I just hope…"

"Please, go on. You hope…?"

Meeting her gaze, Chelsea said, "I hope you won't hurt him."

Lowering her head, Esmeralda sighed. She didn't want to hurt Elliot Brand. But she couldn't promise this woman she wouldn't do just that, because it was obvious to her now what she had to do. If she wanted her home back—or a portion of it, which seemed to be the best she could hope for—she would have to marry its owner. She would have to marry Elliot Brand. And in her time, there was one tried-and-true method for making a man marry you. Well, two, counting true love, which would take too long and be too complicated. She just hoped the oldest trick in the book of womankind still worked.

Elliot was surprised as all hell to glance up from the stable floor he'd been cleaning and see Esmeralda standing in the open doorway. She was looking around, sniffing the air, nodding. He bet the one place she wouldn't see as totally alien to her would be right here. Saddle leather and molasses-flavored grain and horseflesh were the same stable smells she would have known in her own time.

"I am not bothering you, I hope?" she said.

Elliot felt his brows rise. Since when did she ask before bothering him? "Uh, no. No, I was just finishing up."

She stepped farther inside. "I thought I could help you." Shrugging delicately, she said, "I could not convince Chelsea to let me do a thing in the house, even though I told her I am a very good housekeeper."

Now where the hell was she going with this? Elliot managed not to grin as he let her go on. "Are you now?"

"Oh, *sí!* I kept my father's house spotless for him! And he used to say I was the best cook in all of Texas!"

"Really?"

She nodded hard. Her dark hair moved when she did, and the sun behind her made a golden halo around her head. A *misleading* halo, if Elliot were any judge of things.

"I suppose we'll have to convince Chelsea to let you loose in the kitchen, then."

She smiled demurely when he knew full well there

wasn't a demure bone in her body. "I would like that very much." Then she looked up. "But you know that is not all I can do. I was raised on this...on a ranch, after all."

He caught the slip. *This* ranch, she was raised on *this* ranch, that was what she'd been about to say. And she hadn't made any bones about telling him so before. So why skate over it now?

"I can muck out stalls and pitch hay, groom horses and tend sick cattle, and string wire for fence. My father used to say I was as good as any two of his gauchos."

"I'll bet he did," Elliot said. Again she nodded. "So why are you telling me all this?"

Looking up slowly, she shrugged, then looked away.

"You sound like you're applying for a job, Esmeralda. What's up? Hmm? What are you thinking?"

"Nothing." She turned to the side, pretending great interest in the implements that hung from nails and hooks on the back wall. "I just did not want you to think I was...useless. I mean, I can do many, many things, even though I am confused by many others."

"Well, sure you can. I never thought you were useless, Esmeralda."

She peered up at him from huge dark eyes. "You didn't?"

"Hell no. You're smart, and whatever you don't understand, you'll learn. I guarantee you that much. I don't know what you're worried about, Esmeralda, but you don't have to impress me."

"I don't?"

He came out of the stall, set the heavy shovel aside and tugged off his barn gloves as he looked her right in the eyes. "I saw you facing down a pack of killers. Remember?"

She smiled a little, lowering her gaze.

"That impressed me enough to last a lifetime. Okay?"

"*Sí.* Okay."

"Now why don't you tell me why you really came out here?"

She lifted her head fast. "I...I guess I got lonely."

"What, Bubba and Chelsea aren't enough company for you?"

She shrugged. "They don't know the truth about me. I feel...false around them. Always on my guard, you know?"

He nodded, sighing, understanding, but not having a clue what to do to make her feel more at ease. "I'm finished here. What do you say we take a ride together? I'll show you around the place and—"

"*You'll* show *me* around the place?" Her head snapped up as if it had been held in place by a spring that had just given way. "You think I don't know my own ranch like the back of my hand?" As she spoke, her eyes flashed, her nostrils flared and her hands flew expressively. He half expected her to punch him in the nose, but she seemed to catch herself instantly. She bit her lip, lowering her head fast. "I am sorry! *Dios,* what is the matter with me?"

Elliot stood still for a moment, not sure which was the real woman. The flash of fury and anger he'd seen a moment ago, or this recalcitrant lamb. He liked the lamb better, but doubted she was more than an illusion. "Forget it," he said.

"Oh, no, please! I do want to go riding with you,

Elliot. Very much! And…and I want to see how this place has changed over the years.''

Studying her face carefully, for he sensed some sort of a trap, Elliot finally nodded. ''All right then. I'll saddle us up a pair of mounts.''

''Sí, bueno.''

She rode along beside Elliot Brand and wondered how she would manage to get him to bed her. The logical way would be to flirt and tease and tempt him until he gave in to her wishes, all the while believing it was his own idea. But that could take time, and she had no idea how long she would have here. She half expected the skull's magic to come to life from wherever it was and send her back to her own time without a moment's notice. Or maybe it would happen when they found it again…*if* they found it.

No, she had to work fast, and that way was just too slow.

But what else could she do?

Other than getting past that first part of it, her plan was a good one. Elliot put a lot of effort into appearing to be an honorable man. It seemed that he and his entire family valued their good name. And no matter how many things might have changed over the years, one thing couldn't have, could it? A man would still feel he ought to marry a woman if he made her pregnant. Especially a man who considered himself, or wanted others to consider him, honorable.

It was the best bet she could make. She had nothing to lose. She only had to seduce the man into her bed and then claim to be carrying his child. It would, of course, be best if she were actually telling the truth about her condition. In this age, there were likely methods for verifying pregnancy. Yes, she should make sure she became pregnant. It would be easy enough to do. She didn't know what methods women used today, but her own aunts had taught her all about such things. She could figure out the perfect time using no more than her own monthly cycle and the phase of the moon. She would get pregnant. Elliot Brand would marry her, and then she would be entitled to half of her ranch, which was better than none at all.

So the trick was to get him into her bed.

He wanted her. She thought he did, anyway. But he was carrying this "gentleman" act of his so far that he was actually resistant to the idea of despoiling her, for it would ruin the noble facade. The fool.

She'd never in her life encountered this particular problem. How odd.

They rode past the small stream where she'd played as a child, and she eyed the area around it. There were more saplings, and the few trees that had been here had grown to massive proportions. She began to let her developing plan slip to the back of her mind as she looked at the land where she'd been born and raised. "Elliot, look!"

She pointed, and he followed with his eyes. "That tree," she said, and she got off her horse and hurried toward it. "This is where I carved my initials when I was only six years old!" Running her fingers over the coarse bark, she searched around the tree for the spot. When she saw it, she was so excited she forgot about her scheme and barely noticed that Elliot had gotten off his horse and come to stand beside her.

Her fingers traced the letters. *E.M.*

"Esmeralda Montoya," Elliot whispered. "Well I'll be...you...you really did live here."

She stared at the tree, though there was a dampness to look through now. "*Sí*. Did you not believe me?"

"I did. I just...seeing this, makes it real, you know?"

"To me, too. To see how much this tree has grown..." She shook her head, turned around, looking at the low hills and meadows in the distance. "Off that way, about five miles, was where my father first built. It was a small cabin. He abandoned it when he met my mother, and it fell to ruin. That was when he built the big house, on the site where your home now stands. I used to go out to the old cabin sometimes. Even though there was little left but the foundation of flat stones stacked one upon the other."

Elliot nodded. "I've seen them. I always wondered who lived there, who left those stones behind."

She smiled, nodded. "I found a cave near there. It was my secret place. As a girl, I wrote on its walls with chalk."

"Yeah?" he asked, smiling. "I didn't know about any cave. What did you write?"

She lowered her head. "The same as here. My initials...and those of a boy I thought I knew." Licking her lips, she cleared her throat, shifted her gaze and changed the subject. "My mother's grave, and my father's, are just over this way," she said, pointing. "Not too far from here. There is a clearing, beyond the stream. Mama called it her secret meadow. It was her favorite place...." Without thinking, she started forward, moving through the trees, seeking that old familiar spot. But when she got to the place where the graves of her parents should have been, she saw only more trees. Young ones, saplings, sprouting as thick as grass. Looking this way and that, Esmeralda whispered, "Oh, *Dios,* where are they?"

"Now, hold on," Elliot said, coming forward, gripping her hand tight in his. "They must be here somewhere. Let's just look around." He drew her in among the young trees.

But though they searched and searched, Esmeralda did not see her parents' graves. And she grew agitated, angry, more and more enraged with every step. "There were tombstones!" she cried. "Fine granite tombstones! Anyone would have known they were buried here! But no, you and your stinking ancestors, you had to tear them down. You had to wipe out every trace that my family had ever been here!"

"For crying out loud, will you calm down already?"

"No! I will not calm down! I cannot find my family, and it's all because of yours! Damn you Brands to hell! Damn you all!"

She spun around, putting her back to him, covering her face with her hands, and when she did, she glimpsed something through the trees. The grave stones? Could it be them?

"I vow, woman, I've never seen anybody blow up faster than you do in my life. We haven't even looked thoroughly yet, and already you're... Hey, where are you going now?"

"I found them! Oh, they *are* still here after all." She ran through the trees, found the stones and, falling to her knees, embraced them, one and then the other. Then she sat back, examining those granite faces, and shaking her head very slowly as she tried to read the inscriptions.

"See that?" Elliot asked. "My infamous ancestors didn't tear them down after all."

"No."

"And if they had, Esmeralda, it wouldn't have been my fault. You've got to get that through your head."

She nodded slowly. "I suppose you are right," she said in a softer voice. "But your family—your *family*—certainly has done nothing to preserve these graves, have they?"

"What?"

When she glanced over her shoulder at him, he looked confused. "Look at this!" She ran her hands over the tombstones again, and as she did, bits fell away like dust. "Crumbling. Ruined. You can barely read their names here!" She got to her feet, and looked around her. "And there are weeds and saplings and—"

"Dammit, woman, will you slow down a minute!"

She clapped her mouth shut, all but biting her lip to keep her temper in check. Oh, but she was furious. She wanted to strangle him, not make love to him. Which was not going to help her plan one bit.

Elliot could see anger flashing in those eyes of hers. It had sprung out of nowhere, like a freak summer storm. "We didn't know they were here, okay?" he said. "If we had, we'd have kept the plot up. But, Esmeralda, you're talking about two crumbling pieces of granite in a thick patch of scrub brush on a fifty-thousand-acre ranch. We just never saw them there."

She stared at him hard for a long moment. Then the fight seemed to go out of her, and her knees bent. Maybe the fight was the only thing keeping them straight. But she wound up kneeling on the ground, near those gravestones, her head hanging low, her palm still pressed gently to the cool, crumbling granite.

"Ah, hell, I liked you better when you were screaming at me." Elliot knelt, too. He didn't want to, but he took hold of her shoulders anyway, turned her to face him, then brushed the damp tendrils of hair away from her tearstained cheek with one hand and studied her face. Smooth, dark skin, black eyes and thick glistening lashes. He thought she was like all four seasons wrapped in one unpredictable day. She could go from sunshine to blizzard, from heat wave to ice storm, from gentle breeze to lightning bolt, all in the blink of an eye. And he had no idea what sort of weather was coming next.

"I'm sorry," he said, carefully, slowly. His nerves felt raw. Hell, it seemed he was always tense since she'd come into his life. What had happened to his legendary calm? "I...I'd be upset if I found my family's resting place in this condition, too." Tense, he stood waiting as she looked up into his eyes, her own probing and sharp.

"*Sí*, you would. It is not right."

He felt like he was in the eye of a hurricane, just waiting for the storm to kick in again and blow him to kingdom come. It was like tiptoeing through a minefield, talking to her.

"No, it's not right. But now that we know they're here...we can fix it. We can make it right."

Her brows rose. The storm clouds in her eyes seemed to part just a bit. "Fix it?"

"Yeah," he rushed on, sensing he might, for once, have said the right thing to her. "We can." He got to his feet, tugging her up as well and looking around. "We can clear out all this brush," he said, moving his hand in a wide arc to indicate the area around the two dilapidated tombstones. "And rake up the ground, a bit, you know? Smooth it out, chuck the stones out of here." He was into the idea now, seeing it all in his mind's eye as he went along. "We'll plant some grass, some flowers, whatever you want. And then we'll put a fence up around the whole thing. Something pretty. Wrought iron or maybe..." He trailed off then, because he'd glanced at her and noticed the way she was looking at him.

Her head was slightly tilted to one side, and her eyes were wide, and there was a tiny crease between her brows.

"What?" he asked.

Shaking her head slowly, still staring at his face, she said, "You...would do all this?"

"Well, sure. I just said I would, didn't I?"

Her eyes narrowed on him then. *"Why?"*

"Oh, for crying out loud." Elliot took his hat off and ran one hand back and forth through his hair in frustration. "Because it's the right thing to do! Hell, Esmeralda, this not-trusting-any-man-as-far-as-you-can-throw-him routine is getting old, you know that?"

She shrugged, turning slightly away from him, her glance sidelong now, rather than dead-on. "Why *should* I trust a man, eh? I have never known any man worthy of my trust."

"That's bull. It's bull, Esmeralda. A big fat lie. Just an excuse you use for your lousy behavior and your bad manners and your own fear."

Her chin went up, but she kept her face averted. "I have no fear."

"Oh, yes, you do. You're scared to death, Esmeralda. I'm not sure why yet, but I know it's the truth."

"You know nothing!" This time she did spin to face him, her hair flicking over her shoulders, her eyes pinning him to the spot and threatening to toast him to a cinder.

"I do so," he said, daring to face her and tempt her wrath. "And I'll tell you what else I know. You're lying when you say you've never met a man you could trust. Lying right through your pretty teeth, Esmeralda. You know all men aren't bad. You know it because of the one who's buried right there," he said, nodding toward her father's tombstone. "Or are you going to tell me he was a faithless bastard like the rest of us?"

The blaze in her eyes fizzled as if he'd dumped water on it. She looked toward her father's grave. "He was...he was a good man. A fine man."

"Shoot, I know that."

Slanting a damp, sideways glance at him, she said, "How would you know that, Elliot? You never met him."

"No, but I've met his daughter."

Their eyes held for a long moment, and for the life of him Elliot didn't know why the hell he'd said what he had, much less in the tone he had. It had sounded almost...intimate. "I mean," he added, tearing his eyes away and focusing instead on the scuffed toes of his boots, "I mean, you loved him a whole lot. That's obvious. You wouldn't have if he wasn't a good man."

When he peeked up at her, she was staring hard at

the tombstone. "*Sí.* But even he..." Then she slammed her eyes closed tight, shook her head.

"Even he what?"

"Nothing. Nothing. I will not discuss my father with you, Elliot Brand. You are right, he was a good man."

"And you trusted him."

"*Sí.*"

"Then what makes you think he's the only one in the world, huh? Why do you just blithely assume I'm rotten to the core and that every nice thing I do has some ulterior motive behind it? Why can't you give me the benefit of the doubt and assume maybe I'm one of the good guys, like your dad was?"

She drew a long, slow breath. "It is a mistake to trust a man," she said, her voice thickly accented and slightly hoarse, "Even one of the good guys."

Elliot gave his head a shake and wondered how the hell he'd lost what had seemed like a winning argument. "Why do you say that?"

Lowering her head, she shook it quickly. "I...I don't know. I shouldn't have spoken."

He put a hand to her face, cupping it, making her look at him. "But you did say it. And I want to know why."

"No."

She closed her eyes, as if to keep his probing gaze away. And all of a sudden, Elliot glimpsed the truth. She was hurting. Hurting down deep, and not just from her father's death, either. He'd let her down in some way. The one man she'd believed in, the one man she'd trusted, had let her down. Or that was the way she saw it, at least.

"Is it...because he died? Because you know damn

well he didn't have a choice about that, Esmeralda. He wouldn't have left you if it had been up to him."

Those black eyes flashed open so suddenly he almost jumped backward. Their impact when they landed was like a blow every time. "Oh, no? Then why did he send me away, eh? Why did he decide my life for me, and like some mighty king send me to my aunt's in Mexico when my place was with him?" She pulled free of Elliot's gentle hands, turning briskly away. "I should have been here. Fighting to defend our home, right at his side." Her voice broke, wobbled here and there, and Elliot knew she was battling a full-blown crying jag.

He went to her, turned her around, and wrapped his arms around her shoulders, even though she stood stiff as a statue, holding her face frozen like a mask. "You know what I think?" he asked, as she stood stiffly in his embrace. She shook her head. "I think it's not your father you're mad at, so much as it is yourself."

Again, her head moved, but her body was softening in his arms now, head resting on his chest and shoulder. God, her hair smelled like heaven. And her body fit against his as if it was the missing piece of a jigsaw puzzle.

"Why would I be angry with myself, Elliot? He forced me to leave. I had no choice."

"I know that. But you feel guilty all the same. You think maybe, if you'd stayed, he might still be alive."

Her breath rushed out of her all at once, as if he'd punched her in the belly. It came out in a warm whoosh that bathed his neck. "I do think that. I see it, sometimes, you know, in my mind. How I would have killed them all to protect my father and my home.''

''Yeah. I know. I used to think that if I'd been with my parents the day they died, I could somehow have prevented the accident that killed them, too. But that's a fantasy. You know that, right? If you'd been with your father, you'd likely as not have died with him that day.''

''*Sí.* You are right.''

''So you need to figure the way I do. Fate has a plan for you, and dying with your father that day wasn't a part of it. Fate wanted you to live. You weren't there because you weren't meant to be, and that's all she wrote.''

Lifting her head from Elliot's shoulder, she stared into his eyes. ''If Fate wanted me to live, then why did I end up on the gallows facing death, Elliot?''

He lifted his eyebrows. ''You didn't die, Esmeralda.''

''Well, only because you came and…and…'' She blinked her eyes slowly. ''The skull…the skull is said to restore human beings to their proper place.'' She looked at Elliot, then at the trees around them, and the rolling meadows beyond that. ''But…but this is not my proper place. This is a strange new world to me.''

Elliot shrugged. ''It's where you ended up. So to my way of thinking, it must be where you belong. Things happen the way they're meant to, Esmeralda.''

And you were meant to be right here. On this ranch, with me.

Elliot blinked as the odd thought whispered through his mind, and then he rapidly thanked his lucky stars he hadn't spoken it aloud.

"Will you promise me something, Elliot Brand?" she asked, her voice uncharacteristically soft.

Anything. That was what he thought as he looked down into those wide, bottomless black eyes, with their long, thick sable lashes. But he said, "Depends."

"Promise me that no matter what happens...you will never send me away from this place, the way my father did."

He felt a lump come into his throat. "Fair is fair, Esmeralda. And I do promise you that. I just wish I could give you...something more." He bent and brushed the moss off a rotting log, waved for her to sit, and when she did, he stuck his hands in his pockets, and began to pace back and forth. "I believe you when you say your father was swindled out of this place. I mean, hell, how can I not? I met those ancestors of mine face-to-face. It's pretty clear what kind of men they were."

She blinked up at him, looking astonished. "You...you are admitting this?"

"Sure. I just...I don't know what can be done about it now. I mean, it's not our fault that three or four generations ago our ancestors pulled a fast one." He shrugged, shaking his head. "It's not just me that's involved here. It's the whole family. The ranch belongs to all of us. I mean, it's been in the family for a hundred years. And we've added to it, improved it, cleared old forests and planted new ones. There are ponds and wells that never existed in your time, and buildings. Our home, for heaven's sake..." He drew a deep breath, blew it out again. "There are the kids to think of, too, you know? The next generation." Licking his lips, he waited for her to speak, and when she said nothing, he went on. "When our parents died, the ranch was left to all six of us equally. My brother Ben sold his share back to us and used the money to build his martial-arts school in town. The entire upper floor is his home, and it's pretty fabulous. Wes, he sold us his share so he could buy a place of his own. Sky Dancer Ranch, he calls it. He and Taylor raise Appaloosas there. Then Adam sold his share, too, so he could start up his dude ranch on the far side of town."

"So the ranch is owned now by…?" she asked.

He was deep in thought now, pacing and talking, and feeling that she was getting the short end of the stick no matter how thoroughly he tried to explain it all to her. "Garrett, Jessi and I each own a third. We planned to keep it all together, so we could pass it on to the next generation. Little Bubba, and Maria-Michele, and Ben's baby when it comes. You know?"

He looked at her. She lowered her head to hide her eyes.

"I know," he said. "You have as much right to be here as any of us. More, maybe. But how the hell can I explain that to them?"

"I don't know."

"I'll tell you this much," he said. "You've got free run of this place. And you can stay here for as long as you want, come and go as you please. Just like one of the family. I'll make sure of it."

"I…appreciate that." Why did he get the feeling she was gritting her teeth behind those words?

"I wish I could do more. I just don't see how I can."

"Then that will have to be enough," she said, her voice soft. Dangerously soft.

He nodded, expecting an explosion, not getting one. "So, um...how 'bout we ride back to the house, pick up some tools, and come back here to get to work on this spot?"

"*Sí.* Whatever you wish."

She sure was placid all of a sudden. Elliot didn't think he liked it.

"I will bring our horses," she said, getting to her feet and hurrying back out through the trees, in search of the horses, who were, no doubt, grazing contentedly a few yards off. He stayed where he was, feeling like a criminal. Maybe he needed to think on this some more. It really *wasn't* fair.

A second later, Elliot could have sworn he heard a slap, and then the sound of galloping hooves.

He shook himself out of the guilt and hurried out of the scrub lot. And there he saw Esmeralda standing, hands on her hips, looking at the shrinking form of the mare, who'd apparently bolted. "I don't know what frightened her!" Esmeralda said. Then she shrugged and turned to face Elliot. "I guess we'll have to ride back together."

Why did she sound like an overzealous actress in her first made-for-TV movie? Hell, he didn't know. He gripped the remaining horse's reins and reached out a hand to help Esmeralda mount.

Chapter 7

Oh, *sí,* she would be *endlessly* grateful for the meager crumbs Elliot Brand saw fit to throw her way. She would smile and thank him and accept his *permission* to come and go as she pleased on *her own property!* Of course she would!

For the moment.

She was almost relieved. Because, finally, his placating attitude and his humoring of her, his pitiful dismissal of her righteous claim to this land, made it easy to dislike him again. It reminded her that he was her enemy. His family were her rivals. The killers of her father. The thieves of her heritage. The destroyers of her life. And oh, how she'd needed reminding!

For a time, she had forgotten. For a time, she'd seen only the softness and caring in his eyes. The gentleness of his touch. The tenderness in his voice. The strength in his chest and the breadth of his shoulders. She'd begun to see him as a human being, a man, instead of as a Brand. It was good that he had reminded her. Love a man, love his family, her father had always told her. To know a man, just look at his family. Well, she could never care for a man who came from *this* family.

As a Brand, he was nothing more than an obstacle she had to get past. He was the one thing standing between her and her land.

Yet, as she sat in front of him on his horse, it kept occurring to her that seducing this man was not going to be an altogether unpleasant experience.

He'd helped her up, then climbed up behind her, so her body was nestled tight to his, in the V of his legs. One strong arm was anchored around her waist, while the other held the reins in an easy, masterful grip. He said nothing, but she felt him. She seemed to feel him a lot. She was attuned to him in some way, aware of him. She'd never been quite so in touch with what a man was feeling.

So when he stiffened a bit, right after mounting the horse, she felt it. His nervousness, his discomfort with the intimacy of the position. But she also felt it when he relaxed. His arm sliding ever-so-slightly tighter around her waist. His head dipping just a little, so he could inhale the scent of her hair. His chest cradling her back as the horse rocked beneath them. And his hips rocked with the horse, hers rocked with his, and the motion mocked her plan to seduce him, make love to him, and feel nothing. The wind blew, and she let herself relax in Elliot's arms. The silent ride back took on an intimacy that she hadn't expected.

To speak would be to break that spell. He seemed to sense it as she did, and so he didn't speak. She didn't, either. When they finally rode up to the stables back at the ranch, she knew when he smiled, felt the smile in every part of him, and she smiled at the same time.

The mare she'd meanly sent running off was standing in front of the stables, waiting for them.

Esmeralda turned her head, met Elliot's eyes, saw the smile she'd known would be there. But as their gazes locked, his smile faded, and the look in his eyes grew darker, more intense. Something in her stomach tightened, clenched, and she thought his lips inched ever so slightly closer to hers....

But then he cleared his throat, blinked his eyes, averted them. "I'll, uh...I'll get what we need." He dismounted quickly and hurried away, leaving her.

Esmeralda blinked as she watched him go, then gave herself a mental shake. What was wrong with her? She was letting him get to her! No doubt that was exactly what he intended. She was not the only one who could plot and scheme to get what she wanted. No indeed, men were the masters of that game. And Elliot Brand was no exception. Holding her that way! Breathing on her neck as they rode silently back to the ranch. The way his palm had warmed where it lay upon her belly. The way he'd looked at her just now. Trying to melt her heart with his eyes.

Dios!

She got off his horse and walked over to the mare, taking her bridle and leading her back inside the stable. There she fed the horse a handful of grain to placate her. "I am sorry about that little slap," she whispered. "It was necessary. And I thank you for the help."

She removed the saddle and bridle, found a rag on

the wall and rubbed the mare down, following up with a grooming brush. By the time she led the horse out the rear door and turned her loose in the pasture, she was certain the mare had forgiven her.

She simply wasn't certain she had forgiven herself. Even for one moment to let herself feel…attracted…to a Brand. Again. She was sure it was just what Elliot wanted. To charm her into giving up any hope of reclaiming her ranch. Well, he would not succeed. She would be the one to win at this game. She might even pretend to be falling for his transparent charms, but all the while she would be the one charming him. Into her bed—and off her land.

"I think this is everything we need."

She looked up abruptly, torn from her thoughts.

From just beyond the open front door of the stable, Elliot frowned at her, probably concerned by the look of pure hatred on her face. Forcing a false smile to replace it, she walked outside to join him. She quickly examined the items he had tossed into the little cart he'd attached behind his horse. Two pairs of gloves, a gardening spade, shovel and heavy iron rake. A sack of grass seed and some heavy-duty shears. And something big and very odd-looking. Orange and white, with a long snout wrapped in a chain of some sort. "What is that?" she asked, pointing.

Elliot looked where she pointed. "Oh, that. It's called a chainsaw. It's for cutting trees and limbs."

She could not possibly see how that thing could cut anything, much less a tree.

"It's very fast, and very noisy. I'll show you when we get out there."

She shrugged, curious in spite of herself.

"Do you want a drink or anything before we head out?" he asked.

"No, Elliot. If I get thirsty I will drink from the stream. I am eager to repair the damage a century of your family's stewardship has done to my family's resting place."

He sent her a look as he climbed into the saddle, pushing his hat more firmly onto his head and sighing. "You sure do hold a grudge."

She shrugged and reached up a hand.

Elliot frowned. "Where's the other horse?"

"I rubbed her down and turned her out to pasture," she told him, making her eyes as wide and innocent as possible. "I've no use for a mare who runs off and leaves me, anyway." She wiggled her hand at him.

Sighing, Elliot closed his around it and tugged her up. She swung her leg in front of him, settling into position just as before.

Elliot didn't move for a moment. Instead he leaned down, and, softly, his breath tickling her ear, he said, "Esmeralda?"

"Sí?"

"I'm glad you turned the mare out. I like this a lot better."

She turned slightly, met his eyes, and didn't have to remind herself to act sincere when she said, "So do I."

The horse leapt into motion. Elliot's arm held her close and safe against him, and in just a short while, they were back at the site.

For the remainder of the afternoon Esmeralda worked in the hot Texas sun. It didn't bother her. She was used to the hot, humid air. Her skin was dark and tough. She would not burn like some gringo woman.

By noon she had shed the light chambray shirt Chelsea had given her and was working only in the scandalously scant "tank top," as the other woman had called it. And her jeans, of course. But there was no shyness in Esmeralda. If she'd shown any, it would have been false, but as it was, she didn't feel the need to pretend. In the first place, she'd seen the way the women dressed in this time. Especially on the television box. They wore far less, revealed far more, than Esmeralda was doing. Besides, she'd been watching Elliot Brand. His eyes were always on her as she worked. The hotter it got, the more she sweated, the harder he stared. Now it seemed he could barely take his eyes off her.

He'd demonstrated the "chained saw," a crude, noisy, smoke-belching thing that seemed designed—as most things in this century were—to cater to the laziness of the modern man. An ordinary saw or hatchet would have done the job just as well. But this one took away the effort needed.

She was truly surprised that the people of this time had not all gone to fat, as easy as their lives were.

They had cleared a twenty-foot area around the two gravestones now. A huge pile of scrub brush and saplings stood in the nearby clearing, and Elliot was working with a shovel to uproot the larger stumps and roots, while Esmeralda was hacking up the topsoil with the iron rake.

But she stopped when she felt his eyes on her.

Looking back at him, she said, "What?"

"Uh…nothing. I…nothing."

She smiled, and tried to feel smug, because she knew exactly what. He was looking at her, and he was liking what he saw. But it was not so easy to do this, because when she'd looked back at him, she'd liked what she'd seen, too. He'd taken off his shirt. He was digging, muscles bunching and flexing with the effort beneath smooth, tanned, sweat-damp skin.

Esmeralda licked her lips and thought that this really was unfair. She wanted him panting for her, desperate for her...she wanted to make him forget logic and common sense and his love for his home and family all for the sake of one brief moment in her arms. But she was the one who kept seeing illicit images in her mind. She was the one who kept feeling as if her soul had been touched by hellfire and forgetting that it was all just make-believe. An act. A means to reclaiming what was hers.

Dios. She wanted him as much as he wanted her. More, perhaps.

Closing her eyes, Esmeralda knew she was in trouble. Her entire plan was in jeopardy. For her body had no common sense, and it was not listening to her brain. Instead it was yearning to mate with the body of the man who was her sworn enemy.

Traitor.

Elliot was not prepared for this kind of thing. So, okay, he'd drooled over swimsuit models and actresses like every other red-blooded Texas male. But this was different. This was Esmeralda, and she was like every man's fantasy all rolled into one beautiful, sloe-eyed confection. He'd never expected to be this close to heaven before. And if he had, he would never have believed he would be this confused as to what to do about it.

She was slender. Long-limbed. Dark. Strong. Her skin gleamed with a fine sheen of perspiration. Her long, black hair curled and clung to her skin in places. And he was aching like he'd never ached in his life. He wanted to go over there and pull her tight against him and kiss her—right now. He wanted…a hell of a lot more than that, too. Everything in his body was itching to act, to move, to touch.

Everything else in him was telling him not to even think about it. Hell, why did his big brother Garrett have to be so damned determined to raise him up right? Not to take advantage of a woman, not to have casual sex, to be responsible and smart, and to think of the woman first and foremost.

He felt like he was being torn right in two!

He wanted her. But he knew acting on that wouldn't be very chivalrous of him, because he could probably talk her into it if he tried, and he would never really be sure if that was because she wanted him, too, or because she thought it was what was expected of her. That maybe she owed him something for saving her life and taking her in. And then there was the whole hundred-year-old episode that had happened yesterday to think about. A bastard who could have been Elliot's twin had tried to rape her. She'd killed him for it, which was as it should be, as far as he was concerned. But how would she react to Elliot's touch now? Would she be remembering that other S.O.B. and shivering with disgust?

He didn't know what to do, dammit. He just didn't know what to do.

But he knew what he wanted. Two things that happened to be at direct odds with each other. He wanted to make love to Esmeralda. And he wanted to convince her, beyond a doubt, that he was utterly unlike any of the men she'd known before.

And it didn't seem to Elliot, even in his confused state of mind, that he could possibly do both. Hell.

He could have groaned in anguish. But he didn't. He just kept working.

All day they worked, and he never touched her. Never kissed her, never tried anything at all!

What in the name of the blessed mother was wrong with him? How was she ever supposed to get her land back if he didn't marry her? And how was she going to make him marry her unless he made her pregnant? And how was he going to make her pregnant when he wouldn't even touch her?

She'd had him alone, out here in the woods all the day through, and now he was packing the tools back into the little cart, drawing his horse over to it and hitching it up. Soon her opportunity would be over!

"We'll wait for a day when it's not so danged windy to burn this brush," he said matter-of-factly. Just making conversation while he piled the tools into the cart. "But for now, this is good. There's supposed to be a little rain tonight. So the grass seed'll take root right off. We can pick up some flower bulbs and such in town. Chelsea would know more about that than I do, but..."

"Elliot?"

He stopped talking, turned to face her. She stood just about two feet in front of him, and it was clear he was making a concerted effort at keeping his eyes off her chest. And succeeding, damn him.

"It's...so hot. And we've worked so hard. Isn't there a...a water hole where we could go to...ah... cool off?"

"Cool off?" he repeated.

"Sí." She offered a slow smile, tugged the damp shirt away from her skin. "I don't want to go back to the house so sticky. What about the stream?"

"Oh, well, hey, you don't want to go in the stream. It's too damn cold. I mean, uh, you'd have goose bumps the size of…" He blinked fast, gave his head a shake.

"I don't care. I just need to cool off." She turned away, started marching off toward the stream, and called over her shoulder, "You don't have to wait for me, Elliot. You can go on without me. I will walk back to the ranch on my own."

Odd, she thought, how she already knew him well enough to know that he wouldn't consider that an option.

And then that thought led to another. If he was truly too decent to let a guest wander around alone after dark, then maybe he wasn't putting on a big act after all. Maybe he really was nothing like his ancestors.

But that had no bearing on her situation. She needed her ranch back, and the moral character of its wrongful owner didn't matter in the least.

"Now, I can't let you be doing that. I'll come with you," he was saying, and when she glanced behind her it was to see him hurrying to catch up. "Just one quick dip, though. The horse is all hitched up and ready to go. All right?"

"Okay." She blinked at him. "Whatever you say, Elliot."

"Right."

"Is this a good spot?" She'd reached the banks of the stream now and, walking along the edge, had located a place where the stream widened and deepened. A natural pool of crystalline water.

''As good as any,'' Elliot said, sounding genuinely unenthused.

The sun was on its way to setting. A soft pink hue had settled over the sky, just a whisper darker than daylight, but a shade less than twilight still. ''No one will come along, will they, Elliot?'' she asked, feigning shyness…sensing it was called for this time.

He looked at her, said no, then looked again. ''Why would you ask that?''

''Well, I don't intend to bathe in public, silly!'' she said. And gritting her teeth, stiffening her spine, she peeled the sweat-damp tank top off over her head.

Elliot swore and quickly turned away. She pretended not to notice and shucked off the jeans, as well, standing there in only the small panties and bra she still was unused to. And finally she took a step and jumped into the water.

When he heard the splash, her unwilling voyeur looked her way again, probably thinking it was safe now to do so. But Esmeralda was beyond caring what he thought. The water was liquid *ice!* Her body went rigid with cold, and she surfaced, found her footing and hugged herself. Her teeth chattered, and her entire body felt as if it were turning blue. She swore, too. For far different reasons than Elliot had, she suspected. Shivering violently, she walked toward the edge through the waist-deep water.

Elliot grinned at her. ''Told you it was cold.'' He came closer, no longer embarrassed, extending a hand.

She took it. ''You didn't t-tell me it was frozen!'' she said accusingly.

He pulled her up, and she went…right up out of the water and right into his arms. He yelped and would have backed off, but she gripped him and held on. "Don't you dare push me away," she stammered. "I'm *freezing!*"

"Yow!" No doubt the cold water on her body was chilling him, too, but he stood still as she pressed against him, even put his arms around her after a moment. "So, are you cooled off enough now?" he asked her.

"*Sí.* Too cooled off."

"Let me get my shirt for you." He let her go just for a moment, to retrieve the shirt he'd discarded earlier, and then came back to her. Standing in front of her, he draped the shirt over her shoulders, but as he did, his gaze strayed lower. And she saw its heat. His eyes raked over her breasts, their nipples pebbling beneath the bra. And then slid lower, over her belly. And finally he pulled the shirt closed in front, shutting his eyes.

"I'm still cold," she whispered. "Hold me again, Elliot?" She leaned against his chest. But his arms remained at his sides.

"I…don't think that's such a good idea," he muttered.

Lifting her head, staring up into his eyes, her lips only a heartbeat from his, she said, "Please?"

He swore again. Softly. And then he bent his head, and he kissed her. It started out soft, gentle, and she knew he expected her to object. To push him away, or go stiff. But she didn't plan to do that. She planned to kiss him back.

But the moment his mouth covered hers, it didn't matter *what* she had planned.

She melted in his arms when they closed around her. She parted to his mouth when it nudged hers. She accepted his tongue when it slid between her lips. And when his body pressed to hers, hers pressed back. When his hips moved, and his hands urged hers to do likewise, they obeyed. There was no plan, no thought, no will, no conscious action. There was only sensation. A swirling cyclone of feelings. Touch and taste and smell. His skin was hot against her chilled flesh, hard against her softness. She smelled like ice water, and he like horse and sawdust and sweat. And she liked it. She *loved* it.

Her hands touched his hair, running over it and under it and threading through it. She tasted his mouth…he devoured hers. Nothing eased, nothing cooled. It only got more and more intense. His hands pulled her harder against him. His body grew harder against hers.

And he was parting that shirt he'd only just put on her, running his hands over her bare back and over the silky panties she wore. And higher, over her shoulders, and then creeping around one side, all the way around until he cupped a breast, his fingertips rubbing that chilled, sensitized peak. His mouth trailed a hot path from her mouth to her jaw, down to her neck, and lower, and…

And he paused…and she knew he wanted to put his lips on her breast, and she was waiting…aching, longing for him to.

He was so close…she could feel his breath, hot and quick, bathing her nipple. Her hands tightened at the nape of his neck where she held him. Just slightly. Just enough to tell him…

He shook his head, pulled away from her, so that

her hands fell to her sides. He turned his back and
pushed his hands through his hair. "I'm sorry, Esmeralda," he whispered, his voice coarse. Rough. So
filled with regret and still laced with so much passion
that she trembled at the very sound of it. It was like
a touch. Like a rough, gentle touch.

"No," she whispered. "No, Elliot Brand, you must
not be sorry."

"No?" Slowly, he faced her again. And his eyes,
when they roamed over her face, were so...tender. He
reached up, pulled the shirt closed. "You lost your
father a few days ago, were nearly raped after that.
Then you killed a man, were arrested, beaten up and
nearly hanged. Then you were dragged off by someone you probably thought was a ghost, shot at and,
finally, you were whisked through time by some
magic pendant. You telling me you're in any shape
to be thinking clearly right now?"

She lowered her head. "I don't know."

"You don't need to know. I'm not an idiot. I have
a brain, and I do know. This isn't the time for this,
Esmeralda."

Her head snapped up fast. "I want you, Elliot
Brand. That much I do know. I've never...never
wanted a man this way before...." She saw how his
eyes darkened, saw him avert them, and lowered her
head. "You think I am wanton for saying this to
you?"

His hand came to her face, tilting it up. "I think
you're a dream, Esmeralda. A dream come to life.
And I want you, too. So much it's all I can do to keep
my hands off you right now. But..."

"But what?"

"It wouldn't be fair," he said. "Because you are

alone and confused, and maybe turning to me because I'm the only person here who knows the truth about you, or because of what we went through together. I don't know. But…but I can't take advantage of you.''

She nodded slowly, studying his face. ''And what if it is none of those things, Elliot Brand? What if…it is simply that…we want to make love to each other?''

He shuddered visibly. ''Then we will. Make no mistake about it, Esmeralda. We will.''

She closed her eyes, lowered her head until it rested upon his shoulder. ''And how long will you make me wait for you?'' she whispered. ''Until I lose my mind? Until I go up in flames and nothing remains but ash?''

His hands stroked her hair, her back. ''You do wonders for a man's ego, you know that?''

''I speak only what I feel,'' she whispered.

''I need to be sure of something, Esmeralda. I need *you* to be sure of something.''

''I am sure that I want you,'' she told him, nestling closer in his arms. ''What more can there be to know?''

''Oh, a lot more.'' Gripping her shoulders, he set her back just slightly and stared into her eyes. ''Look at me,'' he said softly.

She did. He was a beautiful man. Deep, dark eyes, and hair of russet brown with a rusty auburn light in its depths. Full lips, and a strong jaw.

''I want you to be sure of who I am, Esmeralda. Elliot Brand…not Eldon. Not anything close to Eldon.''

Confused, she frowned at him, shaking her head. ''But I do know that.''

''Do you? Do you really?''

"*Sí!* You are nothing like Eldon."

He nodded. "No, I'm not. And when I make love to you, Esmeralda, I want to know you'll remember that. I don't want you to look at me and suddenly remember him. Or think of him. I want there to be no nightmarish memories. Only you and me."

She nodded, unsure what to say.

"Right now I think it's too soon for that. All that happened to you is still too fresh in your mind to be so easily forgotten. But it will be…in time. You need to rest, you need to heal. And when you're ready…if you still want me…" He stepped back again, to search her face. Then his eyes widened. "Esmeralda? Why are you crying?"

"Am I?" She lifted her fingertips to her cheeks and felt the tears there. She shook her head as if in denial. "I don't know," she told him. "I…I don't know." And, turning her back to Elliot, she walked away to find her jeans, and her sanity, and her plan.

Play TIC-TAC-TOE and get FREE GIFTS!

HOW TO PLAY:

1. Play the tic-tac-toe scratch-off game at the right for your FREE BOOKS and FREE GIFT!

2. Send back this card and you'll receive TWO brand-new Silhouette Intimate Moments® novels. These books have a cover price of $4.25 each in the U.S. and $4.75 each in Canada, but they are yours to keep absolutely free.

3. There's no catch. You're under no obligation to buy anything. We charge nothing — ZERO — for your first shipment. And you don't have to make any minimum number of purchases — not even one!

4. The fact is, thousands of readers enjoy receiving books by mail from the Silhouette Reader Service™ months before they're available in stores. They like the convenience of home delivery, and they love our discount prices!

5. We hope that after receiving your free books you'll want to remain a subscriber. But the choice is yours — to continue or cancel, any time at all! So why not take us up on our invitation, with no risk of any kind. You'll be glad you did!

YOURS FREE A FABULOUS MYSTERY GIFT!

We can't tell you what it is… but we're sure you'll like it!

A FREE GIFT — just for playing

TIC-TAC-TOE!

With a coin, scratch the gold boxes on the tic-tac-toe board. Then remove the "X" sticker from the front and affix it so that you get three X's in a row. This means you can get **TWO FREE** Silhouette Intimate Moments® novels and a **FREE MYSTERY GIFT!**

PLAY TIC-TAC-TOE

YES! Please send me the 2 Free books and gift for which I qualify. I understand that I am under no obligation to purchase any books, as explained on the back of this card.

345 SDL CX7W   **245 SDL CX7Q**
                                    (S-IM-12/99)

Name:

(PLEASE PRINT CLEARLY)

Address: Apt.#:

City: State/Prov.:   Zip/Postal Code:

Offer limited to one per household and not valid to current Silhouette Intimate Moments® subscribers. All orders subject to approval.

PRINTED IN U.S.A.

The Silhouette Reader Service™ — Here's how it works:

Accepting your 2 free books and gift places you under no obligation to buy anything. You may keep the books and gift and return the shipping statement marked "cancel." If you do not cancel, about a month later we'll send you 6 additional novels and bill you just $3.57 each in the U.S., or $3.96 each in Canada, plus 25¢ delivery per book and applicable taxes if any.* That's the complete price and — compared to the cover price of $4.25 in the U.S. and $4.75 in Canada — it's quite a bargain! You may cancel at any time, but if you choose to continue, every month we'll send you 6 more books, which you may either purchase at the discount price or return to us and cancel your subscription.

*Terms and prices subject to change without notice. Sales tax applicable in N.Y. Canadian residents will be charged applicable provincial taxes and GST.

If offer card is missing write to: Silhouette Reader Service, 3010 Walden Ave., P.O. Box 1867, Buffalo, NY 14240-1867

BUSINESS REPLY MAIL
FIRST-CLASS MAIL   PERMIT NO. 717   BUFFALO, NY

POSTAGE WILL BE PAID BY ADDRESSEE

SILHOUETTE READER SERVICE
3010 WALDEN AVE
PO BOX 1867
BUFFALO NY 14240-9952

NO POSTAGE
NECESSARY
IF MAILED
IN THE
UNITED STATES

Chapter 8

Wes was on the porch swing, booted feet propped on the railing, black hat shading his eyes, when they got back to the house. Elliot could see he didn't look happy, even with his eyes hidden. And he figured Esmeralda could see it, too. It was in the angle of his head, in his posture. In his lips. She stiffened a bit. Elliot wished he could soothe her. Poor thing. Wes had never looked exactly friendly, and he must remind Esmeralda painfully of his historical counterpart, the outlaw Waylon Brand.

Sighing, Elliot slowed the horse but didn't get down. He tipped his hat at his brother, intending to head straight to the stable, but Wes got to his feet.

"We need to talk."

"Yeah? About what?" Elliot drew the horse to a halt but still didn't get down.

"Lots of things." Wes leaned backward, pushed open the screen door and called, "They're back."

A second later Garrett appeared in the doorway, and Sara Brand was standing beside him. Elliot blinked. "Sara? Hey, what are you doin' here?" This time he did get down off the horse, forgetting all about Esmeralda as he ran up the steps and scooped the slightly built blonde right off her feet.

When he put her down, she was laughing. "I came to spend some time with my family," she said, beaming. "Don't tell me you're all sick of me already?"

"Hell, no. We lost you for twenty years, hon. That's lots of time to make up for." He hugged her again. Garrett cleared his throat, and when Elliot glanced at him, he nodded toward the woman Elliot had left sitting astride a tired horse. Esmeralda.

Oh, hell, the look on her face right now would burn holes through solid rock. "Ah, shoot, I'm sorry. Sara, meet Esmeralda Montoya. Esmeralda, this is Sara Brand, my cousin."

Esmeralda's eyebrows rose. "Cousin?"

Did he detect a hint of relief in those dark eyes? Then...had that been jealousy blazing there before? No, it couldn't...

Esmeralda dismounted and came forward. Sara took her hand and offered a smile. "So you're the mysterious houseguest I've been hearing so much about," she said.

Esmeralda looked alarmed, and her gaze shot to Elliot's. Elliot shrugged. "That she is. Um, look, I know we have a ton of catching up to do, Sara, but I ought to take care of the horse, and I think Wes here wants a minute with me. How long are you staying?"

"A couple of weeks, if you'll have me that long."

"Shoot, cuz, we'd keep you permanently if we could, and you know it."

He turned as if to go and tend his horse, but Sara's hand on his arm stilled him. "Why don't you let Esmeralda and me do that?" she said.

Elliot turned back again, and frowned.

"It'll give you a chance to have that talk with Wes. And give me a chance to get to know your new friend. Besides, I've been dying to get out to the stables. You know how I love the horses."

Elliot tilted his head. Something was up. He felt an ambush coming on. The hairs on the back of his neck were bristling. He looked at Esmeralda.

She shrugged. "It is fine with me," she said. Then she looked Wes square in the eye. "But in future, Señor Brand, if you wish a word alone with your brother, you need only say so. How long do you wish for the *señorita* and me to play at conversation in the stables, eh?"

Wes blinked in shock, gaping at her. It was seldom that Elliot saw his brother rendered speechless, but he saw it now. He felt his admiration for Esmeralda go up another notch. And he felt proud of her, too.

While Wes stared, Garrett spoke. Only he sounded too serious, and slightly grim. "Ten minutes ought to do it."

She nodded once, firmly. "Fine. I would also add, Señor Brand, that I prefer to be present when I am the subject of conversation. However, I will abide by your wishes in this." Turning sharply on her heel, she walked to the horse, gripped its harness and started off toward the barn.

Sara stood there, looking worried. "Not exactly friendly, is she?"

"I'm not feeling too friendly just now myself," Elliot said. "What's this all about, Wes?"

Wes nodded at Sara, and Sara nodded back, then hurried off after Esmeralda and the horse and cart. When they were out of earshot, Wes said, "Sit down, Elliot."

"I'll stand, thanks. Just say what you have to say and let's get this over with."

"I intend to."

"Now calm down, you two," Garrett said, cutting in. He came down two steps and sat. Elliot stood leaning on the porch rail just to one side of the steps, and Wes stood in front of the swing on the other side, looking poised for a fight. "This isn't any cause for an argument."

"Yeah, well, I'll reserve judgment on that," Elliot said. "What is it, Wes?"

Wes sighed, shook his head. "First off, it's that the artifact is nowhere to be found. Taylor and I have been over every inch of your pickup and the area where you crashed, and there's no sign of that skull anywhere."

"So?"

"So the only two people there were you and this Esmeralda person. We started looking last night, and we've turned over every inch of ground since. It's not there, Elliot."

Elliot straightened away from the rail. "Are you accusing me of something, big brother?"

Wes sighed hard. "Someone took it. Someone had to take it or it would still be there, El. And you know damn well I don't mean you."

"Esmeralda, then."

Wes lifted his brows and his shoulders. "Hey, if the shoe fits—"

"My shoe's gonna fit right up your—"

''Now hold on!'' Garrett got to his feet just as Elliot surged toward Wes. He stood between them, a palm against each brother's chest. ''Elliot, I know you like her. Okay? I know this is gonna upset you, but you have to hear us out on this.''

''Us?'' Elliot blinked at Garrett. ''You telling me Wes has you believing this bull, too?''

''Elliot, there's more,'' Garrett said slowly. ''Look…I ran a background check on her…or tried to. Elliot…there's nothing. It's as if she doesn't exist.''

Elliot closed his eyes, lowered his head.

''You don't seem surprised by that, Elliot,'' Wes said. ''You knew she was using a false name, is that it?''

Shaking his head, Elliot said, ''It's her real name. And she does exist…and she didn't steal the damned skull.''

''Taylor said it was priceless, El,'' Garrett went on. ''To a woman in her situation, it might be awfully tempting to—''

''She didn't steal the skull.''

''No, I didn't.'' Esmeralda's voice came from behind them, and all three heads turned sharply. She stood in the driveway about ten feet away. Sara came running out of the stables after her, but she'd already heard all she needed to. ''I didn't steal the skull, because it was already mine. Given to me by my father before he was killed. But it vanished…and I have no idea where it is now.''

The men stared. Garrett curious, Wes suspicious. But Esmeralda's eyes were fixed only on Elliot's. ''We have to tell them the truth,'' she said. ''It is time, Elliot.''

Closing his eyes, he nodded. "They're not gonna believe it."

"Not gonna believe what?" Wes demanded. "Will one of you please tell me what the hell you're talking about?"

Elliot nodded slowly, sighed deeply and dreaded what he was going to have to do. "Yeah. In a bit. Garrett, you may as well call a family meeting. No sense us going over all this more than once. Come on." He held out a hand to Esmeralda. She walked toward him, came up the porch steps, and took hold of it. She looked offended, and maybe a little bit scared. "Just stay by me," Elliot told her. "It'll be all right."

"M-maybe I should leave?" It was Sara, still standing in the driveway, though she'd come closer now.

"You're family, too, Sara. Come on, you may as well hear this. Hell, you won't ever hear another tale like it, I can promise you that," Elliot said.

Sara tilted her head. "Okay, I'll come, too."

Elliot held Esmeralda's hand tight. Hell, he had no idea how all this was going to work out. But she was right, it was time to tell the family the truth. He just hoped to God they didn't decide to have him committed before he could convince them that he wasn't crazy.

The entire Brand clan gathered in the parlor, and it was so packed there was standing room only. Jessi and her husband Lash shared the easy chair nearest the fireplace, little Maria-Michele playing on the floor at their feet. Taylor had the rocking chair, and Wes stood behind her, his hands on her shoulders. Adam and Kirsten were on the sofa, beside Ben and Penny—and Penny's belly couldn't get much bigger without popping, Elliot thought. She was a week overdue with her firstborn, and Ben was a nervous wreck. Chelsea sat in the recliner, and Garrett had dragged a chair in from the dining room, turned it backwards and was straddling it. He was holding Chelsea's hand. Sara was pacing nervously back and forth. Hell, only cousin Marcus and his new wife Casey were absent, and Elliot figured they would have been there, too, if they'd been given any notice.

He stood beside Esmeralda in front of the fireplace, and since there were no more chairs to be had, he sat down on the stone platform the hearth rested upon. He had hold of Esmeralda's hand, so when he tugged, she sat down beside him, close beside him, her side pressed to his. On his other side was a rack full of fireplace tools, wrought-iron poker, shovel, tongs. Beside those was a round ironwood rack. At his feet, ol' Blue lay sleeping. But when Elliot cleared his throat, even the aging hound dog lifted his ''brow'' and perked up his ears.

''I guess…maybe Esmeralda should start,'' he said.

She swung her eyes to his, and they were wide and dark and uncertain. She was always so forthright, so sure of herself, so outspoken. But it was plain she didn't want to be any of those things right now.

''Okay, then I'll start.'' He drew a breath, sighed, and looked around the room. His family loved him. He didn't have to worry. ''But I have to ask you all to keep quiet until I finish. This is gonna sound like…like something out of an episode of *The X-Files,* and you're gonna be tempted to interrupt and ask questions. Don't. I probably won't know the answers, anyway."

Glancing nervously at one another, the family nodded at him to go on.

"All right. See, Esmeralda lived with her father on a big ranch in Texas. She grew up there. Her mama died giving birth to her and was buried there. But there was considerable...bigotry in this particular town at this particular time. And once Esmeralda changed from a little girl into a young woman, the local boys were prone to...harassing her."

He glanced at her to see if she approved of what he'd said so far. She met his eyes and said quietly, "Harassing me is a very pretty term for what they did. But it will do for now." Then she looked away.

Elliot squeezed her hand. "I know."

She looked up, met his gaze, and he felt a warmth pass between them, a kind of unspoken pact. They were in this together.

"Anyway, her father—Luis Montoya—decided it would be best to send Esmeralda to Mexico to live with her aunt for a while. So that's where she went. While she was away, things went sour on the ranch." He looked at her again, silently asking her to fill in the parts he didn't know.

She nodded. "There were people in town who wanted my father's land. And they conspired to get it. Water holes went dry, because they had blocked the source further upstream. Wells went bad, and crops were lost to prairie fires that started without any apparent reason. Except perhaps arson. Of course, at first my father didn't realize he was being sabotaged. He just thought it was a run of bad luck. He was forced to take a loan from the bank in order to cover the losses. When he shipped his cattle to market in the fall, he would have enough funds to repay the loan in full. He used the ranch as collateral." She blinked and Elliot watched her face carefully, knowing this was all difficult for her to relive. So fresh. Like yesterday, really. "He never would have risked the land he loved unless he was certain he could pay the debt. I know this." The wetness brimmed now. She sent Elliot no more than a glance, and he knew she was in trouble. He jumped in, taking over without hesitation.

"Before he could get the cattle to market, he was attacked by rustlers. Shot in the back, the cattle taken."

"Oh my God!" Chelsea said, rising to her feet. "Was he...?"

"He didn't die...right away. One of his vaqueros got him back to *la casa,* and sent a rider out to bring me back home to him as fast as possible. Somehow...my father held on until I got to his bedside three days later."

Elliot looked around the room, saw Wes lower his head, no doubt feeling guilty for his suspicions about Esmeralda now that he was hearing what hell she'd been through.

"My father had an amulet that he often wore. It had been handed down through the generations of our family, but it was older than any of us and had been on our land long before our people had. It was said to have powers...mystical powers...to return human beings to their rightful place. I never believed it. But my father gave it to me before he died...along with everything else he owned. The ranch hands and I were saying words over my father's grave, which was right

beside my mother's on the land where I had been born
and raised, when the banker came with papers and
claimed he now owned the ranch. He gave me only
a day to clear out.''

''That can't have been legal,'' Garrett said.

''Oh, it wasn't. But the sheriff was the banker's
brother, and the leaders of the outlaw gang of rustlers
were more of the same family. The cattle were stolen,
so the debt could not be paid, and because the debt
was not paid, the ranch was forfeit. But I was determined to fight for my property. And then...'' She
lowered her head, bit her lip.

''She got to be too much of a pest to these men,''
Elliot said. ''Threatened to go over their heads to get
justice. One of them decided to teach her a lesson.
He...um...he grabbed her, took her outside of town
and assaulted her.'' Elliot's jaw went tight as he tried
very hard not to envision what Esmeralda had gone
through. ''She killed him in self-defense. But since
his family ran the town, she found herself behind bars
before she knew it, and facing a death sentence.''

Now Garrett's head came up slowly, and for the
first time Elliot saw skepticism in his brother's eyes.
''Come on, Elliot. No one family would have that
much influence. There would have been a trial, an
investigation.''

Elliot nodded. ''Yeah. Today there would have
been. But all of this happened...'' He drew a deep
breath, looked at Esmeralda.

''It was the summer of 1881,'' she said softly.

There was dead silence in the room. Then finally,
Jessi said, ''Oh, I get it. This is a joke. It's one of
Elliot's jokes, right, El? I mean, come on, you usually
do so much better than this.'' She smiled across the

room at her brother, but when he met his sister's eyes, he couldn't return the smile.

"Taylor found an artifact on a dig, and she asked me to take it to the University for her. Remember?"

Jessi nodded. Taylor's eyes narrowed.

"Okay, so I had it. I was driving along, and I was curious as to what was so important about this find, so I took it out of the box. It was a small piece of quartz, carved into the shape of a human skull. And there was something engraved on the back. Words in some language I didn't recognize. I read it out loud, and there was this flash, and that's when I hit the tree. That skull thing got hot. So hot it left a mark in my hand." He held up his hand, palm out, so they could all see the scar the thing had left. He even got up and walked around the room, giving them each a closer look. "But after the crash, the skull was gone. I got out of the truck to go find a phone, started back toward town, but...well, the town looked odd. And when I glanced behind me, the truck was gone. Just...just gone."

Jessi was shaking her head. "You banged your head in the crash, Elliot. You were disoriented, is all."

"That's exactly what I thought. So I kept walking, heading into town, and when I got there, I saw horses, and wagons, and I thought I was on some movie set. It was like an old western. But there was a gallows in the middle of town, and this woman—" He turned now, looking back to where she sat. "This beautiful woman, with her dress torn and her face bruised, was standing there with a rope around her neck. And the sheriff standing beside her..." He shook his head and eyed his oldest brother. "Garrett, he looked so much

like you he could have been your twin. I thought it
was you, at first, playing some kind of trick on me,
or maybe acting out a role in some hallucination I
was having. But he wasn't. His name was Garrison.
Garrison *Brand*.''

"Oh, come on now, Elliot,'' Wes snapped.

"I didn't believe it, either. But when the guy
shoved her around up there, I knew he meant business. And his brothers, the banker Allen, and the outlaw Waylon—your own twin, Wes—kept calling me
Eldon and acting surprised to see me. Turns out Eldon
looked a lot like me, and he was the one Esmeralda
was about to hang for having murdered. Hell, even
she thought I was him.''

Esmeralda nodded. "I couldn't believe it when I
saw him moving through the crowd. At first I thought
it was Eldon Brand's ghost, coming for my soul. But
then…then he pulled a gun from someone's holster,
and he made them let me go. He put me on a horse
and climbed on behind me, and we rode like the wind.
I couldn't understand what was happening. He was
so like Eldon…and yet, he couldn't have been more
different.''

Elliot gave her a slight smile. "Glad you realized
it.'' She smiled back, but it was nervous, watery.
"We rode hell-bent for leather, with that whole Brand
family on our tails. And we finally had to stop to rest
the horse, and that's when I noticed the necklace Esmeralda was wearing. The family heirloom her father
had given her. It was the crystal skull. The exact same
crystal skull Taylor had given me to take to the University. I asked her about it, and she told me it was
said to have mystical powers.''

Esmeralda nodded. "The next thing we knew, we

were surrounded. They started shooting at us. Elliot begged me to read the words on the back of the crystal skull, to try to make it repeat its magic—even as he was pulling out a gun and risking his life to save mine.''

Taylor was on her feet now. ''This can't be true....''

But Wes was blinking, shaking his head, blinking again. ''I...I felt something when I handled that piece. I should have paid attention. That crazy old Shaman Turtle—he told me never to ignore feelings like that, but I...''

''She read the words,'' Elliot said. ''There was that flash again. And there we were, on the ground, still surrounded by Brands, only they were you guys, and I was threatening to shoot you all with my finger.''

''And the amulet?'' Taylor asked eagerly.

''It was gone,'' Esmeralda said. ''But look...it left the same mark on my skin that it did on Elliot's. It grew very hot...and it burned me.'' Parting the collar of her shirt slightly, Esmeralda got up and came to the center of the room where Elliot now stood. She turned in a slow circle so they could all see the mark left by the amulet.

Garrett was shaking his head in disbelief. ''Okay. Okay, I...I don't know what happened to you two...but this is all...well, it can't be what you think it is. There has to be some logical explanation. It's all just...well, you're just mixed up. I mean, Elliot hit his head and, Esmeralda, you might well have been hurt in that accident...maybe in some way you don't even remember.''

''It would be very rare for two people to hit their

heads and have the same hallucinations from the injury, Garrett,'' Chlesea said softly.

"Chelsea's right,'' Jessi put in. "No, this isn't a
delusion…it's some kind of a scam.'' As she spoke,
her narrow-eyed gaze raked over Esmeralda. "Rest
assured, honey, you aren't going to put one over on
this family. And just because my brother can't see
through you doesn't mean the rest of us can't. I don't
know what you're up to, but—''

"She's telling the truth, Jessi.'' It was Wes, once
the biggest skeptic of them all. Now studying the
ways of the Shaman he was born to become. "I don't
know how or…or why any of this happened…but I
believe her.''

"My God, Wes, do you know what you're saying?'' Taylor asked. She was a scientist, his wife. And
her eyes were huge. "We're talking about *time travel*
here.''

Wes met her eyes and nodded. Taylor held his gaze
for a long moment.

Adam said, "Hell, Einstein believed it was possible.''

"You guys have all lost your minds!'' Jessi said.

"It will be easy enough to check out, Jess.'' This
was Penny, who had a private investigator's license
and planned to open up an office in town once the
baby was old enough. "I mean, all the details given
here can be checked out. Like the names of
those…those so-called Brands. What town was it
again, Esmeralda?''

"It was this town,'' she said softly. "It was Quinn,
Texas.''

Penny nodded. "And the ranch…?''

"Jeez-Louise, Penny, don't you *get it?*'' Jessi

shouted. "It was *this* ranch. It was the Texas Brand. And she's come here with this far-fetched fairy tale to try to scam us out of it. She wants our home, can't anyone see that?"

Every eye in the room turned to Esmeralda. She lifted her chin slightly, facing them all. "My story is not a scam...it is not a lie. But Jessi Brand is right about one thing," she said, her voice shaking but loud. "This ranch you call your own rightfully belongs to me. And if I could possibly do so, I would take it from you."

She lowered her head then.

Elliot reached out, closed his hand around hers. "That took a lot of courage to admit to this crew, Esmeralda. And if they have half as much, they'll admit that if they were in your shoes, they'd feel exactly the same way."

She looked up at him, a slight frown puckering her brows, her eyes searching, surprised and confused.

"I want that woman out of this house," Jessi said. "Hell, better than that, I want her in jail! Garrett, surely some part of this dog-and-pony show she's concocted must be illegal?"

Garrett shrugged helplessly, glancing at his wife for advice. But before Chelsea could speak, Esmeralda did. "I do not blame you," she said. "I will leave tonight."

"The hell you will," Elliot said. His hand tightened on hers, and he faced Jessi dead on. "You gonna have her sleeping out in the street, Jess? Huh? Her claim is over a hundred years old, and even then it was made to look bogus. What the hell do you think she's gonna do, take us to court with this story? You think a judge in the world would believe it?"

Jessi glared at him as if she thought him an idiot.

"She's no threat to us. But that doesn't change the fact that her claim is legitimate. I *know*. I was *there*, dammit. She's staying. She's got free run of this place, and she's damned well staying. Because if she goes, *I go*."

"Oh, for Pete's sake, Elliot—"

"I mean it. I'll go."

He saw the stunned expressions on every single face in the crowd. Well, most looked stunned. Garrett looked worried, too. Chelsea thoughtful. Penny curious. Wes looked shaken, but Elliot detected support there. And when he glanced Ben's way he saw approval. A slight nod, strong eye contact that told him that Ben, at least, thought he was doing the right thing. Always quiet, Ben would stand by him in this.

"That's the story. That's the truth. That's why the amulet vanished, and it's why Esmeralda screamed bloody murder when she saw the television for the first time. It's why I had to drive fifteen miles an hour bringing her back here that first day. She damn near got carsick, even then. She'd never been in a car before, never even seen one. It's why she was wearing the clothes she was wearing. It's why she was so afraid of you all when she saw you—because you look just like those other Brands, the ones so bent on killing her. It's all absolutely impossible, but it's the truth. I'm your brother. I wouldn't make something like this up and I'm not fool enough to be tricked into believing tall tales. You know that. You ought to take me at my word. That ought to be enough for you, but if it's not, then take a ride tonight. Out past the east fence line just past the ridge. Cross the stream, where it vanishes into that scrub lot. Take a look at what's out there. We've been here all our lives and never noticed it. But Esmeralda took me right to it. You check that out if you need proof.''

He lowered his head. "I'm tired. I'm going up to shower and head to bed. I'll give you until morning to decide what you want to do." He turned to Esmeralda. Held out a hand.

She looked at it, then lowered her head, shook it slowly. "I...think I'll go walking. I'm too tense to sleep just yet."

He frowned, wondering if walking was what she really intended to do. "Esmeralda, don't run off, you hear?"

Her lips thinned. "It's clear I am no longer welcome in this house, Elliot."

"You're welcome with me," he said. "And I'm not gonna let you go off alone after...after today." He looked toward the window. Dark outside, now, and the air would be chill. "I'll get us a couple of jackets, and we'll both go walking, okay?"

She nodded quickly. "*Sí.* Okay."

Elliot raced up the stairs, determined not to leave her alone with his family for more than a minute or two. Even that might be too long. Damn that Jessi, when she felt her family was threatened she was like one of Penny's bulldogs with a hangnail. She would tear Esmeralda apart if he gave her half a chance. The rest of the family might be willing to hear him out, give him the benefit of the doubt, give Esmeralda half a chance.

But not Jessi. She was too damned hot-tempered and overprotective, particularly of him. If he didn't know better, he would think maybe Jessi was jealous of him and Esmeralda.

And Esmeralda was like a firecracker on a hot plate. Hell, if the two of them ever went at it, he would hate to see the results.

Chapter 9

She felt like a lamb in a den of lions for a moment as they all stared at her. But then she reminded herself of who she was. She was Esmeralda Montoya. She was the lion. *They* were the lambs. She had not been afraid to take on their bloodthirsty, ruthless ancestors. What had she to fear from them? They were soft. The men could not bear the thought of raising their voice to a woman, much less killing one. They strove to be honest, honorable, all of them. She could conquer this entire family if she used her mind. She had no qualms about doing whatever was necessary—and *that,* combined with the fact that she had nothing to lose, made her the certain victor in this battle.

Elliot had defended her. Against his own family, he had stood on her side. A quiver of guilt threatened her resolve. But then she met Jessi Brand's eyes and chased that guilt away. The girl hated her, suspected her of the very worst, automatically. Without cause or reason.

She might as well live up to the *chiquita's* expectations.

"What's out there, Esmeralda?" Adam Brand asked. He looked so much like the banker who had swindled her father that Esmeralda nearly snapped at him. She had to remind herself that this was not Allen Brand. He was not a banker. And might even be a decent human being in spite of the sinners' blood running in his veins.

"The graves of my parents," she said softly. "So overgrown with neglect that at first I thought they'd been destroyed. But we found them, among the brush and saplings, covered in vines and weeds. Elliot…he brought tools. And we spent the day clearing out the spot." She shook the sadness from her mind, met Adam's eyes, then Jessi's. "You can go out there right now with a lamp and see for yourself. The names and dates on the tombstones are right there. You can still make them out."

"Oh, I'll do that. Don't you worry," Jessi said.

Her husband put a hand on Jessi's arm. "You're gonna feel really rotten if it turns out she's telling the truth, hon."

"Yeah, but I'll be too busy watching the pigs fly overhead to notice," she replied, her words dripping ice.

Wes shook his head slowly, glanced at his wife. Taylor held his gaze and slowly nodded. Esmeralda blinked. So Taylor and Wes were believers. And Ben, the large, quiet one, he seemed to believe, as well. Garrett the lawman, and Penny, the pregnant wife of Ben, seemed skeptical. Not disbelieving, but needing proof. Adam seemed wary, Jessi downright hostile, Lash, uncertain but leaning toward doubt. Adam's wife, Kirsten, was almost as quiet as Ben, but she also seemed doubtful. Chelsea was just accepting. Maybe not even caring if it were the truth or not. She would be kind to a rabid dog, should one show up slavering at the door, Esmeralda suspected.

The one person she could not read was the young woman—Sara. Sara was timid, thoughtful, and showed nothing but amazement on her face. Every other person seemed to feel one way or another about Esmeralda's story, her very presence, but Sara was either a master at hiding her feelings or truly didn't know yet how she felt.

"I don't know what you're planning," Jessi said, interrupting her thoughts. "But I'm warning you, Esmeralda, don't mess with my brother's feelings. You can try your damnedest to take this ranch, you can sneak out in the night and rob us blind, or you can burn this place to the ground. But you hurt my brother, and I promise, I'll come for you."

Esmeralda swallowed hard. "Your brother is a grown man, Jessi Brand. A strong man. A smart man. I do not think you need to stand over him like a mother over her little child, do you?"

Elliot came back down the stairs, a flannel shirt over his T-shirt and another one in his hand. He looked at Jessi, then at Esmeralda, and back again. "Jessi?" he said.

She snapped her eyes to his, then rolled them, shook her head and looked away. Just for an instant, Esmeralda thought she glimpsed tears in those angry brown eyes. But then Elliot was slipping the shirt over her shoulders, followed by his arm, and then he eased her through the room and out of the house.

The moment the screen door creaked shut behind them, she felt the tension begin to ebb. And as Elliot walked beside her, down the porch steps and out across the lawns, it ebbed more and more. Cicadas whirred and nightbirds cooed as the stars glittered from a cloudless black-velvet sky. The breeze was cool, bracing, fresh. Esmeralda stooped once, to take off her shoes, and then walked on, the cold green grass cushioning her feet.

"Are you all right?" Elliot asked her softly.

"*Sí,*" she said. Then he stopped walking, turned her to face him and lifted her chin in his hand so he could search her eyes. And she said, "No." Her throat hurt; it felt tight and raw, and her eyes burned.

"I didn't think so."

"I can not go back there, Elliot," she whispered. "They hate me."

"No, they don't. They feel threatened. And…and they tend to be a bit overprotective of their own. They'll come around."

She shook her head. "I don't think they will." And why should they? she thought. They were right. "I can not sleep in that house, Elliot."

"Then where do you think you're gonna sleep?" he asked gently. "Hmm?"

She took a breath that stuttered into her lungs and stuttered out again, in spite of her efforts to contain it. "I don't know…in the stables…with the horses."

"Esmeralda—"

"Please don't argue with me, Elliot. I would not be able to close my eyes in that house tonight. I will be fine in the stables. Perhaps even get some rest, no?''

He looked at her, his face sad. "I'm sorry they made you feel so unwelcome. Maybe...maybe I was wrong to tell them the truth.''

She shook her head. "It had to be done.''

"Yeah, but it didn't help matters any.'' He reached out a hand, stroked it through her hair. "I'm so sorry you had to go through this. After everything else...''

"Do not feel sorry for me, Elliot Brand. I am strong.''

"So you keep telling me.''

"I will survive. I always survive.''

He nodded. She was trying very hard to hold her tough shell in place. Not to let him in. And yet she could not help but feel all sorts of emotions bubbling up inside her. Physical longing for this man. It burned in her every time she thought about her mission—to bed him and wed him as fast as possible. To make love to this man—the images in her mind would not leave her alone. It would be more than a means to an end. It would be...it would be madness. Passion. Fire. Yet she must do it.

And more...more troubled her soul. That he was so good to her, that he had first risked his life to stand by her in the face of his murderous ancestors...and that now he had stood against his own beloved family for her sake. It was more than any man had ever done for her. No one had shown this much concern or compassion for her since her own father. No one.

Until Elliot Brand. Her enemy.

Somehow, he felt like her only friend.

"I need to be alone, to think,'' she told him, in all

honesty. "I need…oh, Elliot, please, just let me go to the stables for the night. Please."

Searching her face, he finally nodded. Reluctantly, though. "Do you promise you'll still be there in the morning?" he asked her. Their walk had brought them to the front doors of the stables, and they stopped outside them. He held both her hands in his now.

"I promise that much to you," she said. "I will be here. I will not run away. Oh, Elliot, but I could not run even if I wanted to. Where would I go in this world that is so strange to me?" Her voice broke a little on that last sentence.

She saw him swallow hard. "Nowhere," he said. "You stick by me and I promise, you'll be fine." He dipped his head, brushed a soft kiss over her mouth, drew away.

Esmeralda trembled, and her hands crept around his neck.

Closing his eyes, Elliot swayed forward again, almost as if he couldn't help himself. He kissed her slowly, deeply, and for a long, long time. Her body was held in a gentle, possessive, protective embrace. His was warm and solid and strong. He wrapped her up tight in his arms, and he kissed her like a man would kiss a woman he loved.

And finally he straightened, pulled away, tipped his hat and rasped, "Good night, Esmeralda."

Her lips formed the words, "Good night, Elliot." But no sound emerged. Or if it did, she could not hear it beyond the frantic beating of her own heart.

"Jeez-Louise, would you look at that?" Jessi swung away from the window and stomped a foot.

"What's the *matter* with him, anyway?"

Several others heads were crowded around this window, and several more at the next, and those who wouldn't fit had gone into the dining room or kitchen to peek out those windows. Jessi had no doubt every single member of the family had witnessed that passionate kiss her brother had just bestowed upon that con artist out there.

As he headed back toward the house, they all moved away, curtains fell back into place, and the strays regrouped in the parlor. "I thought you were the resident expert on such things, Jessi," Wes said. "Looks to me like Elliot's in love."

"Oh, hell, that's not love. That's heat."

"Yeah," Adam said. "Seems like Elliot's always behaving this way, bringing home strays, defending them against the family." He was being sarcastic, and Jessi knew it. Truth was, Elliot had never acted so damned oddly in his life.

"She's no good for him," Jessi said. "Dammit, she's gonna break Elliot's heart right in two. I'm telling you, I can see it coming."

Chelsea got to her feet. She was nowhere near old enough to be the family matriarch, but as Garrett's wife, she'd taken on the role all the same. "Jessi," she said, "you know you and Elliot have always been closer to each other than to anyone else. Always took each other's part against the grown-ups. Always covered each other's butts in times of trouble."

"So what's your point?" Jessi asked.

Chelsea shrugged. "Well, couldn't it be that you're feeling a little bit…jealous right now?"

Jessi made a disgusted noise and rolled her eyes.

"I have a husband, a baby, a business and a home of my own, Chelsea. You think I don't have anything better to do than chase off my baby brother's girlfriends so I can keep him all to myself?"

Chelsea shrugged, eyeing Jessi, as if to say, *you tell me.*

Jessi stomped a foot. "You're wrong."

"Maybe," Garrett cut in. "And maybe not. But I'm still head of this family, and I've got something to say."

"About time," Ben muttered.

Garrett eyed him, but said nothing. He returned his attention to the whole group of them, glancing toward the kitchen and the back door every once in a while in case Elliot should return. "Sure as shootin' this all sounds flat-out impossible. But stranger things have happened. Hell, Wes and Taylor both experienced stranger things than this! Now, I know it's hard to do, but…but Elliot's one of us. A Brand, dammit, and I say we give him the benefit of the doubt. It's what's right. We ought to be supporting him here, not doubting him. And I'll tell you something else, too—if he loves that woman, then throwing around accusations about her is just the same as kicking Elliot right in the belly. You think about it, Jessi. You remember how you felt when we were all ready to string up Lash for getting you pregnant."

Jessi lowered her head, a hint of shame creeping through her.

Lash said, "If it's all the same to you guys, I'd prefer *not* to think about that."

Everyone laughed, but it was uneasy laughter.

Then Sara rose. "I know I'm the newcomer here,

but maybe that makes me a little more objective.''
She shrugged. "I *like* her."

Jessi felt her own eyes widen. "You *what?*"

"I like her," Sara said. "And I think Garrett's
right. Why not assume she's telling the truth until you
have proof otherwise? Trust your brother. Hell, I lost
my brother once, and I'll tell you, I'd rather believe
any tall tale than have that happen again.''

Garrett nodded.

Penny spoke up then. "That's not to say we can't
do a little checking in the meantime. I mean, it
wouldn't be hard to verify some of the things she
mentioned. Like the names of those alleged Brands,
and who owned the ranch back in 1881. And if it
changed hands that year, and if so, under what cir-
cumstances.''

"And those gravestones," Ben said softly.

"Yeah." Wes nodded. "I have a feeling we're
gonna verify everything she told us. And I'll tell you
something else...what she said about the legend surrounding that pendant. What were her exact words?
'It restores human beings to their rightful place'?"
Wes lifted his brows. "I think you'd all better prepare
yourselves for the chance that's exactly what it did.''

"What are you saying, Wes?" Jessi asked.

"I'm saying that if some ancient artifact with mystical powers put that girl here, then maybe there's a
reason. Maybe here is exactly where she belongs.''
He gave a nod, slammed his hat onto his head and,
taking Taylor's hand, headed for the door. Leaving
the others staring after him, wide-eyed, contemplating
and confused.

Elliot knew damned well someone would hear him.
Oh, Wes and Taylor had gone home, as had Jessi,

Lash, and the baby. Adam and Kirsten headed out, and Ben and Penny shortly after them. Only Garrett and Chelsea remained, and little Bubba and Sara. And he thought they'd taken to their bedrooms, but he wasn't sure, and he didn't care.

He wasn't going to lie warm and snug in his bed, under his roof, while Esmeralda slept in the cold, in the dark, all alone outside.

She didn't even have a nightgown.

He located one, a nice heavy one of softest fleece. White. Something Jessi used to wear in the wintertime. He snagged the blankets off his bed, rolled them up, tucked them under his arm and grabbed a couple of pillows for good measure. It all made a pretty large bundle, but hell, he didn't have to walk far.

He walked down the stairs with his gear, through the kitchen to the back door.

"You got a free hand there, cousin?" Sara asked him just as he gripped the doorknob.

He turned, glancing her way. Then he had no choice but to smile. Sara stood by the stove, a recently filled Thermos in her hand. The aroma of hot cocoa reached him, and he noted the roll of blankets sitting in a kitchen chair nearby. "Looks like we had the same idea," he said.

"Not *exactly* the same idea," Sara said. "I was planning to deliver the care package and then come back to my own bed."

Elliot felt his face heat, averted his eyes. "She's not what Jessi thinks she is, you know."

"I know," Sara said. She crossed the kitchen, slipped the Thermos's handle over Elliot's fingers. "Besides, I think you look cute together."

He sighed. "I wish Jessi thought so."

"She'll come around."

"I don't want to lose her over this."

"Don't worry," Sara said. "I'll talk to her. She doesn't want to lose you, either, you know."

"Yeah, well…"

"Go on. Poor Esmeralda's probably freezing by now." Sara reached past him to open the door, then held it as he went out.

"Thank you, Sara," he said.

She smiled at him. "You have a good night, Elliot," she said, eyes twinkling. Then she closed the door.

She lay in the hayloft, wide awake, burrowed in the hay but still cold, and jumping at every sound. She half expected one of those Brands to come out here and try to slit her throat in her sleep.

And part of her wouldn't blame them for it.

Dios, what was she doing here? She'd been rescued from death not once but twice by Elliot Brand. He'd taken her into his home, welcomed her, defended her against his own family…and what was her thanks to him? This ongoing plan to wrestle the ranch from his grasp? To take from him that which he loved?

She wasn't even certain she could go through with it now.

But if she did not, then what would she do? Where would she go?

The door below creaked softly, and her thoughts ground to a halt. Esmeralda sat up straight, eyes straining in the darkness as she tried to see. But she couldn't. The stable was inky. But she could hear…the soft shuffling and munching of the horses below. She could smell the hay, the sweet molasses-scented grain, and the aroma of horseflesh. Good, all of it. And she could feel the itchy hay and chilly night air on her skin...and the gooseflesh rising on her arms because of the fear.

What was that? Footsteps?

"Who's there?" she demanded, trying to sound fierce.

The footsteps stopped. "It's just me, Esmeralda. It's just me."

Elliot. Oh, what was he doing out here?

His movements brought him closer. Up the ladder, into the hayloft. "Where are you?" he asked.

"Over here," she told him, and he followed her voice. In a moment he was beside her, sitting down in the hay.

"I should have brought a light," he said. "But I had all I could carry as it was."

"Why did you come, Elliot?" she asked, and if she sounded disheartened, she was. He should not be here. Not when she was still so torn, so confused about what she should do.

"Hell, Esmeralda, I couldn't leave you out here all alone. I brought you a nice warm nightgown. Here." He pressed the soft cloth into her hand. "And blankets and pillows, too," he added. "Go ahead, get changed."

She sat perfectly still, not moving a muscle.

She could hear the smile in his voice when he went on. "It's not like I can see you, Esmeralda. Go on, change. I'll make you up the best hay-bed you've ever seen. And then we'll have some hot chocolate, okay?"

She felt her lips pull into an unwilling smile. "You are a very strange man, Elliot Brand."

"Am I?"

"*Sí.* I am a grown woman, tough as a grizzly bear and twice as mean. And yet you...you comfort me as if I were but a frightened little girl."

He reached out a hand, unerringly cupping her cheek. "You're not fooling me in the least, you know. Part of you *is* a frightened little girl. And the rest of you—that tough, mean part—I think its sole purpose for existing is to protect that little girl in you from being hurt again. But you know what?"

She blinked, glad he couldn't see the sudden moisture in her eyes. My God, why did those words seem to pierce her so deeply? "What?" she asked.

"I'm not gonna hurt you, Esmeralda. I promise you that."

A sob welled up in her throat, so huge she nearly choked on it, and she averted her eyes, even though she knew full well he couldn't see the tears. "You are so full of mud, Elliot Brand," she muttered in a voice almost too hoarse to speak. But in some dark corner of her soul a frightened little girl seemed to smile softly and sigh in long-overdue relief.

Chapter 10

Elliot smoothed out the loose hay in the darkness and spread one of the blankets over it.

"You should have brought a lamp," Esmeralda said softly. He could hear the sounds of cloth slipping and brushing against skin as she changed clothes. He was trying real hard not to think about that. Not to imagine what she was taking off...just how undressed she was at any given moment...a few feet away from him in the dark, hay-strewn barn.

Ah, hell, he was thinking about it anyway.

"There's a light switch on the wall," he said. "But only a tenderfoot would use it."

"*Que?*"

Elliot smiled in the darkness. "Jessi and I used to do this all the time when we were kids. Slip out here in the pitch-dark with our bedrolls and a few snacks. Sit up half the night telling ghost stories and trying to scare the hell out of each other. First one to turn on the light was a coward.''

"Ah." He thought he heard laughter in her voice. "So we see who can stand the darkness longer, eh?"

"We could."

"And are you going to try to frighten me with ghost stories, Elliot?"

He finished smoothing the blanket. "Only if you want me to. You dressed yet?"

"*Sí*." She crept closer. He heard her movements in the hay, felt her warmth, smelled her. "Oh," she whispered, reaching the blanket. "*Sí*, this is much better." And a second later she was sitting cross-legged, close beside him on the blanket.

Elliot pulled the second blanket over their laps. Then he reached for the Thermos and unscrewed the lid. As he poured, she sniffed. "Mmm, what is that?"

"Hot chocolate. Sara made it. In fact, she was planning to bring it out here to you when I showed up in the kitchen with the same idea."

"No," Esmeralda said softly as Elliot found her hands and pushed the cup into them.

"Oh, yes. She's a sweet girl, and she likes you."

"I do not know what she finds in me to like. I could not be more different from her."

"Maybe that's what it is. No one wants somebody just like them. I mean...take me for example."

She sipped, made a sound of delight, and then resumed the conversation. "What about you?"

"Well, I'm the most easygoing person I know. If I'm known for anything at all, it's my laid-back approach to life, and maybe my sense of humor. I never get upset over much of anything."

"I do not believe that."

"No?"

"No." She sipped again. "Everyone gets upset about things. Some simply hide it better than others."

Frowning, Elliot tilted his head to one side. "I suppose that's true about some. But not me."

She sighed. "You haven't been exactly calm since I've known you, Elliot Brand."

"No, maybe I haven't. In fact, you're right, I absolutely haven't been myself. But that's just it. I mean, here I am, this calm, unflappable guy without a care in the world. And then you come along. You're like a hurricane, blowing in and stirring everything up."

He felt her stiffen beside him as she set the cup aside. "Is that how I seem to you?"

"That and then some. Everything is a major deal with you. You seem to feel things a thousand times more than most people do. More than I do, at least. And I think it's contagious, because since you've been here, it's been rubbing off on me."

"Well, forgive me for having emotions!" she snapped, turning her back to him.

Elliot curled his hands around her shoulders. "See what I mean? I make a simple observation and you get furious over it. I wasn't insulting you, Esmeralda. I…I like that you're completely unpredictable. Keeps me on my toes. It's…it's exciting being around you, never knowing what's going to happen next."

Her head turned, her chin brushing over his hand on her shoulder. "You find me exciting?"

"Hell, you already know that." Elliot drew a breath, let it out slowly. "This probably wasn't such a good idea, my coming out here tonight."

"I…I think it was a very good idea," she whispered. And when he would have taken his hands away, she bent her head, brushed her cheek over his knuckles, and then her lips.

"Esmeralda…"

"Shhh," she whispered. Slowly she turned around to face him. Her palms closed on his face, and her lips found his in the darkness. Elliot felt the shudder that worked through him when those warm, wet lips touched his, parted, pressed closer. He groaned just a little and slid his arms around her, pulling her tight and kissing her hard.

When he lifted his head, he whispered, "I want you so much, Esmeralda…but we shouldn't…"

"I want you, too, Elliot. And I know you want to wait…but I don't think I can."

"I swear to God, Esmeralda, this isn't what I had planned when I came out here tonight. I wasn't expecting…"

"I thought that was what you liked about me?" she said softly. "Never knowing what to expect?" And with those words she pulled back, out of his arms, her movements rapid. A second later she pressed against him once more, but she wore nothing now. He felt her skin, warm and smooth and utterly bare against his hands, his cheeks, his neck. Catching his hand in hers, she pressed his palm to her lips, and then to her breast. "Touch me, Elliot."

He felt her against him. Softness, heat, and the hard pebble of her nipple growing taut against his palm. He shivered all over, fire pooling in his belly, in his groin. "Dammit, Esmeralda, I'm only human, you know." Drawing back, he yanked at his shirt, popping buttons as he wrenched it off and tossed it aside. And then he pulled her to him again, his chest naked against hers this time, and her hands were on him, sliding up and down his shoulders, tracing the length of his back as her mouth trailed fire down his neck to his chest, to his belly.

Kneeling there in the hay, he tipped his head back, grated his teeth, and lost himself to need as her tongue painted hot trails over his belly, and her hands clasped his buttocks and squeezed.

The jeans. He had to get out of the jeans.

Her cheek brushed over his hardness, and then her fingers were busy at the button. He caught her hands, stilled them. "Wait," he managed.

She stopped what she was doing immediately. Elliot took her shoulders in his hands and pushed her backward, until she was lying on her back. He wanted to give pleasure, not just take it. He knew instinctively that no man had ever done that for her before. And he wanted to be the one to show her how it could be. Slowly, gently, he stretched out beside her.

"Why did you stop me?" she asked, confused.

"Because you were going too fast," he told her. Then, leaning down, he kissed her slowly, deeply, and his hands ran up and down her spine as he did. He brought one hand around, between their bodies, and he touched her, opened her, and stroked gently. Her sudden gasp told him she had not expected this. And the subsequent ones told him that she approved. He bent his head to kiss her mouth again, and then her neck, and then lower, to kiss her breast. He kept his attention there, sucking and tugging at the tender crest as his hand continued to caress her below. And Esmeralda trembled, her breaths coming faster and her heart pounding against his chest. Her hands curled in his hair, and her legs parted.

"Elliot," she whispered, "Elliot…"

"Right here. I'm right here." He shimmied out of his jeans, kicking them away as quickly as possible, and then he rolled on top of her, cradling her gently in his arms. "Are you sure you want this?" he asked her.

"Oh, *sí, sí!*" she cried, and, clutching his hips, she pulled him into her.

Elliot went stiff and still, closing his eyes in rapture as he felt her tightness envelop him. But only for a moment, for she began to move, and he had no choice but to move with her. It would have been death not to, he was sure. Oh, she felt good. Her hands, her mouth, her body, felt so good. Soft and warm. So responsive to his every touch, his every breath.

She moved faster, and he did, as well, sliding deep inside her, withdrawing, plunging still deeper. She held him, and clawed at his back, and her teeth closed on his neck. He thought she was drawing blood, and he didn't care. It was good. It was all good, all of it. The pain, the pleasure. Her smells and her sounds. He strained harder, moved faster, held her tighter to receive him, and finally his body seemed to explode inside hers. Even as he grated his teeth and pumped his seed into her, she screamed his name and sank her nails into his back, arching so hard against him that he thought he'd melded with her somehow.

And then, slowly, so slowly, her body uncoiled, relaxed. And his eased, his taut muscles softening as his body seemed to melt atop hers. He slid slightly to the side and wrapped his arms tight around her waist. She lay with her head on his chest, and he felt moisture there.

"Are you crying, Esmeralda? Did I hurt you?"

"I don't know what you did to me, Elliot Brand. But it was not hurting me at all."

He smiled very softly. "You never…felt that way before?"

"I didn't know anyone could feel that way," she said.

He stroked her hair. "You've had selfish lovers in the past."

She lifted her head, and he sensed her looking into his eyes, though he could barely see her face. "I have had no lovers, Elliot. Men have used me. But never loved me."

"Then they were fools," Elliot said softly and, cupping her head, he drew her back down to rest on his chest. They lay silent for a moment, and Elliot battled the thoughts that kept coming into his mind, finally deciding just to voice them. "Esmeralda?"

"Mmm?"

"If…if you didn't know there could be pleasure for you in…in this…then why did you want it to happen?"

He could feel her lashes brushing his chest when she blinked. "I felt desire for you, Elliot Brand," she told him. "Just because I didn't know it could be so thoroughly quenched doesn't mean that I did not feel the desire all the same."

"Oh." He thought about that for a moment.

"I had other reasons, too," she finally said. Her words sounded like a confession. "But they matter no more. They matter no more."

Elliot nodded. He didn't like thinking it…didn't like feeling it, but man, there was something awfully big coming to life inside him. Some huge, over-whelming feeling about Esmeralda Montoya. The biggest feeling he'd ever felt in his life. He thought maybe this was what love was like. Bigger and more powerful and more frightening than he had ever imagined. And he thought it was no wonder his brothers had all temporarily turned into blithering idiots when it had happened to them. He barely knew what to do next, what to say, what to think. Should he tell her? Was he even sure yet?

No. No, not yet. He needed to think about this some more first.

He snuggled close to her, held her in his arms, and thought this must be the closest to heaven he would ever be.

No one was more in tune with her cycle than Esmeralda. Her aunts had explained it to her more than once, and since coming here and concocting this plan, she had been absolutely certain when she would need to seduce Elliot in order to bear his child.

As she lay there in his arms, feeling more cherished and protected than she ever had in her life, she felt her eyes widen as she remembered her plan. Her carefully calculated plan.

Her hand pressed to her belly, and she blinked three times in quick succession and tried to remember the date…and then she peered through the window high in the hayloft at the moon, in its first quarter and waxing. Oh, no! What had she done? What had she done?

She'd followed through on her plan, that was what. And now she didn't know if it had worked, and she wouldn't know for a couple of weeks yet, and already Elliot was stroking her face, kissing her again, beginning to rekindle the fire she'd never known lived inside her—the one that must have been sleeping there all along, just waiting for the right man to ignite the flames.

Elliot. Oh, *Dios,* what had she done to poor Elliot? And how would she undo it now?

Elliot woke her gently before dawn, kissing her eyelids until they fluttered beneath his lips. "Shhh," he said. "It's just me. Better get dressed, honey. I don't want the others walking in on you like this."

"Oh. Oh, *sí,* I will." She sat up, stretching, yawning. When Elliot started to move away, she said, "Where are you going?"

"I'm gonna slip back into the house before anyone stirs awake," he explained. "They don't need to know…about this."

She was quiet for a second, and he didn't know why. Then she said, "You are very wise. If they knew you had been with me this way, they would be very disappointed in you, I am sure."

"Hey…" Elliot hurried back to her, knelt in the hay and gripped her shoulders. The sun was starting to rise now. Beams of deep orange crept in through the single window in the peak to paint her coppery skin and bathe her hair in fire. Elliot stared into her face and suddenly realized what he'd missed by leaving the lights out last night.

Didn't matter. He would see her, drink in every inch of her with his eyes, next time. And he knew beyond any doubt that there would be a next time.

"Don't think what you're thinking, Esmeralda."

She lowered her lids, hiding her eyes. "What do you mean?"

"You think I'm ashamed or something. I'm not.

You hear me?'' He gave her a little shake, so she looked up into his eyes again. "I'm not. I was only thinking about you. I don't want you feeling embarrassed. It's none of their business. Not yet, anyway.''

"*Sí*. If you say so, Elliot, then I—''

"It's the truth.''

She shrugged, and it was pretty obvious she didn't believe him. "Hell, I'll just have to find a way to prove it to you, then, won't I? Hmm?''

She peered up at him, doubt still shadowing her black eyes. "You need to prove nothing to me, Elliot Brand.''

"I think I do. But you let me worry about that.'' He leaned close, kissed her lips gently. "You, um…you thought any more about…about going back?''

She shrugged her shoulders. "The pendant is gone,'' she whispered. "Even if I wanted to go back, I could not, not without the pendant. And even if we did find it, it might not work its magic again.''

"That's all true,'' Elliot said. "But if we find it, and if it would work…would you want to go back?''

She searched his eyes, then lowered her head. "I don't know what you are asking me. I… To go back might well mean facing death. But I don't intend to remain an unwanted guest in your home, either, Elliot. That's what you really want to know, yes? Don't worry. I am strong. Even in this time, I can find a way to get by. And I will.''

"Oh, hell,'' he muttered. "You get something in your head, you're just like a bulldog with a steak, you know that, Esmeralda?''

Her dark brows rose.

He shook his head. "Give me a few minutes, and

then come in. I'll be in my shower by then, and no one will be the wiser. Much as I'd like to stay out here and talk some sense into you, I have to get cracking. It's my turn to make breakfast.''

She lowered her head, shook it slowly. "Your family does not want me at their breakfast table.''

"Yeah, well, *I* want you there. Besides, it'll just be Chelsea and Garrett, Sara and little Bubba. The rest won't be around for hours yet.''

The sun climbed higher, lit her face better. Elliot saw her clearly. She looked scared. Scared and sad and alone, in spite of her tough talk.

"Please?'' he asked.

Lips thinning, she finally nodded. "Oh, all right.''

Elliot grinned. "Good. See you in a few minutes, then.'' He bent down, kissed her again, and then scrambled down the ladder and into the house.

The Brands' idea of breakfast was, Esmeralda thought, enough to feed a working man for a full day. Around the table, everyone seemed strained. Well, everyone except Sara, who bubbled with excited conversation that seemed sincere. And Bubba, of course, who told silly jokes he'd learned from one of his uncles.

"What do Bozo the Clown and Kermit the Frog have in common?'' he asked, grinning.

Since he aimed the question at her, Esmeralda said, "I don't know. What?''

"They have the same middle name!'' Bubba shouted. "Ha! Get it? Bozo *the* Clown, and Kermit *the* Frog? Ha ha!''

Elliot slapped his hands on the table and laughed

out loud. Chelsea smiled weakly at her husband, who said, "That's a good one, son."

Esmeralda only shrugged and tried to figure out why Sara was laughing as hard as Elliot was. "I have to tell that one to my class, Bubba. They'll love it," Sara said.

Then the laughter died, and things went back to being strained. Chelsea smiled often and tried to make conversation, but her worry was plain in her eyes each time she glanced Elliot's way.

Garrett, too, seemed very concerned about his brother. He looked ill with worry. And as for Elliot, he couldn't have been more obvious, though Esmeralda was certain he didn't mean to be. He was so cheerful this morning, smiling nonstop and heaping food onto his plate as if it was going to be a long hungry winter. His eyes met hers often across the table, and they always stopped there, lingered there, darkened.

Lord, he even hummed or whistled between eating and talking.

No wonder his family looked worried. Oh, sure, they had seen through Esmeralda from the start. They knew what she wanted. They'd been right.

But she had changed her mind. No land was worth breaking the heart of a man as decent, as kind, as wonderful as Elliot Brand. She was going to let it go. She was not going to force him to marry her. Not now.

It felt good to have finally figured out the right thing to do. And yet it hurt, too. Because she knew she was going to have to leave here. A frightening prospect, yes, in a world she knew so little about. But a sad one, too…for the idea of leaving Elliot Brand did odd things to her heart.

The back door burst open, and Jessi Brand came charging through. "Well, I don't know how you did it, Esmeralda, but you sure were thorough in your research!" She slammed a fat sheaf of papers down on the kitchen table.

Esmeralda looked at them, then at Jessi. "I don't know what you mean," she said.

"Research," Jessi snapped. "Study. You studied everything about our family history, every detail, just so you could make this insane story of yours seem authentic."

Esmeralda shook her head. Elliot got to his feet. "Jessi," he began, a warning tone in his voice.

"Don't you 'Jessi' me, it's all right here. Everything she said, it's right here! The names of the Brands who lived in Quinn in 1881. Garrison was sheriff, and his brothers Waylon and Blake were part of an outlaw gang. Allen owned the bank, and Eldon, the youngest, was murdered by a young Mexican woman in an argument over property. A woman who was sentenced to hang for her crime, but who escaped justice. Everything is right here. Even her name, Esmeralda Montoya, and her father's name. He owned the ranch, but he was killed by unknown bandits, and when the mortgage wasn't paid off, the bank took possession of the property. It's been Brand land ever since."

Taking a deep breath, still glaring at Esmeralda, Jessi sank into a chair. "So there. You see?"

Elliot came to stand right behind Esmeralda's chair, his hands closing softly, reassuringly, on her shoulders. "All I see is proof that everything she and I told you last night is the truth."

"Oh, for Pete's sake, Elliot," Jessi snapped. "What you ought to see is that it was all a matter of public record, and that she could have gotten this information just as easily as I did!" Shaking her head, she shot Garrett a look. "She's claiming to be a woman who murdered one of our ancestors, Garrett. If you can't arrest her for pretending to be someone she's not, then arrest her on a hundred-year-old murder warrant that's still outstanding."

"Now, Jessi, just—"

"That's it." Elliot's voice was suddenly so deep and so angry that even Esmeralda felt a chill. "That's it, I've had all I'm gonna take from you, Jessi Lynn Brand. Now it's my turn to talk and your turn to listen, you hear?"

Eyes widening slightly, Jessi nodded once. "Say what you want, Elliot. You'll never convince me this wild tale of hers is true."

"Then maybe you'll believe this. I love this woman."

Dead silence. Esmeralda heard her own gasp, and she saw Jessi's jaw drop. The woman looked as if she'd been hit between the eyes.

"And what's more, I'm gonna marry her."

Chapter 11

"*You're what?*"

Everyone in the room shouted the same words, or similar ones, but no one quite as loudly or with as much impact as Esmeralda. She was so stunned by Elliot Brand's foolish declaration that she leapt to her feet as she asked the question, sending her chair over backward behind her. Elliot jumped out of the way of the chair, but he would not escape the woman as easily. Esmeralda whirled to face him, poking him in the chest with her finger as she said, "You have some nerve, saying such things!"

"But—but I—"

"But nothing! You don't even *know* me, Elliot Brand. What makes you think you love me, eh? And even if you did, what makes you think I want to marry you?"

He lifted his brows, and she felt a pang, because

there was a bit of hurt in his eyes, but mostly confusion. "You mean...you don't?"

She flicked both hands open, palms up. "The light dawns," she said. Then she turned away, facing his family. "You can stop your worrying now, *muchachos*. You keep your precious stolen land and your brother and your opinion of me. I want none of it! My father once told me that to love a man is to love his family—to marry a man is to marry his family. To be loved by a man is to be loved by his family. Well, it is all too plain this family wants no part of me, and I want no part of it!" She turned and strode out the door, slamming it none too gently behind her, and she kept right on walking.

This family—they were *loco!* All of them! First they accused her of making up stories, then they found proof that what she'd told them was true and somehow decided it was proof instead that she'd lied. They refused to believe their own blood when he told them what happened and, in the same breath, vowed to do harm to anyone who might hurt him. And as for Elliot...*Dios,* he was the most *loco* of them all. Unlike any man she had ever known! First he told her he didn't expect sex as payment for his aid, and then he made love to her anyway, and the next thing she knew, he was claiming he wanted to marry her!

Marry her!

She slowed her pace a little, glancing over her shoulder nervously. Back along the winding, dusty road, the big white house stood watching her go. No one followed. No doubt they were all relieved she'd finally gone. Perhaps even Elliot.

Marry her. Imagine that. It was exactly what she'd planned to make him do. It had all been so simple in her mind. Get pregnant, or claim to be so, should his seed not take root in her after all. She knew he would do the honorable thing by her then. He would marry her. And then she would claim a portion of his land when she demanded a divorce.

So simple.

But everything had changed, hadn't it? He was just too damned good, too kind to her, too…too wonderful. He was nothing like his bloodthirsty ancestors. And, damn him, he thought he was in love with her.

Her. A scheming, conniving woman who'd planned to use him and steal his land…exactly the way his ancestors had used and stolen from her.

And yet he wasn't coming after her. Why not?

She rolled her eyes heavenward and started walking faster again. It wasn't as if she *wanted* him to come after her. Besides, that *loco* family of his was likely grilling him endlessly just now, demanding to know what his intentions were. Probably they would take his portion of the land away from him now, just in case he should find a way to bring her into the family. Just to protect the ranch from the likes of Esmeralda Montoya.

Well, to hell with all of them.

The creak of the screen door in the distance made her look back quickly, and even as she did, she ducked low. A clump of sagebrush near the roadside gave her cover as she looked back. Elliot stood on the porch, looking down the road. Cupping his hands around his mouth, he called her name. Her throat went dry. She licked her lips and wondered why her eyes were burning.

"I am sorry, Elliot Brand," she whispered. "You do not deserve what I was planning to do to you. The rest of your family… *Sí*. But not you. And so I go.'' Her throat growing too tight to speak, she added softly, ''*Dios, papa,* I wish you were here!'' Then she crept away, down the slight slope beside the dirt road and into the thicket nearby, keeping low until she was well out of sight. Knowing, even then, that Elliot would come looking for her.

But he would not find her. No, not where she was going.

Elliot walked and called and felt just about as low as he could ever remember having felt. The only time it had been this bad, he thought, was when he'd been knee-high to a cricket, and Garrett had gathered the whole family together to tell them that their Mama and Dad wouldn't be coming home anymore.

Esmeralda had lost her father, too. And to her that pain was fresh and new. She would want to be close to him.

Okay. So the first place Elliot would search would be the tiny burial ground.

''El?''

He stopped short on the dirt road, bristling at his sister's voice. Not turning to face her.

''El, I'm sorry. I didn't…I didn't know you were that serious about her.''

Slowly, he turned. ''You know, when they all wanted to beat Lash bloody, I stood up for him. I stood up for you. That's the way it's always been with us, Jessi. You and me, just like this.'' He held two fingers up, side by side. ''But not anymore.''

He started to turn away. She caught his shoulder. ''Elliot, please! I just don't trust her, is all. I didn't mean to—''

"I know you don't trust her," he said slowly. "But you're supposed to trust *me*, Jess." He shook his head slowly. "You let me down. I mean, of everyone in this family, you were the one I was sure would take my side." He shook his head once, then pulled away from her touch and kept walking.

"Elliot!" Jessi shouted. "Dammit, Elliot, I'm sorry!"

He heard tears in her voice and almost broke, but he held firm. He didn't turn back.

He didn't turn back.

Not for a long while. He walked over acres of the ranch, through the wooded parts, across the open parts. He went to the grove where the tombstones of Esmeralda's parents stood, crooked and crumbling. But she wasn't there. He searched near the stream, but he didn't find her there, either. Hours passed as he walked the ranch, calling her name, hoping she would calm down and come back.

Hell, he supposed he had been a little bit crazy back there at the breakfast table. Just blurting everything out the way he had. He hadn't even known he was going to say it. But the minute he did, he knew it had been a mistake. He'd been driven by the need to strike back at his family—to shock them the way their lack of support had been shocking him since all this had started.

And yes, there was more than that. He truly did feel *something* for Esmeralda. Something potent and hot. He wanted her to distraction. He was all wrought up all the time since she'd come into his life, and he *liked* being that way. It was an exciting kind of feeling.

Hell, when all was said and done, it made perfect

sense that she ought to marry him. The farther he walked, and the more he thought about it, the more reasonable it seemed. Even if this thing was too new to call love, it was still...*like*. At least *like*. Right? Hell, she had nowhere to go, and he wasn't involved with anyone or likely to be. He'd never felt even passingly fond enough of a woman to think about wanting to settling down.

Except Esmeralda. He was way beyond passingly fond of her. And he wanted to make love to her every single night of his life. And he was damned well going to, whether she married him or not, and from her response last night, he kind of thought she might agree with him on that. So they might as well do the deed. Make it legal. Tie the knot.

It would solve all her problems. She would be a Brand then, and the ranch would be as much hers as it was his own, and so that problem would be solved, as well.

Man, the more he thought about it, the more sense it made.

Of course, blurting it out the way he had...and with her temper being what it was...and then the whole family looking at her like she'd come to destroy every living Brand on the planet—well, it was no wonder she'd run off. She tended to overreact to everything, anyway.

He smiled to himself, thinking of the way she looked when her temper heated up—as it often did. Her eyes would widen and flash, and her nostrils would flare just a little. Her chin would come up, and her shoulders would square. Her spine would go rigid, her legs would seem to lengthen, and her hands would curl into tight little fists. He liked to watch that…the way she reacted with every part of her being.

She'd been like that when they'd made love, too.

Her voice deepened and slowed, and she muttered soft, breathless words in Spanish. Her body softened and lengthened and heated. Her breaths came shorter and faster, while her heart beat fast and hard. Her every sensation was reflected in her face, in her eyes, in her movements, in her touch.

Oh, hell. He had to find her.

She couldn't have gone very far on foot. He almost smiled again at the irony of that thought. The two of them had come a hundred years on foot, so he supposed…

Oh, no. What if she'd decided to try to go back?

His heart jumped and pounded, making it hard to breathe. But she couldn't, he told himself. Not without the pendant.

Right. Not without the pendant. In fact, I'll bet that's where she is right now. Out by that big old oak tree on the River Road, looking for the pendant.

He nodded hard and turned to head back toward the ranch. He would get a horse…or the pickup. No, no, a horse, because she was on foot, and she wouldn't be likely to stick to the beaten paths. He would be more likely to find her on a horse.

Unless it's already too late. Could be, you know. She might have already found that stone skull and zapped herself right back where she came from.

The image of Esmeralda as Elliot had first glimpsed her filled his mind. Standing tall, proud and undefeated, on the gallows, a noose around her neck, the wind in her hair.

He tried to force the nightmare away as he broke

into a run. And as he did, he saw the sky darkening to the south and the roiling shapes of storm clouds gathering.

She wasn't at the crash site looking for the pendant. Elliot scanned the ground for the stupid, cursed thing himself, but he didn't find it. And he knew he probably wouldn't. Wes had looked…hell, so had Taylor. And she was prone to finding things like lost villages buried under a century or two of dirt and time, so if *she* hadn't found it, Elliot figured his own chances were pretty slim.

As were Esmeralda's.

God, he hoped so, anyway.

Thunder rumbled nearer, and a look at the sky gave him a shiver. The storm clouds were moving in fast from the gulf, and even now the wind was picking up. Hanging his head, he mounted his horse, a long-time friend of his. Trigger was named for the smartest horse in history, so far as Elliot was concerned. He'd always been a stickler for trick ponies and rodeos. And he'd taught Trigger a thing or two in their years together.

"Don't suppose you're any good at tracking runaways, though, are you, Trigger?"

The smallish mare shook her mane and blew, just as if answering.

"She isn't," a voice said. "But you know good and well that I am."

Elliot looked up to see Jessi mounted on a dingy white crossbreed Appaloosa named Sugar. And beyond her was Garrett, sitting tall on Duke, Wes riding Paint, Adam seated upon a horse he called Sundance, and Ben riding a sibling of Duke's that he'd long ago claimed as his own and insisted on calling Horse. Ben always had been a little different.

Elliot sighed, lowered his head. "I take it she hasn't showed up back at the house, then," he said.

"Not yet. But Sara and Chelsea are there waiting, in case she does," Jessi told him. "Lash is asking around town."

"Meanwhile, Taylor's gone to the university to dig up anything she can find on that crystal skull," Wes said.

"Yeah," Ben put in. "And in case you're still worried, don't be. Nancy Drew is on the case, as well."

Elliot smiled. Ben's sleuthing wife, Penny, was one of a kind.

"She drafted Kirsten to help her," Adam said. "Even little Bubba's pitching in. He's keeping watch out his bedroom window with that toy telescope of his."

Elliot nodded. "So the family's decided to help me find her, after all?" He eyed each of them.

"Well, all except Sara," Jessi said. "She's still ensconced in the attic, digging through the family history. But the rest of us…yes, Elliot. We want to help."

"And what about *when* we find her?" Everyone looked at him, then at each other. Elliot waited, but no one spoke. "Look, this is real. It's not some scam to steal the ranch, and it's not a hallucination. I was *there*. I saw all this happen. Now, you either believe me or you don't. Which is it?"

Wes looked at his siblings, shook his head slowly and nudged the dark Appaloosa with the white, spotted rump forward. When they reached Elliot's side,

Wes turned Paint around to face the others. "I'm with you, Elliot."

Ben was next. He held Elliot's gaze for a long moment, then nodded hard and lightly kicked his horse's tawny sides. "I guess if my Penny could come back from the dead, then anything's possible," he said. "Besides, I know better than to side against love. It always wins anyway."

Now Elliot was flanked by two of his brothers. Adam looked at Garrett, and Garrett at Adam. "It's just…it's just that we all know time travel isn't possible," Adam said. "But…if Elliot says it happened…"

Garrett nodded. "He's our brother. If he says it's snowing in Guadalupe on the fourth of July, then we got no choice but to believe him."

"Right." Adam nudged his horse ahead, and Garrett followed. "We're with you, Elliot. But if you tell anyone, I'll kick your backside."

"You'll try," Elliot said.

Adam sniffed. "Hell, to tell you the truth, I'm a little relieved. Never quite got over you telling me you'd marry Kirsten yourself if I let her get away from me."

Elliot lowered his head, smiling softly. He'd only been half-kidding, but he would never say so. Finally only Jessi remained. She met Elliot's eyes. Drew a deep breath. "I don't want to lose you to some crazy woman…from this time or any other," she said. "But I guess if I don't ease up on you, I'm likely to lose you anyway, huh?"

He nodded.

Thinning her lips, Jessi nodded back. "Okay, then. I believe you. All right?"

He held her eyes, searched them until she looked away. "I think you're lying through your teeth, Jess. But at least you're making an effort."

"Doin' the best I can," she muttered. "Come on. Let's get back to the ranch and see if she left any sign."

Elliot nodded. If anyone could pick up a trail, it would be Jessi. "Thanks, Jess."

Jessi nodded and whirled her horse around. As she did, she, too, looked at the sky. The storm was going to break any time now. It hovered overhead as thick and black as coal oil, dark clouds tumbling over one another in an agitated boil. Elliot could feel the tension in the air. It almost crackled. The storm was ready to break loose. And Esmeralda was out there somewhere, alone and afraid.

Esmeralda was warm and safe, and quite pleased with herself. She'd spent the day exploring the land that felt as if it were the last remaining member of her family. Revisiting old haunts that hadn't changed in a century...exploring the places that *had* changed. And rediscovering her favorite spot in all the world. Oh, she wasn't exactly in the lap of luxury here, but she was glad to see that she could get by, even in this strange world. Because some things hadn't changed.

The cave, for example, was still here. Right where it had always been. The same spot where she used to come as a child. It hadn't been so far from the old house she used to like to visit. The house had been little more than a cabin. Four walls and a loft, her father had told her. Later it had gone to ruin after her father had built the big house, on the same spot where the Brands' home now stood. But this place...this had been first. It was a part of her family history, of her heritage.

The log cabin was no longer there, of course. She'd looked for the stone foundation that used to be there and seen only one small patch of stones, four feet long and two high. The rest of the foundation had been scattered long since. But the cave remained. Long ago it had been only a stone's throw from the cabin. Her father said that when he was a single young man just starting out, he used to store milk in there to keep it cool in the natural spring that ran through the deepest recess.

She hadn't gone back that far. She'd seen the storm coming and had crept just far enough into the cave to ensure she would stay dry. She'd brought an armful of twigs and dried leaves with her. It had taken longer to locate a piece of flint, but that particular stone was plentiful here. She sparked a fire to life easily. Lord knew she'd done so many, many times before on her father's hearth, or that of her aunt. Or on the trail between the two. She could have blocked the cave's entrance with pine boughs, had she wanted to, but she preferred that the smoke from the fire have a clear way to exit. Besides, the opening was small, and not much wind or rain would come through. She'd even had time enough to gather a nice pile of fallen leaves into her haven. They made a fragrant and utterly soft bed for her.

A good thing, for it looked as if she might be here the night through.

The storm she'd sensed, then seen approaching finally broke loose, making the darkness fall early. Esmeralda curled into her leaf bed, beside her snapping fire, and watched the dark rain pour down. All the day through she'd managed to avoid thinking about Elliot Brand. Even now, she tried to elude him, but he kept invading her mind. When she turned her head sharply, as if averting her inner eye, she saw him yet again.

The spot on the wall was faded and dull, but her eyes picked it out, even in the winking firelight. EM loves EB. A crooked, lopsided heart surrounded the silly, little-girl sentiment. She'd spent hours, she recalled, digging the letters into the stone with her father's hammer and his hunting knife, which she'd used as a makeshift chisel. He'd been furious when he'd seen the blade. Honestly, she'd ruined the thing. But she never told him how, or why.

As a little girl, she'd fancied herself in love with Eldon Brand. Then he had changed. His parents had been killed, his eldest brother had run off, the rest of the boys had been farmed out to any family who would take them, and Eldon had changed. He'd become a mean, heartless, cruel man without a soul. A man she could never love.

Only now did she realize…it had never really been Eldon in her heart at all. It was Elliot. It was Elliot all along. Somehow…her heart had known. It had recognized a shadow of Elliot in Eldon…a kernel of him…somehow. And it had known.

Just as she knew now what was really eating at her soul.

Elliot was who he was because of his family. Everything he had become—everything that made him a man she could so easily love—was due to them. The Brands. The family she'd hated all her life and vowed on her father's grave to destroy. As much as she disliked them—or wanted to—she could not deny that.

If she stayed in Elliot's life, she would come between him and his loving family. Without that loving family...well, he would cease to be Elliot. Just see how differently Eldon had turned out when his family had fallen apart. Think of little Bubba, and Jessi's child, Maria, and the one Penny would give birth to at any time now. How would their lives turn out if Esmeralda broke the bonds of this family?

No, family was too important. She knew that far better than anyone else could.

Sí, Esmeralda. And what about your own child, eh?

Blinking hard, she looked around, as if seeking the source of that voice, even though she knew it had come from within. She pressed a hand to her abdomen. "It was only one night," she whispered to the empty cave...to the carving on the wall and to the dancing flames. "It was only one night, there will be no child."

Even to her own ears, the words sounded like lies.

He was soaked to the skin, it was pitch-dark, and Elliot had seen no sign of Esmeralda yet. He was even more worried than he'd been before. The night was cold, not bitter, but cold. And the storm was working itself up into a real frenzy. Hell, where could she be?

"Thank goodness you're back," Chelsea said, hurrying to greet the soggy crew of failed searchers at the door. She was tugging Garrett's raincoat off him almost before he closed the door behind him. Last one in, as always. He'd seen to it that they all put up their horses, rubbed the animals down and fed them, and then he'd hustled every one of his siblings through the door ahead of him. Father figure. It was his way.

Chelsea shook the rain off his slicker and hung it on a peg near the door. "There's coffee and cocoa waiting," she said. "Go on in by the fire. You're soaked through."

She was on Elliot even before she finished speaking, tugging his coat off, shaking the rain from his hat. Mother figure. That was Chelsea.

"I'm goin' right back out," Elliot said. "Just need some dry clothes and a hot drink. Five minutes, tops." He heeled off his soggy boots, and his damp socks left footprints on the floor as he headed into the parlor.

Chelsea, now rubbing at Jessi's hair with a towel, said, "Well, there's been no word from her here."

"I keep tellin' you, Mama," Bubba said, stomping his foot. "Emmer-elda's hidin' in the secret castle."

"I know, hon. I know." Chelsea ruffled Bubba's hair, and turned to Elliot again. "Sara has some news you'll all want to know about."

Elliot was standing with his back to the blessed heat of the fireplace and feeling guilty as hell for soaking up the heat when Esmeralda was probably freezing somewhere. He looked up at Chelsea. Wes, Ben and Adam had managed to get their own coats off and escape her coddling hands. Then Sara came in, a tray of steaming mugs in her grip. Garrett spoke before Elliot could.

"What is it, Sara? Chelsea says you have news?" Garrett asked, taking two mugs, handing one to Elliot.

"Pretty old news, actually. Look at this...." Setting the tray down on the coffee table, Sara bent to the stack of very old, very time-yellowed papers beside it. Turned out they were actually newspaper pages, each one carefully attached to a cardboard page of a scrapbook. And even the scrapbook looked aged and worn.

Quinn Town Cryer, the paper's banner read. And beneath that, 6 June, 1881. Sara said, "Let me read you the lead story. The headline says, Mexican Murderess Escapes Justice." She cleared her throat, and read on.

"Esmeralda Montoya, daughter of the late Luis Montoya, former owner of the Double-M Ranch, was sentenced to hang today for the murder of Eldon Brand. Montoya, an unmarried, unchaperoned, undiscliplined harridan up from Mexico to see to her father's burial, has been disputing the Brand family's claims to the ranch and making a scandalous nuisance of herself around town. After knifing the unarmed Eldon Brand in the gut and leaving him alone to die, Montoya faced the gallows today. Her hanging never took place. Aided by an unknown outlaw who burst in on the execution waving a gun, Montoya escaped justice on a stolen horse. Though the sheriff and a posse gave chase, the pair somehow eluded them. One source claims the posse had them surrounded at one point, but none of the men involved will comment on how the pair managed to escape. So far, Montoya and her unknown accomplice are still at large. Eldon Brand, her victim, will be buried tomorrow at the Quinn Town Cemetery."

Sara cleared her throat. "The byline is Jeremiah Brand. Hardly an unbiased reporter, hmm?"

"Biased or not, that's not exactly proof," Jessi began, then she bit her lip. "I mean, I believe Elliot anyway. I don't need any proof. But if I did, this wouldn't qualify."

"Oh no?" Sara asked, and she turned the cardboard with the clipping attached and at the same time yanked a magnifying glass from her hip pocket. "Check out the photograph, cousin Jessi."

Jessi sighed, moved closer, and took the page. Then, frowning, she held up the glass and looked closer. "Oh...my...*God.*"

Lifting her head slowly, blinking, wide eyed, she said, "Where did you *get* this?"

"In the attic, with a bunch of stuff your parents and their parents had stashed away up there. I can't believe you guys have never gone through it. Your entire family history is up there. Even old Wanted posters with Waylon Brand's mug on them—he looks just like Wes!"

Shaking her head slowly, Jessi looked at the newspaper photo again. "This can't be...." she said.

Having had enough, Elliot gulped down the last of his cocoa, and took the page from his sister's hand. And there was Esmeralda, just as he'd first glimpsed her. Standing on the gallows. The dress torn, the bruise on her cheek, her hair loose...and that stupid pendant hanging around her neck.

Seeing her face, even in the poor-quality, time-faded photo, made him ache for her all the more. He handed it to Garrett, shaking his head. "So you have the proof you said you didn't need," he told Jessi. "And in case you didn't notice, that's the selfsame dress she was wearing when she arrived, right down to the rips and tears in the same places. And that's Tay's pendant around her neck. And I don't rightly care about any of this. I just have to find her.''

''Look in the castle, Uncle Elliot,'' Little Bubba said.

''Yeah, I will pal.'' Elliot started for the door. But Bubba yanked his shirtsleeve hard.

''How? You don't know where it is!''

''I'll find it.'' He didn't want to hurt Bubba's feelings, not for the world, but he was in a hurry. It was cold and dark and…

''I can show you!'' Bubba said proudly, eyes big and round, as Elliot looked down at him and tried hard to conceal his impatience. ''In my 'scope…out my window…I can show you.…''

''Now, Bubba, bud, it's too darn dark outside to see anything out your window,'' he said. ''And Uncle Elliot's got to hurry and go find Esmeralda, because it's raining and cold outside.''

Making a face that suggested Elliot was a complete idiot, Bubba said, ''But she's not gettin' wet, 'cause she's in the secret castle! An' she's not cold, 'cause of the fire…that's why I can see from my window, Uncle El! 'Cause of the fire.''

Nodding, he patted Bubba on the head and turned toward the door. Then he stilled and turned back to the little boy again. Fire? He could see a fire from his window? ''Maybe you'd better show me after all, Bubba.''

Grinning widely, Bubba took Elliot's hand and they raced through the room to the stairs, then up them to his bedroom.

Chapter 12

"I'm going alone," Elliot said.

His family had crowded into Bubba's room to take turns looking through My First Telescope to the tell-tale light of a distant fire. Bubba said there was a cave out there that he'd discovered on one of his many excursions with his dad, and that he called it the secret castle because that was what it looked like to him. Garrett remembered the place once Bubba reminded him. And Elliot remembered that Esmeralda had mentioned a cave, too, a place where she used to go as a girl, to dream of some fellow she'd been sweet on. Yet another man in the long line of them who'd managed to let her down, or hurt her in some way. He remembered that, too. Had sensed it at the time.

He didn't plan on doing the same.

"Elliot, come on. The more of us that go with you—"

"The more of you that go with me, the more likely

Esmeralda will be to take off again. You guys haven't been exactly hospitable toward her, you know.''

''Well, how the hell could we have possibly known she was for real?'' Jessi argued.

''Because I told you she was.''

Jessi's head lowered, and she looked guilty.

''Elliot's right,'' Chelsea said. ''Besides, he could probably use some time alone with her to explain why he decided to issue her the world's clumsiest and most poorly thought-out marriage proposal.''

''More decree than proposal,'' Sara said.

Elliot took a minute to glare at Chelsea, then he shook a finger at Sara. ''Don't you forget that you're single, too, and sooner or later I'll have the chance to get even with you for that remark.''

She grinned. ''I'm holding out for Prince Charming,'' she said. ''So I imagine you're gonna have a long wait.''

''Go on, Elliot,'' Jessi said. ''Go get Esmeralda. When she comes back we'll all apologize and maybe we can…I don't know…start over with her. If she'll let us.''

Elliot nodded and hurried out of the room. His clothes were still damp. He didn't rightly care. He slung his wet slicker on, clapped his damp Stetson on his head and ran out the door. Boots slapping mud, rain pounding him all the way, he raced through the darkness to the stable and saddled up a fresh horse, and then he was out of there. He kept telling himself to take it slow. That Esmeralda was—according to Bubba, at least—in a warm, dry spot, sheltered from the storm. Probably safe.

Probably.

Probably wasn't good enough. He'd at least taken

time to snag a flashlight on the way out of the house, and he flicked it on as he rode toward the distant cave. He worried all the way about what he would find when he finally got there.

Esmeralda lay in the soft, fragrant leaves. The cave was toasty-warm, and that made her sleepy. She was hungry, too, but she supposed that would have to wait until morning. Then she would see about finding some food. For now...

She closed her eyes and told herself not to think about Elliot.

But she thought about him anyway. She imagined him finding her here, striding through the cave's small opening, rain-damp and tired. He would say, "I've been so worried about you. Are you all right?" And she would lower her eyes and nod and say she was fine. And then he would come the rest of the way inside and sit with her near the fire, in her leaf bed, and he would tell her he was sorry about the way his family acted. He would say it didn't matter what they thought, that he loved her and wanted to marry her all the same.

Esmeralda shivered a little as she lay there, eyes half-closed, imagining his dark eyes and the emotion in them as he told her that. She thought that would be the time when she would have to tell him the truth. That she'd been planning to trick him, that she'd only wanted to sleep with him so she could get pregnant, make him marry her, and then lay claim to at least part of the land. But she would hurry on to tell him the rest. That she'd changed her mind. That she couldn't go through with it.

In her mind, Elliot was angry at first. But within a

few minutes his face softened, and he forgave her. He said what she'd planned didn't matter. He said he loved her anyway....

She opened her eyes wider, then rolled them at her own foolishness. "*Sí*, that's exactly the way it will happen!" she snapped at herself in the darkness. The fire snapped, too, as if in agreement. "Not only does he not love me—he doesn't even know me. And if he cared even one tiny little bit, he wouldn't have stopped searching for me so soon."

Not that she wanted him searching for her at all. Because she didn't, and she didn't know why she was letting her mind conjure all these silly scenarios, anyway. They all ended the same. With him sweeping her into his arms and kissing her. It was nothing but a craving. Nothing but lust. She was in a cave with a storm raging outside, while he was safe in his bed in his big fat house, surrounded by his big, cruel family. That should tell her all she needed to know about Elliot Brand.

The sound of her name floated to her, faint and distant, brought to her by a sudden gust. The flames shot upward, and sparks flew. Frowning, Esmeralda whispered, "What was that?" and sat up slowly.

She strained her ears...and in a moment, she heard it again. Closer this time. But still faint, and muffled by the rain. "Esmeralllllldaaaaaa!"

Creeping fast on all fours, she rounded the fire and knelt in the cave's opening. There the wind buffeted her face, and raindrops pinged like bullets. "Elliot?" she asked the wind.

The shout came again, and she saw it. A light, small but bright. As she stared at the distant spot, a silhouette grew sharper against the storm; a man on

a horse. He was bent in the saddle, curving his back
in defense against the elements as he rode onward.

He *had* come after her! Oh, *Dios,* suppose he truly
did love her?

Her heart lurched a little. So many questions. Was
she carrying his child? Would he forgive her for that,
and for what she had planned? Could he? Did
she...did she love the man? Was it possible to love
a man she'd known for such a short time? Oh, but it
felt as if she had known him forever.

But what about his family? They hated her! They
would never accept her. And her father had insisted
that...

Oh, but what did it matter? She was getting too far
ahead of herself. She didn't even know for sure it was
him.

He called to her again. Elliot's voice, no mistaking
that. Turning, Esmeralda drew a flaming limb from
her small fire, and then stepped out of the cave and
waved it slowly back and forth over her head.
"Here!" she called. "I am here, Elliot!"

The small light aimed toward her. The horse began
to move faster. Thunder ripped through the sky, and
lightning cut a jagged path. Blinding, it was, and
striking so hard she felt the ground beneath her feet
vibrate and sizzle, and she heard the sound of the
strike like a gunshot—deafening, frightening and
sharp.

The horse reared, and she thought Elliot tumbled
from its back, but she couldn't be sure. She took two
steps forward. "Elliot?" He was still a hundred yards
from her, up on the hillside. Lightning flashed again,
a bare instant after the first strike, and she saw more
clearly. Two things were illuminated in the night to

her questing eyes and pounding heart: the riderless horse, galloping back the way it had come…and the huge, ancient tree, leaning slowly toward the ground where the horse had been. Then leaning more. Groaning and leaning even more.

Esmeralda lunged forward, her torch still in her hand. "Elliot!" Where was he? It was dark again. She couldn't see him. But the tree gave one last groan, and then cracked loudly and toppled. It crashed to the ground, splitting and creaking as it broke. The sound it made was deafening. A groaning, creaking, snapping, and then a dull roar as it hit.

And something else. Something that could have been a man's cry.

She ran, heedless now of the rain drenching her, or of her bare feet slipping and slapping in the cold mud. She just ran. That tiny light was her guide, though it lay still on the ground. She followed it, let it guide her, and called Elliot's name over and over again.

Then she saw him. He lay on his back in the mud, hair plastered to his face…and it looked as though a tree with a girth the size of his horse's lay right across his body. From the waist down she couldn't even see him for the trunk and the limbs and leaves.

"Elliot!" she cried. She dropped to her knees in the mud, looking around frantically and jamming her makeshift torch between two nearby limbs to free her hands. She pressed her palms to his wet face, bent closer. "Elliot, Elliot, wake up! Wake up!" Her lips pressed rainwater kisses to his face, quick, desperate kisses that were like prayers. "Elliot, please!"

He was crushed. He must be crushed. She must see for herself, try to help him. Thunder laughed at her, a deep, vicious gust of ridicule. Lightning slashed ar-

rows at her, as if threatening to strike her down, as
well, should she remain too long within its reach.
Wind howled its menace like a hungry wolf.

Gently she lowered Elliot's head and took her
hands away. They were bloody. Frowning, she scrambled for the fallen light, the one he had brought, and
she shone its beam on his head. There was a rock just
beneath him. She moved him off it and knew he'd hit
his skull hard on that stupid rock when he'd fallen.

And the tree...

Turning, she aimed the light at the place where it
crossed his body. Then she blinked and crawled
closer. *"Gracias, Madre de Dios, gracias!"* she
cried. For there was space. The trunk was not lying
on his body. She could put her entire hand between
Elliot and the bark. The tree's huge limbs were keeping it up off him, though how long they could hold,
she did not know.

She had to get him out from underneath.

"Elliot? Elliot, I have to move you. You understand?"

Nothing. No response.

Esmeralda moved around behind him, sliding her
hands underneath his arms, trying to be very careful
of his head. Bending her knees, she pulled with all
her strength.

Elliot slid just a bit, and then her feet slipped in
the mud and she landed hard on her backside. The
thunder roared, amused by her pathetic efforts. "To
hell with you," she shouted in defiance. Gripping Elliot, she tried again, and again, and again, moving his
body inch by painstaking inch, until finally he was
clear of the tree. It must have hit him hard on the way

down. His left foot lay oddly, the toe of his boot pointing straight to the left.

He was soaked, covered in mud. So was she at that point. She had to get him back to his home, to his family. He needed a doctor, a warm bed. But how could she move him? She could not carry him!

"Esmeralda...?"

She swung her head around, eyes wide. "Elliot! Oh, you are awake, *gracias Dios,* you—"

"Call...my horse...back."

She frowned. "Call...your horse? But how?"

He was struggling to stay conscious, struggling to form words. She could see that. "Whistle..." he finally managed.

"Whistle. *Sí, sí,* I will whistle." She licked her lips, put her fingers to them and tried to whistle in the way she'd seen Elliot do. It took three tries to make a sound loud enough for the horse to hear—maybe. If it hadn't run too far.

She was rewarded, though, only moments later, by the sound of hoofbeats and finally a soft nicker, as the poor, wet horse stood on the other side of the huge tree, looking over it at his former rider.

"You'll have to...lead him...around," Elliot managed.

"I know. I will only be a moment." Scrambling to her feet, Esmeralda made her way over the fallen tree to the other side, scraping her elbows and knees on the rough bark as she went, scratching her face on tiny branches, too. She gripped the horse's bridle and quickly led the animal all the way to the end of the tree's massive reach, around the other side and back to Elliot. There she looped the reins over a limb, just to be safe, and quickly knelt beside Elliot again.

"Can you get up?" she asked him.

"I...I don't know."

"I will help you." She bent to him, sliding her hands beneath his body, palms to his back, and eased him up into a sitting position.

Elliot closed his eyes and seemed to sway from side to side as he lowered his head into his hands. Rain pounded down like a waterfall on their heads.

"It's all right," she whispered. "Come, you must stand. Just get on the horse. That's all you have to do, just get on. I will do the rest. Come, Elliot, you can do this!"

He nodded, lifting his head, his arms. He grabbed hold of a limb. She moved behind him, wrapped her arms around his waist. "Ready?" she asked, and when he nodded, she lifted for all she was worth, as Elliot used the limb to pull himself upright. "Good, good." She let go of him, and he clung to the tree. Coming around in front of him, she said, "I'll bring the horse closer." He nodded, but the moment he put weight on the crooked foot, he cried out and very nearly went down again. Instead, he wound up with his arms grasping her body like a padlock, hugging her hard about the shoulders as his entire body trembled. "Dammit to hell!" he rasped, looking down at his leg and turned-out foot. "It's broken."

"I was afraid it might be. Hold on, my love, I will take care of you, I promise you that."

He snapped his gaze to hers, even as she hurried to pry his arms away from her and guided them to the tree for support. "What did you say?" he asked her.

"I said I will take care of you. This is all my fault. You shouldn't have come after me, Elliot." She left him there and hurried the three steps to the horse, then led it closer. "Lean on me," she told Elliot. He did, and somehow she managed to help him, pushing, pulling and tugging, to get into the saddle. But he didn't sit upright. He leaned forward over the animal's mane, his hands gripping the wet, slick pommel.

"Come, pony. We go slow, eh? Be careful with him." She climbed onto the horse behind Elliot, one arm around his waist to keep him from sliding off, the other guiding the horse. They began the slow, plodding course back toward the ranch.

It grew wetter and colder every single step of the way. And every step, she was more worried for Elliot. For though she shook him now and then, and spoke to him constantly, he never replied. She didn't think he opened his eyes again, either.

Damn.

It was a full hour before the house finally came into sight. Esmeralda was shivering so hard by then that she could barely hold the reins. Her knuckles throbbed, and the rest of her hands had gone numb. She felt as if she were soaked in ice instead of rainwater. Her feet were like lead blocks of throbbing agony. She rode the horse right up to the front porch, stopping at the foot of the steps. Then, lifting her head in the pounding rain, she yelled for help as loudly as she could.

There was a commotion, the door flew open, and the next thing she knew, a half dozen Brands were tugging her from the horse, tugging Elliot from the horse. Someone ran inside shouting "Call Doc," while Garrett carried Elliot into the house, and Wes—

she thought it was Wes, the dark one—scooped her up and carried her inside, as well.

When Esmeralda next opened her eyes, it was the dead of night. She was clean and dry, and her feet were blessedly warm. She lay in a bed, covers thick and piled atop her. Pillows, soft and cloudlike, were beneath her head. The room was dim, but a faint light glowed from the hallway. Beside her bed the meanest Brand, the one called Jessi, was slumped in a chair, sound asleep.

Elliot, Esmeralda thought. He'd been hurt. Where was Elliot?

Blinking the sleep from her eyes, remembering everything, she sat up and flung the covers back. She was dressed in the white fleece nightgown they'd given her. It was thick and warm and soft as down. White stockings—the kind they called "socks," hugged her feet to keep them warm.

For a family who hated her to the core, who had seen through her schemes from the start, and who were determined to protect their brother and their home from her, they certainly had taken good care of her.

She didn't deserve their kindness.

Getting to her feet, she winced inwardly when a rush of heat and prickly pain rushed through them. She had to go still for a long moment, sitting on the edge of the bed, gritting her teeth, fighting not to cry out at the sensation as the blood flowed into those poor, abused appendages once again. They'd been warmed, but they came to life more with use. Eventually she managed to stand on them, and, as quiet as a mouse, she tiptoed to the door, opened it very slowly and crept out of the room. Bit by bit she made her way down the darkened hall to Elliot's bedroom, and there she saw light coming from beneath the door and heard hushed voices.

"Doc said he'd sleep the night through," Garrett whispered. "Come on to bed, hon. He'll sure holler if he needs us. You know Elliot."

"All right." That was Chelsea. "Let's leave the door open, though, so we'll be sure to hear him if he wakes."

Neither of them said the words Esmeralda desperately wanted to hear. That he would be all right. That his injuries were not serious ones, and that he would recover.

She flattened herself to the wall as they emerged from Elliot's bedroom. She didn't want to see them, couldn't face them. Surely they would hate her now more than ever. She had caused all this. She had hurt their brother just as they had feared she would.

Oh, but she hadn't meant to!

When Garrett and Chelsea had vanished into their own bedroom farther down the hall, Esmeralda dared to breathe again. She had to stiffen her spine and force herself to move on. She was so afraid of what she would find when she stepped into Elliot's room.

Bracing herself, she did. They'd left the light on, dimmed, but on. Esmeralda stood for a long moment in the doorway, just staring at the only man besides her father ever to claim he loved her.

Elliot lay on his back in his bed. Some sort of rack had been positioned over the bed, with pulleys and cables, and this rack held his injured leg up, so it dangled above the mattress. From the knee down, Elliot's calf was encased in a plaster cast that made it appear twice its size. Only his toes stuck out the end. The rest of him was all covered in warm blankets, just as she had been. His head cradled on pillows, a big white bandage taped to the back of his skull. Snuggly warm, he was. Except for his poor toes. How cold they must be, without a thing to warm them.

Creeping closer, Esmeralda put her hands on his toes. "Like ice," she whispered. She held them there, between her hands, for a long moment, letting her body heat warm them. Eventually she took her hands away and, bending down, peeled off one of her socks, and then carefully put it over his toes, to keep them warm.

Elliot stirred just a little. Esmeralda stilled, lowering her eyes to his face. His eyes remained closed, his body relaxed. She moved closer to him, pulling a chair up beside the bed to sit down. "Elliot? Can you hear me?"

"Mmm."

She pressed a hand to his face, and found it warm. A bit too warm. He was feverish, no doubt. And no wonder. "*Dios,* I hope you're going to be all right. You *must* be all right, do you hear me?"

He moved his head slightly, turning it toward her, and then tucking in his chin, almost as if in an effort to nod.

"*Sí,* you must be all right. I could not bear it otherwise. You never should have come after me, Elliot Brand. You are a foolish man to risk so much for a woman like me."

Her throat seemed to tighten. She cleared it forcibly. She had things to say to him, and she didn't know when she would have the nerve to say them again. "Only a fool would believe he could love a woman such as I am. I am no good for you, Elliot. No good for you. Your family, they were right about me all along. You should have listened to them.''

She put a hand over his. He turned his and weakly closed it around hers. Yes, he was hearing her; he was aware of her here.

''I had a plan, you know,'' she told him softly. ''I planned to seduce you, Elliot. To take you inside me only so that I could become pregnant with your child. I was going to trick you into marrying me and then divorce you and claim the right to take part of this ranch away from you.'' She lowered her head, her eyes watering now. ''But I could not go through with it. And that is why I had to leave. Now you know the kind of woman I am. Now you know the truth, Elliot. I used you. That's all that was between us. A lie. My lie, and my scheme. My need to avenge your ancestors' crimes upon you. And now I've realized you...you are nothing like them. You are a good man, Elliot Brand. A good man.''

The hand holding hers eased its tentative grip. Esmeralda leaned forward and pressed a kiss to Elliot's cheek. But he weakly turned his head away. And she thought there was a dampness at the corner of his closed eye that hadn't been there before. ''I am so sorry I hurt you,'' she whispered.

Then she turned to hurry away, back to her own room. She would stay until daylight. Just long enough to ask one of the others about Elliot's condition. No longer. Then she would go away and never again torment the sweetest man she'd ever known.

Jessi woke to find Esmeralda gone, and she didn't figure it would take a rocket scientist to figure out

where to find her. Hell, there was *something* going on
between Esmeralda and Elliot. If she wasn't trying to
scam him out of the ranch, then maybe it was just
gratitude. Or something.

She didn't want to think about the "or something"
right now.

But when she got to Elliot's door and heard Esmeralda's tormented voice speaking softly from the
other side, she got a whole earful of "or something."
And she leaned softly against the wall, listening, and
feeling more and more ashamed of herself.

"Land sakes," she whispered. "She's in love with
him. And I don't even think she *knows* it!"

When Esmeralda said her goodbyes to Elliot, Jessi
straightened up and hightailed it back to the bedroom
that had once been her own. She got to the chair beside the bed, slouched down and slammed her eyes
shut tight just before Esmeralda came creeping back
into the room. Jessi tried hard to look as if she'd been
sound asleep the whole time. Then finally, Esmeralda
crawled back into the bed, pulled up the covers...and
proceeded to cry herself to sleep.

Jeez-Louise, what a mess, Jessi thought fiercely.
Ah, hell, it was tugging at her heart to hear the soft,
sobbing sounds the woman poured out into her pillows. She was hurting...seriously hurting. Now that
Jessi knew she'd been right all along about Esmeralda's plans...she thought maybe she'd been dead-
solid wrong about the woman herself. And much as
she hated to admit when she was wrong, particularly
since it was such a rare event, anyway, she had to
admit she'd probably messed up big-time in this case.

Well, hell. At least it wasn't entirely too late to fix
things.

She hoped.

Sometime near dawn Elliot came awake to a splitting headache, a throbbing shin bone, and a bad, bad feeling in the pit of his stomach.

Then he thought back, remembering, piecing things together. And he remembered it.

All of it.

Culminating in Esmeralda's bedside confession last night. She'd never really wanted him. Never truly cared for him at all. She'd only been using him. She'd slept with him as part of her plan to trick him, and then she'd changed her mind.

It hurt. It hurt more than the damned broken leg, and it hurt more than the knob on the back of his head. It felt as if it would be fatal, as a matter of fact. He'd loved the woman. He'd stuck up for her, defended her to his entire family, vowed to turn away from them all if they didn't ease up on her....

And she'd been lying. Plotting. Using him.

Faking everything? That night together...my God, it couldn't have been make-believe, could it?

Why the hell had he let himself fall for her? Why? God, he'd been such a fool. She'd told him as much last night, hadn't she? That he was a freaking fool to have fallen for her little game.

Damn her.

Damn her.

Chapter 13

"Morning, Elliot."

The cheerful voice of his sister brought his attention slightly away from the bleeding, gaping wound in his pride and the even bigger one in his heart. "Morning, Jessi."

"Hell of a night, huh?"

"Guess so."

Jessi came in, carrying a tray loaded down with sick-folk food. Tea, toast, juice, fruit. "What the hell do you call that?"

"You've been running a fever. So you get a light, healthy breakfast, lots of liquids, and a dose of aspirin. Like it or lump it, brother."

He muttered under his breath, eyeing his leg as he struggled into a sitting position. Jessi set the tray on his lap and plumped the pillows under his back. "You suck at playing the hero, you know," Jessi said, pulling up a chair and sitting down as if she planned to stay a spell.

"Why's that?"

"Heck, you went off to rescue Esmeralda and instead, *she* wound up hauling *your* sorry butt back home."

"Hmmph." He didn't want to discuss Esmeralda. "So the leg's broken?"

"Yup, clean through. You're lookin' at six weeks in that cast. And the first one flat on your back in bed."

He nodded. "We'll see about that. And the head?"

"Doc said you were lucky to be born with a hard one. Brand trait, he says." She grinned. "Eat your toast."

Lowering his head a little, Elliot wondered if Esmeralda had been hurt at all. With the storm and the rain…that tree falling. Hell, he didn't remember a lot.

"I'm just glad Esmeralda came back," Jessi said, sounding cheerful. Disgustingly and suspiciously cheerful. "I mean, I sure don't intend to be the one waiting on you for the next week or so."

"Yeah? What makes you think she'll be sticking around that long?"

"Duh."

He searched Jessi's face and finally dropped the rapidly cooling toast back to the plate and sighed. "You were right about her, you know."

"What?" Jessi blinked at him with her wide, doe-in-headlights expression—the one that fooled lots of folks into thinking her harmless and innocent. It didn't fool him for a minute.

"You know exactly what I mean. She was using me. Planning to scam me out of the ranch. That's all she wanted me for. Nothing else. You knew it all along. You were right, I was wrong, and that's the first and last time you'll hear me say those words, so enjoy them."

"Really?" Jessi asked, not sounding at all surprised.

"Yeah." Elliot had to pause a minute to breathe. His voice wanted to crack, and that would give away too much. "She, uh…she came in here last night and confessed everything."

"How would you know? You were out cold, between that lump on the head and the pain meds Doc gave you."

"I was…partly awake." He lowered his head so she couldn't see his eyes. His sister knew him too well to be looking him in the eye at a time like this. If she knew how much Esmeralda had hurt him, she would be out for blood. And even though he was angry, he didn't want to see the woman harmed. "I was lucid enough to understand what she was saying to me, at least."

"The words maybe."

Elliot lifted his head, studied his sister's face. Elfin and mischievous…and slightly worried right now. "What's that supposed to mean?"

"Means hearing and understanding are two different things, El. And you barely managed to do the one and were sure as hell in no shape to do the other."

He shook his head. It hurt when he did that, so he stopped. "You don't make any sense. I just told you, Jessi, you were right. I was wrong. She confessed. It's over." Picking up the toast again, Elliot dipped a corner of it into the sweetened tea and forced himself to take a soggy bite.

"Hmm. That's...odd, isn't it?"

He swallowed and fought nausea. "It's cold. It's miserable. It's rotten. But I wouldn't call it odd."

Jessi shrugged. "Drink your tea."

He took a sip to oblige her.

"I just think it's strange that she would admit it, at this point. I mean...well, I assume that means she decided not to go through with this...plan of hers."

"Apparently."

"That's what seems so odd. I mean, she pretty much had you right where she wanted you, didn't she? You said you were gonna marry her. Right in front of everyone. So...if that were all she was after the whole time...well, then it makes darn little sense for her to run away like she did. Doesn't it?"

Elliot shrugged.

"Wonder what made her change her mind?" Jessi mused.

He had to avert his eyes. Being reminded of his passionate, if poorly thought out, declaration—made in front of the whole fam-damily—was painful. And humiliating. "Don't know," Elliot said. "Don't care. I just want her out of here."

"Well, sure you do. I mean, it's not like she went out in a raging storm, pulled your broken body from underneath a tree and hauled your sorry butt all the way home or anything. Not like she saved your life. I mean, it wasn't that big a deal. Her feet weren't that badly cut, and there was no *real* frostbite. Sure, they were blue and all, but Doc said she'd be okay. And the bruises and scratches on her face were fairly minor. And sure, she was soaked to the skin, chilled to the bone and covered with mud from head to toe, but that's nothing a hot bath didn't fix right up."

Elliot felt his stomach clench into a tight knot as his sister talked. And every word conjured up an image. Strong, determined Esmeralda facing down the fury of a storm to help him. Cradling him in her arms, kissing his face and promising him that it would be all right.

"Is she...is she okay?" he managed to ask.

"Hell, Elliot, I don't know. She cried herself to sleep last night. Right after she left your room."

He lifted his head. "She did?"

"I was wrong about her, Elliot," Jessi said.

"No. No, you were right. She told me everything."

"I know." Jessi smiled a little sheepishly. "I was listening outside the door. But the only thing I heard was a woman telling a man that she loved him too much to hurt him."

"That's *not* what she said," Elliot told her quickly.

"No. No, it's not. But tell me this, Elliot. Why do *you* suppose she couldn't go through with it? She had what she wanted. You offered to marry her. So why did she suddenly change her mind?"

Elliot lowered his head, closed his eyes. "I don't know." Then he lifted his gaze to hers again. "And I don't want to know. I believed in her so much, Jessi, and she let me down. She made a fool out of me. I'm sure as hell not going back for seconds."

She nodded. "Maybe...maybe there's something I can do."

"Like what?" He shook his head hard, ignoring the pain. "Listen, Jessi, I don't want you getting involved in this. Just let me alone, okay? Stay out of it. Please."

Jessi leaned over and stroked his forehead. "Oh, Elliot, darlin'...you really ought to know better than to think I could do a thing like that!'' She kissed his cheek, got to her feet and hurried out, leaving Elliot with cold toast, weak tea and a badly bruised heart. He lay there staring hard at the door and forbidding his mind to think too hard on the things Jessi had said. He wasn't going to go softening up toward Esmeralda again. He wasn't going to set himself up for another blow. Hell, she'd made herself pretty damned clear last night. He would have to be a fool to forget that.

But even as he lay there, staring, banishing her face from his mind, the door opened slowly, and the phantom beauty stood there, looking back at him. Her hair tumbled over her shoulders. Her eyes were wide and black. In them he saw a bit of worry, a bit of fear, a lot of regret.

''What do you want?'' he asked her.

She shrugged delicate shoulders and came farther inside. ''To see if you were all right. You seemed so...so weak last night.''

''I'm fine. You don't need to worry yourself about me.'' He knew he sounded like a petulant kid. He felt like one. ''And you didn't need to come in here, either. You could have asked someone if you gave a damn how I was doing.''

She lowered her head. ''I...am not exactly in favor with your family right now, Elliot.''

''Yeah, well, you're not in favor with me just now, either.''

She drew a breath, sighed deeply. ''So you *did* hear what I told you last night.''

''I heard.''

''And as I thought you would, you hate me now.''

She lowered her head. "So I guess it is time for me to say goodbye, Elliot Brand."

"Oh no it's not. Not just yet, it isn't. I want to know something, and I think you owe me the truth after all this. Why did you change your mind? Why did you decide not to go through with your clever little plan?" he asked her. He hadn't intended to, had deliberately told himself not to, but suddenly he needed to know.

She only shook her head and turned toward the door.

"Dammit, answer me. I deserve to know!"

She kept going, stepping over the threshold. Elliot lunged from the bed, forgetting his leg, his cast, his cables and pullies, and his tray of food. As a result, he and all the rest of it wound up crashing to the floor in a tangled, wet mess.

"Elliot!"

Esmeralda was back at his side instantly, her hands strong and sure, gripping him, helping him up and easing him onto the edge of the bed even as she brushed the mess of food off him. Her hands pressed to his face, her wide eyes searching his…and they were damp. "Are you all right?" she asked. And it seemed she was scared to death that he'd injured himself again.

Dammit, why was he so freaking determined to see things that were not real? "Fine," he muttered, averting his eyes. He couldn't look at her. He was too soft, and she was too beautiful.

"Well, what have you done to him now?" Jessi called from the doorway. She stomped in, surveyed the mess and shook her head, hands on her hips. Turning to glance behind her, she said, "You see what I was saying?"

Entering behind her, Chelsea sighed. "Yes, I guess I do. Once again, Jessi, you were right."

And behind Chelsea, Sara entered the room. "I'd offer to stay and help, but I have classes to teach. There's just no way..."

"That's all right, Sara," Jessi said. "Esmeralda made this mess, she's just going to have to stay long enough to clean it up."

Elliot narrowed his eyes on his sister. When he slid a glance Esmeralda's way, she was looking confused. "I...I don't know what you mean," she said.

"What I mean, Esmeralda," Jessi said, striding forward and bending to pick up the toppled pulley apparatus that was supposed to be supporting Elliot's leg, getting it upright and untangling its cables, "is that we have jobs, families and lives, all of us. Plus this ranch to run, and now we're not only short a hand, we've got an invalid to take care of."

"I'm no invalid!"

"And it's all your fault," Jessi went on, ignoring Elliot as if he hadn't spoken. "Now, I know you told Sara you were planning to leave today, and I just don't think that's fair. You can't make all this trouble and then just walk out and leave us to deal with it. We need your help right here."

"Oh, no..." Elliot tried to cut his sister off, because he could see, very clearly now, where she was going with this.

Lifting her chin, facing Jessi like a martyr facing the flames, Esmeralda said, "You are right. I've been thoughtless and rude. Of course I will take over Elliot's share of the chores until he is well again."

Jessi seemed taken aback. She glanced at Chelsea, who looked at Sara, who shrugged and looked at Jessi again. Hell, Elliot thought. They were all in on this?

"That's not going to help. The men can take up the slack with the ranch chores, Esmeralda. What we need is someone to take care of Elliot."

Esmeralda looked at him swiftly. "But…but I cannot do that. I will tend the cattle. Or the horses. I know horses, believe me. Let someone else care for Elliot—"

"Oh, come on, Esmeralda. What do these men know about caring for an invalid?" Jessi asked.

"I'm no damned invalid!"

"Shut up, Elliot," Jessi snapped. She turned her gaze right back to Esmeralda again. "Doc says he has to be flat on his back in that bed for a week. After that he can start trying to get up and around again, but he'll have to take it slow. He'll be on crutches. It's going to be tough going for a while, and we just don't have the time to take proper care of him. If you won't do this, I'll have to hire a nurse, and—" Jessi broke off, rubbing her chin, shaking her head. "Here's a thought. We'll pay you."

Esmeralda shook her head. "No."

"We'll pay you in land."

Slowly Elliot looked at his sister. "Have you lost your freaking mind, Jessi?"

"We're going to need her full-time, twenty-four hours a day, seven days a week, for what will probably stretch into two months while we get you back on your feet, little brother. It's worth any price." She eyed Esmeralda. "I still hold title to one third of this ranch," Jessi said slowly. "I'll give you part of it if you'll stay."

"Of course she'll stay," Elliot snapped. "The land is all she's wanted the entire time she's been here."

Esmeralda's head snapped around, and her eyes blazed and her nostrils flared. "Is that what you think? After all that was between us, is that what you really think?"

"Of course it's what I think! It's what you told me!"

"It is not what I told you, you stupid man!" She was still crouching on the floor, where she'd been cleaning up the mess. But she rose now, straightening to her full height and tearing her furious gaze away from his to look at Jessi. "I will stay," she stated, her voice practically snapping with electric rage. "But not for your stinking land. I don't want it. It's poison now. Desecrated by blind men and their descendants."

Jessi lifted her brows. "We're not all bad, Esmeralda. But I suppose that discussion would do better if we held it another time. So what do you want? We'll have to come to some kind of arrangement."

Her chin went higher, hair snapping with the motion. "I will ask but one thing in return for my work. When he is well—" this with a quick snap of her head toward Elliot, all done without so much as glancing at him "—I want to go far away from here. Perhaps you will help me find a place to live, a job so that I can support myself and my…" She bit her lip fast, lowered her head. "That is all I ask."

Jessi nodded. "It's not anywhere near enough, but let me worry about that. As a base price, it's agreed."

Esmeralda nodded. She didn't look happy about it, but she nodded. "I never thought," she said softly, "in my wildest dreams, that I would be working for a Brand."

Jessi smiled slowly. "My married name's Monroe, if it makes you feel any better."

"And I was a Brennan before I married into this clan," Chelsea put in.

"Yeah," Sara added. "And until pretty recently, I thought my last name was Jones." Esmeralda tilted her head at that. Elliot thought she must be wondering why they were speaking in kind, friendly tones to her now that she had agreed to stay.

"It's a long story," Jessi said, her eyes fixing to Esmeralda's. "She'll tell you about it some time. So, will you stay?"

Their gazes held for a long moment. "I will stay."

"Good."

Then Esmeralda waved her hands. "Then go about your own jobs. I have work to do."

Nodding, the three women backed out of the room, all of them looking rather pleased with themselves, Elliot thought. Esmeralda, largely ignoring him, acting as if he were no more than a piece of furniture that needed to be moved so she could clean underneath it, tugged back his covers. "Into the bed, then."

Swallowing hard, Elliot glared at her. "You never answered my question. Why did you change your mind?"

She bent down, lifted his cast-encased leg carefully. "The leg is going back into the sling contraption," she told him. "If you don't turn in the bed, it's going to be very painful." And she started to carry out her threat.

Elliot turned so his back was to the headboard, and Esmeralda eased his leg into the sling, very gently, despite all her threats. Then she tugged the covers over him...all except for the suspended leg. Looking around the floor, frowning, she swooped down and came up again with the sock he'd been wearing on the wounded foot.

"I changed my mind," she said, gently easing the sock over his exposed toes, "because I thought you were too decent a man to be tricked in such a way. But now I think perhaps it was just that I am too decent a woman to do it to you. Heaven knows you deserve far worse."

But he wasn't giving her words all that much thought. He was too busy remembering...remembering last night, when she'd taken that sock off her own foot and put it on his, and it had still been warm from her body heat. And more...before she'd done it, he recalled, she'd cupped his cold toes in her hands, warming them.

"Does that answer your question, Elliot Brand?"

He blinked, looked up at her. Could a woman who didn't care about him in the least really be so tender? Especially when she'd thought he wouldn't know the difference?

"No," he said. "I have another."

She lifted her brows and shoulders at the same time, as if she couldn't care less about his questions, and bent to pick up the fallen tray, the toppled teacup, the spoon, the little plate. She stacked them all together, and the clattering noises the dishes made seemed as angry as she had suddenly become.

"Why did you turn down Jessi's offer just now? If all you ever wanted from me was the land, then—"

She slammed the tray onto the bedside stand so hard he almost jumped out of the bed. "I *never* said that was *all* I wanted from you, Elliot Brand. *You* said that. And the reason I turned your sister down is because I want to be far away from here. Far away from *you!* You think what? I will build a house and live beside you every day, knowing what you think of me? I told you what I was planning, and I told you how wrong it was, and how badly I felt for ever thinking of doing such a thing to you. I apologized for ever taking the notion. I felt lower than your stinking ancestors for what I intended to do. But even then, I was never as bad as you believe me to be!''

''Now wait a minute—''

''No, Elliot, you wait a minute. You have insulted me to my soul. For you sit in judgment of me and brand me a harlot…and no matter what I say, you believe it to be the truth.''

He was speechless. He sat there, gaping. But when she snatched up the tray and started for the door, he knew he had to talk, and talk fast. ''I *never* said that about you, Esmeralda. I never—''

''You believe it.'' She went to the door, gripped the knob.

''But I don't. I swear, I don't.''

''*Sí.* You do. Only a harlot could be with a man the way I was with you if all she wanted from him was his land. I thought I could make love to you to trick you out of this land, but I found I could not do it. I could not. When I gave myself to you, this stinking land was the furthest thing from my mind, Elliot Brand. And yet you believe that is all that motivated me. So you call me a harlot.'' She shrugged. ''And I call you a fool.'' Then she glanced at the spilled tea and scattered food on the floor. ''I will be back to clean that up.'' And jerked the door open and stepped through into the hall. Then she turned and gave that door a slam that rattled the windows and Elliot's teeth along with them.

Elliot fell back on his pillows, feeling as if he'd just attempted to have a logical conversation with a cyclone. Esmeralda Montoya blew full force from so many directions all at once that he couldn't hope to make sense of her. First she said she'd been trying to trick him into marrying her so she could have his land, then she said that wasn't the reason she'd slept with him, then she said she'd changed her mind because she thought he was decent, and *then* she called him the lowest form of pond slime ever to live and said she couldn't wait to get away from him.

Hell, he was dizzy, and he didn't think it had a damned thing to do with the concussion.

Why was she so mad at him? What the hell did she want from him, anyway? And why had she turned down Jessi's ridiculous offer?

That was what really had him baffled. If she had gone to all this trouble to get back the land she believed she'd been cheated out of…then why the hell had she turned down the best chance she'd had of getting it?

Chapter 14

It hurt her far more than it should have to know that Elliot honestly believed she had never felt a thing for him. That he thought she had been pretending that night in the stables. That he thought she was so accomplished a liar that she could pretend something as powerful as what she felt for him.

What she *had* felt for him.

She stayed, but it burned at her, ate at her. And she cared for him, bringing him food and drink and aspirin for his leg. She brought him water to drink, and to wash with, but she refused to help him bathe. His sister could do that herself, or he could stay dirty. She did not particularly care one way or the other.

He wasn't obeying her orders, but she told herself she didn't care about that, either. He would get up at will and hobble, somehow, into the bathroom attached to his bedroom. He did this a couple of times each day. She caught him hopping back to his bed now and then, so she knew. She also knew that to stand up and have the leg lowered brought on excruciating pain. So he didn't stay up long.

When a week went by and this was still the case, she could see his frustration, and she was fool enough to feel sorry for him.

When she came in that morning, he wasn't in his bed. Assuming he was in the bathroom, she waited…and then she heard a clattering sound, followed by Elliot cussing under his breath.

Without shyness or a hint of hesitation, she opened the bathroom door, half expecting to find her charge toppled on the floor.

Instead, Elliot was braced against the small basin. The cast was propped on the nearby toilet seat's lowered lid, as Elliot balanced on the other one, apparently trying to shave. His face was coated in lather, and his razor lay on the floor.

She couldn't help the wave of feeling that rushed into her. Or the wave of nausea that came with it. But *that,* at least, was unpreventable. She'd been ill three mornings in a row. Her time was late. She was not an idiot. She knew full well what that meant. The plan she had abandoned, the one she could not carry out, had worked.

Softening toward Elliot, she pulled his arm around her shoulders and turned him away from the basin. "Come. It pains you too much to be on your feet. You must lie down."

"I haven't had a decent bath or a shave in a week," he argued, but he didn't fight her as she helped him back toward the bed.

"That is my fault. I am sorry, Elliot. My anger with you has made me neglect the job I agreed to do.

Come, get into bed. I will take care of this for you.''
She eased him onto the edge and quickly lowered his
leg into the sling. Then she hurried into the bathroom,
located a small basin in a tall closet and filled it with
warm water. She carried this back to the bedroom,
left again, and returned this time with a washcloth, a
towel, a bar of soap and the razor.

His face was still covered in foam. He eyed her.
''You have some shaving cream on you,'' he said. He
reached out, swiped it off her cheek with a finger.

''Gracias.'' She tried not to feel the shiver of
awareness that passed through her at his touch, and
dipped the razor into the water, then lifted his chin
with her forefinger and began shaving him in slow,
even strokes.

''I guess…I owe you an apology,'' Elliot said. He
managed to speak without moving his jaw much, all
the while watching her.

She shrugged in that I-could-care-less way she had
mastered—or hoped she had—rinsed the blade, and
shaved some more.

''I never thought you were…what you thought I
thought you were.''

''A whore?'' she asked.

Elliot winced. ''Esmeralda, I never…''

She shaved a little harder.

He covered her hand with his. She took his hand
away and kept shaving. He sighed. ''All right, so
what was I supposed to think? You hurt me, Esmeralda. I thought I was falling in love with you, and
then you up and tell me it was all part of a plot to
steal my land. What the hell was I supposed to
think?''

She lifted her brows but kept shaving, saying nothing.

"What am I supposed to think now?" he went on.

Finished, she snatched up the towel, wiped his face clean of foam. "I don't care what you think now."

"Well, I do. I want to know the truth, Esmeralda. Did you feel something for me? Did you...do you still?"

She met his eyes but quickly averted hers, not wanting him to see. A second later, he clamped his hands around her head, drew her face to his and kissed her.

His mouth was warm and fresh. She stiffened her body, willed herself to pull free of him, but for some reason she didn't pull at all. In a moment, as his lips moved against hers, coaxing, soothing, she felt herself soften and yield. Her body trembled, hungered, yearned for his just as it had before. Just as it had truly never stopped doing.

Dios, how she still wanted him. Still...still loved him...even knowing how little he thought of her.

Elliot's fingers moved gently through her hair as he ended the kiss. She kept her eyes closed, ashamed of her weakness, unable to face him.

"My God," he whispered. "Are those tears?" His thumbs ran over her cheeks.

Her stomach heaved. She shot to her feet, ran into the bathroom, with barely time to spare, and retched so hard she fell to her knees. She was still there, leaning over, eyes watering, when she felt his hands on her shoulders.

Gently, he helped her to her feet, and she knew it hurt him to be up, out of bed, and wished she could think of some reason why he would put himself through any pain at all for her.

Still, he stood there, all his weight on one leg, the other sort of dangling, toes barely making contact with the floor. Elliot searched her face. "You're not fully recovered from that little adventure of ours, either, are you? Dammit, Esmeralda, you should have said something."

She shook her head. "It is nothing."

"It's not nothing."

It wasn't. But he didn't know that. "I'll be fine."

"You're right, you will. Go on, go lie down until you feel better. I mean it, Esmeralda."

She looked at him, nodded once, and hurried out of the room. Because if she looked into those eyes of his much longer, she sensed he would see through her lie to the truth she was hiding so carefully inside.

She didn't look...well. Elliot didn't like it. He didn't like that he cared, either, but there was no denying that he did, and her non-answers and cryptic criticisms made him think that maybe she *had* felt something for him once.

The way she'd responded to his kiss made him think maybe she still did. Not the vomiting part. But before that. The shaking, the softening, the opening of her lips to his.

Ah, hell, he was probably setting himself up for another fall. A hard fall this time. Not that it hadn't been a hard fall last time...just not quite hard enough to knock any sense into him. Must not have been. Because he still wanted her. He still felt all soft and squishy inside whenever her eyes met his. And now that he realized she wasn't feeling up to snuff, he was as worried as he would have been if it had been little Bubba or Maria-Michele sick.

He was still in love with that damned stubborn, quick-tempered woman. Esmeralda. All raven hair and ebony eyes and emotions made of nitroglycerin. He was in love with her.

And he didn't have a clue how she felt about him or what the hell to do next.

He waited until she was busy someplace else—knowing damn good and well that she wouldn't have gone to her room to rest as he'd suggested—and got out of bed. He was sick of this room, sick of being on his back, and pain or no pain, he was finished with it. Besides that, with Esmeralda sick, he wasn't going to have her running up and down the stairs all day to look after him. He snagged the crutches that had been left in his room for when he was ready and hobbled into the hall.

At the top of the stairs, he stopped. He looked down. Then he looked at the crutches. Then he looked down again. He'd better think of something soon. Gravity was already making his leg start to throb. Licking his lips, he tugged the crutches out from under his arms and lowered himself until he was sitting on the floor. Then, laying the crutches beside him, he proceeded to thump down the stairs, bump by bump.

"What in the Sam Hill is all that—" Chelsea asked, coming into the living room in reaction to all the noise Elliot was making, then stopping in her tracks when she saw him, sitting on his butt, cast out in front of him, three steps from the bottom. "Elliot!"

"Ah, hell, Chelsea, don't panic. I'm fine. Just got sick of being cooped up in the bedroom is all. And I don't think it's any too good for Esmeralda to be running up and down the stairs waiting on me all day.''

Chelsea frowned hard and folded her arms over her chest. Elliot figured that was probably because she needed to grip herself to keep from running over there and trying to help him up. He thumped to the bottom, stood the crutches up and, gripping them in the middle, used them to lever himself up to his feet, er, foot. Then he hobbled over to the biggest, softest recliner in the room and dropped into it.

Man, who would have believed it would take this much effort just to get down the stairs? He was hot, breathless, and his leg was throbbing like a big bass drum.

''Here,'' Chelsea said, apparently unable to restrain herself. She pulled a footstool over and lifted up his leg to lay it gently on the thing.

Elliot sighed out loud, the relief was so palpable.

''You should have hit the sofa instead of the chair.''

''I'm sick to death of lying down. This'll be fine.''

''Right.''

She didn't look as if she believed him. Elliot didn't particularly care. ''Where is Esmeralda, anyway?'' he asked her.

Chelsea frowned. ''I thought she was upstairs with you.''

''You mean she's not down here?''

Chelsea shook her head. Elliot lowered his, cupped his chin. ''Damn. She must be sicker than I thought.''

''She's sick?'' Instantly concerned, Chelsea glanced up the stairs as Elliot nodded hard.

''I told her to go lie down for a while, but I didn't really expect she'd do it. She must have been feeling worse than I realized.'' He shook his head, as Chelsea turned to scan his face.

"So what's wrong with her?" she asked.

"Damned if I know. I thought it must have been something to do with that night, the storm and the rain and all. But I'd expect her to have pneumonia from all that, not some stomach ailment.''

Chelsea tilted her head to one side. "Stomach ailment?''

Elliot nodded.

"She was…um…ill this morning?"

"Yeah."

Drawing a deep breath, Chelsea closed her eyes. "Yesterday, too. I heard her, early, before anyone else was up.''

Sighing hard, Elliot said, "Poor thing. You know, I'll bet it's the same thing as what's been ailing Taylor. Must be something going around.''

"Well, of course it's not the same thing," she said, smiling and shaking her head. "I guessed what was wrong with Taylor over a week ago, and it's not…" She stopped there. Blinked. Looked at Elliot, then up the stairs again.

He saw Chelsea's eyes go wider. Saw the way she gaped at him for a minute. Then she swore, saying a word Elliot had never heard her use before. He automatically looked around for Bubba, but the little fellow must have gone out this morning with Garrett, so he wasn't in earshot of his mamma's uncustomary language.

"Well, what's the matter?" Elliot asked, totally confused.

Chelsea anchored her hands on her hips, tapping

one foot and glaring at him. "Have you slept with that woman, Elliot Brand?" she demanded.

He battled a grin, but it tugged at one side of his mouth anyway as he turned his face away from her. "I'm not gonna discuss my love life with you, Chelse. Sorry."

"Hell and damnation," she cussed, and she stomped into the kitchen, leaving him clueless. He heard her dialing the phone, but he had no idea who she was calling. Who could figure women out, anyway?

For the second time in just over a week, someone had called a Brand family meeting. Elliot had divided his time between the armchair and the sofa all day, even made it as far as the front porch once, to sit in the swing with his leg propped on the railing for a little while. Esmeralda had seemed to perk up by afternoon. She'd had lunch with him out on that big front porch in the sunshine. She had eaten as if she hadn't been fed in a week, which he thought wasn't likely to do her stomach bug much good, but he decided not to say anything.

Anyway, halfway through the afternoon, the family started trooping in. Poor Penny, walking tilted backward with her belly leading the way, both hands underneath it, as if she needed to hold it up. Two weeks overdue now, if Elliot's count was right. Ben came beside her, looking as if he hadn't been sleeping well. Garrett and Chelsea were already inside, but they'd been deep in conversation in the kitchen, muttering under their breaths to each other and making Elliot wonder what the hell was up. Adam and Kirsten arrived looking gorgeous. Those two always looked gorgeous. Barbie and Ken go country, he thought. Jessi showed up with little Maria-Michele riding piggyback on Lash. Sara had been stacking cookies on a big tray, and she brought them in to set on a table. If Sara had one passion besides teaching and family, it was food. And finally Wes and Taylor arrived. Taylor looked worn-out. Rings around her eyes, and she seemed pale.

"You still don't look up to snuff," Elliot observed when she came to his chair to ask how he was feeling. "Jeez, I hope to hell this isn't food poisoning or something."

"It's not," she said, and she smiled a little oddly.

"Are you sure? I mean, it's hanging on, whatever it is." Everyone was settling in now, finding seats, and the conversation was dying down.

"I'm sure," Taylor said. "Chelsea called me this morning and just about chewed me a new belly button for not having gone to the doc already." She shook her head slowly. "I just never thought..."

"Well, *I* told you to go see Doc over a week ago!" Elliot said. "So what did he say?"

Her smile grew. "It's sweet of you to worry about me so much."

He gave her hand a squeeze. "I am worried about you, sis. But it's more than that. Whatever you have, I think Esmeralda's coming down with it, too, so if you know what it is, I wish you'd spill."

The room went dead silent. Every single head turned his way, and Taylor looked as if she were going to faint. He glanced past her at Wes. Wes looked like he was going to come over, yank Elliot out of his chair and throttle him.

"What?" Elliot asked. "What did I say?" He

glanced around the room, and it looked to him as if every single person was in on some secret he had yet to figure out. He finally found Esmeralda. She'd gotten to her feet and was backing slowly out of the room. She'd made it all the way to the arching doorway to the dining room, and when he met her eyes, she turned and fled. He heard her run out the back door. Heard the screen bang closed behind her.

Shaking his head slowly, he brought his gaze back to Taylor's again. "Will somebody please tell me what the hell is going on here? Taylor, what's wrong with you? What's been making you so sick?"

Taylor glanced at Chelsea. Chelsea shrugged. "Tell him."

Looking at Elliot again, Taylor came closer, perched on the arm of his chair and put her arm around him. She gave him a gentle hug. "Oh, Elliot, hon. I'm not sick. I'm pregnant."

She sat back just enough to look at him. He searched her face, happy for her for just a second before the rest of it hit him. She was smiling at him, but worried, too. And he only vaguely heard Jessi saying she'd guessed days ago, and Adam and Kirsten congratulating Wes.

Taylor had been ill and pale, sick in the morning, but better in the afternoon, for days now. Jessi hadn't been that sick when she'd been carrying Maria-Michele, nor had Penny all through her pregnancy. But Elliot knew some women could be miserable for the first few months.

Now…there was Esmeralda. Sick lately, but only in the morning. Pale. She didn't look as if she'd been sleeping well, and she'd seemed hungry as a horse at lunchtime.

What if she wasn't sick at all. What if...?

"Oh my goodness, oh-my-goodness, oh-my-ow-ow-*ow!*"

Every head in the room swung again, this time toward Penny, who'd cut loose with a string of exclamations that made no sense at all. Elliot looked, too. Penny had shot to her feet, belly first. And her brows were up and she was biting her lips and clutching her belly with both hands.

"Penny?" Ben asked. "Hon?"

"I...think...maybe..." Penny scrunched up her face and made a horrible sound, like a balloon makes when you pinch its neck and let the air squeal out of it. It made the hairs on Elliot's neck stand up.

"Oh my God," Ben said. The next thing Elliot knew, Ben was scooping Penny right off her feet and heading for the door. And it was a darn good thing Ben was a big fellow, because at this stage Penny was no pixie. Plus she was squawking and not staying any too still. Ben looked over his shoulder, and his eyes were huge, his skin pale, his expression shell-shocked. "Baby," he said. "Now! Hospital!"

Then he was out the door. There was one moment of stunned silence before the family burst into motion, and then there were Brands running in a hundred directions. It was a whirlwind, one of those wonderful, chaotic moments Elliot knew he would always remember. Everyone talking, yelling, at once, grabbing keys, hats, kids, handbags. And then, like magic, they were gone.

Elliot sat alone in the living room. The screen door bounced twice and went still. Car engines came to life and faded. And there was silence. Dead, lonely, silence.

Elliot figured they would get to the hospital, get settled into the waiting room, get to pacing, and then realize they'd run off and forgotten him. Hell, he'd been through this before. He had loads of time to get to the hospital. Hours and hours.

So he figured he'd best use that time to wrap his mind around things here. Around the situation... the...the *very slight* possibility that maybe...

Shoot, he couldn't even say it.

Could he?

He closed his eyes and thought on it for a minute. He tried to picture Esmeralda with her belly swollen out to the size of Penny's. He tried to picture himself laying his hand on that bulge and feeling that amazing miracle squirming around inside her, the way he'd done when Jessi was carrying Maria-Michele. He tried to picture Esmeralda lying in a white bed, with her raven curls spilling around her, and her black eyes gleaming and moist as she cradled a tiny dark newborn in her arms.

Shoot. He sniffled, blinked his eyes dry, told himself he was just emotional because he was about to become an uncle again. But he knew better. Reaching for his crutches, he hobbled to the door, stepped out onto the front porch and looked around. She wouldn't have run off again. He knew that much. She'd promised to stay and care for him until his leg was healed up, and she had too much pride to go back on her word. Besides, she wouldn't want to risk him chasing after her and reinjuring himself.

"Esmeralda?" he called. Very carefully, he moved along the porch, faced the barn. "I know you're out here somewhere. Don't you think it's best we talked, you and I?"

There was no answer. Just the dust, slowly settling back now that the vehicles had all sped away, and the sun had hunkered down on a distant hillside in the west, fixing to settle in for a good night's sleep.

"I guess you know what it was Taylor wanted to tell us all. I guess everyone pretty much had it figured out but me. She's expecting a baby." Lowering his head, he shook it slowly. "Everyone was pretty excited. We Brands, we…we think pretty highly of little ones. Hell, there's not much can make us happier, I guess, than adding another member to the family."

He moved toward the steps, stopped at the top. "Esmeralda?"

Still no answer.

"You should have seen it. No sooner did Taylor break the news than Penny started hollering. She finally went into labor! Then everyone ran off to the hospital. I…I ought to head over there myself, by and by. I imagine before the night's out there's gonna be one more Brand in this bunch."

Still no sound. But she was out there. Watching him. He could feel that dark gaze on him like a touch.

"Don't know how I'll get there, though. I'm not even sure I can make it down these steps." Drawing a deep breath, he squared his shoulders. "Guess I gotta try, though. If you're not gonna come to me, then I'm damn well gonna come to you, Esmeralda. 'Cause I have a question that needs an answer, and you're the only one who can give it."

He gritted his teeth, and began to hobble down the porch steps. But at the second one, he deliberately tipped sideways. He yelled on the way down, landed on his back, hard enough to knock the wind out of him. His crutches went sailing off in opposite directions.

In about half a second Esmeralda was on her knees, gripping his shoulders and spewing a Spanish scolding that he figured would burn his ears if he understood it.

He smiled at her. "It worked."

"You did that on purpose!" she cried. She sat back on her heels, shaking her head at him. "You could have hurt yourself even more than you already have!"

"It would have been worth it." He gripped her shoulders and flipped her over fast and easy, planting himself on top of her, straddling her hips, his hands still on her shoulders. "There. Now maybe I can keep you still long enough to talk this out."

"Let me up!" she cried, twisting under his grip.

"No. No way, Esmeralda. Not until we get a few things straight between us. Now, you tell me right now. Are you carrying my child?"

She closed her eyes, averted them by turning her head to the side.

He gripped her chin and made her face him, though she kept her eyes shut. Bending his head, he kissed her mouth.

Her eyes flew open in anger. She pounded his shoulders, but he just gripped her wrists in his hands and pinned them to the ground. "Turn away or close your eyes, and I'll kiss you until you open them again. And I'm fully prepared to stay right here until you talk to me. Answer the question, Esmeralda."

Pursing her lips, she glared at him. "I don't know. I could be." He stared at her. She sighed. "It's too soon to tell for sure, Elliot. I think...I think so."

And just like that, the possibility was real. He felt

light-headed…awestruck, and he eased back, released her wrists and looked at her. He put his hand on her abdomen…closed his eyes. "My God," he whispered.

"Now you know why I have to leave."

His head came up fast. "No! Hell, Esmeralda, if this means anything at all, it means you have to *stay!*"

She shook her head.

"Dammit, Esmeralda, I love you. I want to marry you!"

"Do you? I don't think so, Elliot. I don't think you can love a woman you believe could trick you the way I planned to do." Sighing, she shook her head. "For all you know, this is exactly what I planned."

"I don't believe that."

"Don't you? And how do I know that?"

"I told you, Esmeralda, I love you. I want you to be my wife."

"Because of the baby."

"I asked you to marry me long before I knew about the baby."

"But you changed your mind when you knew what I had planned to do."

He blinked, shook his head. "*You* changed *your* mind about going through with that plan! You couldn't do it to me, Esmeralda. Because you love me, too! Admit it!"

She lowered her eyes, shook her head. "I would never know if you truly believed that, would I, Elliot? I would never know for sure that you didn't think this child I carry was the very weapon I planned to use against you. And you…you would never know for sure I didn't marry you just to get my hands on the land.''

He shook his head in denial. ''Tell me you love me, Esmeralda. Say it once, and I'll believe you.''

She shook her head. ''No, you won't. You'd be a fool to believe me.''

''Then I'm a fool,'' he said. ''Because I do believe it. Even though you won't say it, I believe it. That's why you couldn't go through with your plan. That's why you wouldn't accept Jessi's offer. That's why you ran away. You love me, Esmeralda Montoya.''

She closed her eyes. He kissed her again. And, slowly, she kissed him back. But when he lifted his head away there were tears on her cheeks. Gently, he got off her, helped her sit up, stroked her hair. ''Give me tonight, Esmeralda. Give me tonight. Come with me to the hospital. Be with the family. Share this miracle night with me...with us...and tomorrow, I swear to you, I'll find a way to make this work. I swear it. Just please, promise me you won't run away again. Twenty-four hours, Esmeralda, that's all I ask. Can you promise me that?''

She searched his face, and her eyes seemed so hopeless. So certain he was dreaming of the impossible. But at last, she nodded. *''Sí,''* she said. ''I will promise you that. It is the least I can give you in return for all you have given me, Elliot Brand. You...and your family...you are nothing like your ancestors, you know that?''

''I know that. I'm just glad to hear you finally do.'' He took her hand in his, drew it to his lips. Then he smiled. ''For now, let's find a way to get to the hospital.'' He nodded toward the one remaining vehicle in the driveway. ''You up for an adventure?''

She looked at the pickup truck, then at him, brows lifted. "What sort of adventure?"

"Your first driving lesson?"

Her eyes widened, and then she smiled. "You want *me* to try to drive that iron horse?"

He nodded.

"You must want to get to this hospital very badly, Elliot Brand."

"We can't miss this. You need to see what you'll be missing if you leave me, Esmeralda. There's nothing quite like a Brand family birthing."

Chapter 15

Esmeralda had never seen such a place as the hospital. It was big, yes, but so…so clean. Everything painted white, and so many gleaming metallic surfaces and fixtures…so many machines. So many *people!* All of them hurrying this way and that in their white coats.

Many of them seemed focused on the simple birthing of Ben Brand's child. An event so ordinary seemed today to be something of great concern. Penny was wheeled from one room, which they called the "Labor Room," into another, which was called the "Delivery Room." As they moved her along on a bed with wheels, so many Brands crowded around her that Esmeralda felt certain Penny would be stranded in the hallway, unable to go any farther. But that wasn't the case. She was wheeled through them all, into the room, her husband Ben beside her, holding her hand, while the others elbowed their way to the door that closed on them and tried to peer through the glass.

All except for Elliot. And that was a good thing, for his leg had to be hurting him. He sat now in one of the padded seats in the "Waiting Room." Esmeralda hovered in the hallway, partly watching the others at Penny's door, partly wondering why all this excitement caused her such pain.

Oh, but she knew why. It was so simple, really. She, too, was carrying a Brand child. But she would never be a part of the glorious chaos that was the heart of this family. They would not greet her news with joy and excitement, nor would they all come tumbling and jabbering into the hospital to see her child born. She would be alone, and far away from all of them when her time came. Unless...

"Esmeralda?" Elliot called.

She turned her head to see him sitting there in the waiting room, watching her, an odd, pained look in his eyes. Sighing, wishing things could someday be different, she walked in there to join him. Before she sat, she shoved the small table closer to where he was, and he smiled his thanks and put his leg up on it.

"I think I've come up with a solution," he said. She frowned and tilted her head to one side.

"I don't see how—"

"I have no choice, that's how. Now, the way I see it, we have two problems. First, you want to know for sure I don't just want to marry you because of the baby."

"*Sí.*" She sat down beside him, deciding to hear him out, even though he couldn't possibly overcome the obstacles that lay between them.

"Okay, well here's your proof of that. One," he

said, ticking off the number on his fingers, "I asked you before I knew about the baby. Two, I still don't know for sure if there *is* a baby. And three..." He reached into his pocket and pulled out a small box. "I've been carrying this around since...well, since before I got hurt. And if you don't believe me, you can check the date on the receipt...er...right after I tear off the part with the price on it."

Esmeralda sat there, still, frozen, wide eyes focused on the small velvet box he held. She was afraid to touch it. Sighing, Elliot opened the box to show her the golden ring with its winking diamond shooting fire, the way it felt as if her heart were doing.

"But when did you have time to...?"

"I didn't go into the house to shower that morning," he said. "You know, after the night we spent together. I went into town, instead, woke up Fred... that's the jeweler...and made him open up his shop for me. Took one look at this ring and bought it. Then I came home again before you even knew I'd been gone."

"Elliot..." she began.

"Then you ran off, and I got hurt, and I sort of shoved this to the back of my mind. But it's here now. And I hope you'll...you'll want to wear it. Soon."

He snapped the box closed and shoved it back into his pocket. "The second problem is how can I be sure you're not just marrying me for the property, right?"

Meeting his eyes, she nodded.

"I can tell you I'm already sure of that, but that's not going to cut it, is it?"

She shook her head from side to side.

"Then the only thing left to do is give you the property."

Blinking twice, she furrowed her brows. "What?"

"I'm going to sign my share of the ranch over to you, no strings attached. It's yours, and I'll make it legal first thing in the morning, the second I can call a lawyer."

Shaking her head, Esmeralda tried to make sense of his words and couldn't. "I don't understand. You would give me your share of the land in return for—"

"In return for nothing, Esmeralda." Elliot turned so he faced her on the cushioned bench of the waiting room. He clasped both her hands in his. "It's yours, free and clear. You can keep it, you can sell it, you can give it away. And you'll know it's yours, free and clear, no matter what you decide about...about us. Whether you marry me or not."

She felt her eyes widen, sat back a bit and searched his face. "I see. You give me the land so I will have no reason to marry you."

"Except love."

She lifted her brows. "Or gratitude." She shook her head slowly. "I don't know, Elliot...."

Her words trailed off as a sudden burst of activity and noise came from the group crowded outside the delivery room door. Ben stuck his head out, grinning from ear to ear. "It's a boy! A big, healthy boy, by God!"

His eyes gleamed, and his smile seemed to split his big face, it was so wide. "Come on, come on!"

"Wait a minute!" a nurse cut in, frowning as she opened the door wider and stepped out into the hall. "One or two at a time."

"Hell, sugar, it's a Brand family tradition!" Ben yelled, and, stepping back, he held the door wider.

The poor nurse was nearly trampled as the pack of smiling Brands surged into the room.

Esmeralda heard the sudden hushing of their excited voices. The exclamations of joy became soft coos and tender sounds before the door swung closed again. A lump came into Esmeralda's throat, and her eyes burned. "Come," she said to Elliot. "I'll help you. You should be in there with your family."

"You are my family."

She closed her eyes as he got to his feet. Her face averted, she handed him the crutches. She walked with him as far as the door, opened it and held it for him.

And for just a moment she looked in at that family. All gathered round Penny in her hospital bed. Penny wasn't one of them by blood but by marriage. Yet the love in their eyes and in their voices was every bit as real as if she were.

"Look at that," Garrett said softly. "We're so proud of you, Penny."

"You've given this whole family such a precious gift," Adam said, holding his wife Kirsten's hand. "First you came back to us, and then you brought little…little…hey, what are you going to call him, anyway?"

Everyone laughed softly. Wes kept looking at the baby and then at his wife, Taylor, and he looked near to tears himself.

"Zachary Orrin Brand," Ben said, his voice proud. "After Penny's father, and ours."

Esmeralda stayed in the doorway as Elliot moved forward and knelt beside the bed, reaching up to stroke the baby's cheek. He seemed entranced.

Swallowing her tears, Esmeralda backed out of the

room, unnoticed. She hurried to the exit and through it, and finally let the cool night air soothe the burning tears on her cheeks. Finally she knew why none of Elliot's solutions would make things all right between them. It was because her father was so, so right. Marry a man, marry his family. She could hear him saying it now, how important family was. She would never be accepted into the Brand family. Not the way those other women had been. They would never welcome her child as they did Penny's. Never. Not when they would all know the truth of its mother. That she'd plotted and schemed to get herself pregnant. That she'd had to be bought with a gift of land. Maybe it wasn't true, but it would be the way they would see it. And she didn't blame them.

"Esmeralda?"

She dashed at the tears with the backs of her hands, not turning toward the sound of Elliot's voice. In a trembling, hoarse tone, she said, "It won't work between us, Elliot. I…it turns out I am not pregnant after all. My monthly time…has come. And so there is no need."

He came closer, his boot clicking over the parking lot's pavement. "There's every need."

"Please, don't make this harder than it already is. I…I am leaving in the morning, Elliot. I need to find my own way in this world of yours. I need to start over, fresh. Without shame. You have a wonderful family. Someday you will find a woman you can be proud to bring into it, a woman they will love as they love you. I…I just do not belong here."

He said nothing. Maybe he couldn't speak, she didn't know. She walked away.

She heard murmurs, not from Elliot, and she

glanced over her shoulder. The entire Brand family stood in front of the hospital's entrance. All except for Penny. Even Ben had left his wife's bedside, though Esmeralda didn't know why.

"See?" Sara said. "I told you she was leaving."

"She's not leaving," Elliot said. Esmeralda stood very still. "Garrett, I'm turning my share of the ranch over to you. Effective immediately. We can get the papers drawn up tomorrow."

There was a moment of stunned silence. Even Esmeralda didn't know what to say.

"Well, sure, El, if that's what you want," Garrett finally said, speaking slow, in the deep, thoughtful tone he always used. "But why?"

"Because I'm in love with Esmeralda. And I want to marry her. And she's convinced everyone will believe she only married me for the land if she accepts."

"Well, that's just silly," Jessi said, speaking loudly. "Anyone can see the woman's in love with you."

"Sure she is," Chelsea said. "But you know, much as Esmeralda will deny it, I think the opinion of this family means an awful lot to her. I mean, you all heard what she just said, didn't you? Doesn't it, Esmeralda?"

Her spine stiff, Esmeralda turned slowly to face them. "*Sí.* It does. I know I am not worthy of the love of such a family as yours. I know I have only proven myself lacking in your eyes, time and time again. First I plot against you, and then I run away and cause Elliot to be injured...."

She had to pause, to breathe. It was Wes who walked forward slowly. "It's not like the Brands did much better by you, Esmeralda," he said softly.

"First they cheated your father out of his land and killed him. Then they attacked you and abused you and tried to have you hanged for murder."

"Yeah," Jessi said, taking over. She came closer. They all did, as Jessi spoke. "And then the modern branch of the family thought the worst of you from day one, never giving you a fair chance, and only seeing the truth when it was too late and you'd already made up your mind to leave."

"Right," Sara said. "So then they had the nerve to lay a big guilt trip on you and lie to you about not having time to take care of Elliot's injuries just so you'd stay and give them a chance to make it all up to you."

Her brows bunching together, Esmeralda said, "You...you did what?"

Chelsea, Sara and Jessi, all of them crowded closer, surrounding her. "We wanted you to stay, and that was the only way we could think of," Chelsea said. "We had plenty of people on hand to take care of Elliot."

"That's not all we did, either," Jessi said. "We...finished that project you and Elliot started. You know, out where your family is buried?"

Tears sprang anew into Esmeralda's eyes. She couldn't speak. Her hand flew to her breast.

"We planted some flowering shrubs and rose-bushes. And the boys put a gorgeous picket fence around it, with a gate," Sara said.

"Oh, we're not finished yet," Jessi said. "We wanted to order some new headstones, too, but we thought we ought to let you pick those out."

Esmeralda fought to breathe. "Why? Why would

you do all of this for me? Is it…because of the baby?'' she asked, one hand pressed to her belly.

"We did it to show you how sorry we were, and to convince you to give us another chance, Esmeralda,'' Jessi said. "And we started all this long before we even suspected about the baby.''

"There is no baby,'' Elliot said softly, his head lowering. "That's for the record, folks. She's not pregnant after all, and I want to marry her anyway.''

"She most certainly *is* pregnant,'' Chelsea said softly, her eyes on Esmeralda's, almost daring her to deny it. When Esmeralda said nothing, Chelsea went on, even as Elliot's eyes widened, and he searched her face. "We've never seen Elliot as happy as he's been since you came to us, you know.''

"That's right,'' Jessi said. "I'm closer to him than anyone. And I'll admit, I was jealous as hell of you at first. But…but I love him. I want him happy. If you leave him, Esmeralda, it's gonna break his heart. And you love him. I know you do. It's plain as day.'' Jessi shook her head. "I just don't see what the problem is.''

Esmeralda lifted her gaze, and she looked at the Brands all around her. "I guess…I have always believed that nothing is more important than family. And I thought I was not welcome in this one. I blame myself for that, not you.''

There was a murmuring beyond the three women. Adam, Ben, Wes, Lash Monroe and Garrett leaned close to each other. Meanwhile, Taylor and Kirsten crowded closer, to stand beside the other three women. Taylor said, "I know I want you in this family. I mean, I study the past for a living. There's so much you can teach me. So much I want to talk to you about." Then she smiled and rubbed her own belly. "And our babies...they're going to be born so close to each other. They'll be best friends. Maybe...maybe their mothers will be, too."

Esmeralda could hardly speak. Kirsten reached out to take her hand. "Penny and I have discussed this, you know. And we both feel the same way. I owe Elliot a lot...he helped me through the hardest time of my life not too long ago. And I think you're the best thing that's ever happened to him."

Someone cleared his throat, and when Esmeralda looked up it was to see the Brand men gently moving their wives and sister aside as they crowded closer. Cars came and went behind Esmeralda. Other people passed, looking at the crowd of Brands oddly. None of them paid any mind. The women cleared a path, and soon the men all stood right in front of Esmeralda. Garrett gripped Elliot's arm and moved him front and center. And then Garrett said, "I heard you say that to marry a man is to marry his family," he told her. "So..." And then, at his nod, he and the other four men dropped to one knee. Those who were wearing hats swept them off, and together they all droned, "Esmeralda, will you marry us?"

"Say yes!" a voice yelled from a distance, and when she looked up, Esmeralda saw Penny Brand at her hospital-room window, a nurse at her side, smiling. She cradled her newborn in her arms.

Tears streaming down both cheeks now, Esmeralda looked up and directly into Elliot's eyes. "I cannot believe all this..."

"Is it true?" he asked her. "What Chelsea said, I mean. There really is a baby?"

"*Sí,*" she said. "It is true. I...I didn't think you would let me leave if you knew."

"Hell, *señorita,* I wasn't plannin' to let you go either way." He slid his hat off, held it in his hands. "And at this point, I don't think the rest of them are going to, either." Tossing his hat aside, he took the little box out of his pocket once again, opened it and took the ring out. His brothers had all inexplicably started to hum some silly tune. "So...what do you say? Will you marry me?" Elliot asked.

Sniffling, dashing her tears, vaguely aware that passers-by and traffic were now stopping to observe, and that doctors, nurses and patients were peering through every window, she nodded. "*Sí,* Elliot Brand. I will marry you!"

A full-volume Texas whoop went up from the surrounding Brands. Hats flew into the air. Hugs were exchanged. Horns blasted, and pedestrians applauded.

Elliot clasped her hand and slipped the ring onto her finger. Then he got to his feet and swept her into his arms for the kiss she knew she would remember for the rest of her life.

Far away, an old oak tree stood with a recently acquired scar scuffing up its beautiful bark. At its feet were skid marks, bare earth showing through the green grass, left there by a distracted driver a little over a week ago, just before his pickup truck crashed into the tree's massive trunk. A few yards beyond the tree was a crystalline stream, and in the stream, resting upon a flat stone on the bottom, lay a crystal pendant cut in the shape of a skull. As the sun hit the pendant, it winked and gleamed beneath the water.

It had been resting in this very spot for several days

now, but suddenly a shift of the current set it free. The water lifted the small stone pendant up, into its chill embrace, and the crystal skull tumbled and bobbed as it was swept away, downstream, toward the Gulf of Mexico.

* * * * *

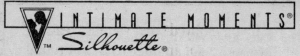

If you enjoyed what you just read,
then we've got an offer you can't resist!

Take 2 bestselling love stories FREE!

Plus get a FREE surprise gift!

Clip this page and mail it to Silhouette Reader Service™

IN U.S.A.	IN CANADA
3010 Walden Ave.	P.O. Box 609
P.O. Box 1867	Fort Erie, Ontario
Buffalo, N.Y. 14240-1867	L2A 5X3

YES! Please send me 2 free Silhouette Intimate Moments® novels and my free surprise gift. Then send me 6 brand-new novels every month, which I will receive months before they're available in stores. In the U.S.A., bill me at the bargain price of $3.57 plus 25¢ delivery per book and applicable sales tax, if any*. In Canada, bill me at the bargain price of $3.96 plus 25¢ delivery per book and applicable taxes**. That's the complete price and a savings of over 10% off the cover prices—what a great deal! I understand that accepting the 2 free books and gift places me under no obligation ever to buy any books. I can always return a shipment and cancel at any time. Even if I never buy another book from Silhouette, the 2 free books and gift are mine to keep forever. So why not take us up on our invitation. You'll be glad you did!

245 SEN CNFF
345 SEN CNFG

Name	(PLEASE PRINT)	
Address	Apt.#	
City	State/Prov.	Zip/Postal Code

* Terms and prices subject to change without notice. Sales tax applicable in N.Y.
** Canadian residents will be charged applicable provincial taxes and GST.
   All orders subject to approval. Offer limited to one per household.
   ® are registered trademarks of Harlequin Enterprises Limited.

INMOM99   ©1998 Harlequin Enterprises Limited

Don't miss Silhouette's newest cross-line promotion,

Four royal sisters find their own Prince Charmings as they embark on separate journeys to find their missing brother, the Crown Prince!

The search begins
in October 1999 and
continues through February 2000:

On sale October 1999: **A ROYAL BABY ON THE WAY**
by award-winning author **Susan Mallery** (Special Edition)

On sale November 1999: **UNDERCOVER PRINCESS**
by bestselling author **Suzanne Brockmann** (Intimate Moments)

On sale December 1999: **THE PRINCESS'S WHITE KNIGHT**
by popular author **Carla Cassidy** (Romance)

On sale January 2000: **THE PREGNANT PRINCESS**
by rising star **Anne Marie Winston** (Desire)

On sale February 2000: **MAN...MERCENARY...MONARCH**
by top-notch talent **Joan Elliott Pickart** (Special Edition)

ROYALLY WED
Only in—
SILHOUETTE BOOKS

Available at your favorite retail outlet.

Visit us at www.romance.net

SSERW

Celebrate Silhouette's 20th Anniversary

With beloved authors, exciting new miniseries and special keepsake collections, **plus** the chance to enter our 20th anniversary contest, in which one lucky reader wins the trip of a lifetime!

Take a look at who's celebrating with us:

DIANA PALMER

April 2000: SOLDIERS OF FORTUNE
May 2000 in Silhouette Romance: *Mercenary's Woman*

NORA ROBERTS

May 2000: IRISH HEARTS, the 2-in-1 keepsake collection
June 2000 in Special Edition: *Irish Rebel*

LINDA HOWARD

July 2000: MacKENZIE'S MISSION
August 2000 in Intimate Moments: *A Game of Chance*

ANNETTE BROADRICK

October 2000: a special keepsake collection, plus a brand-new title in
November 2000 in Desire

Available at your favorite retail outlet.

Where love comes alive™

EXTRA! EXTRA!

**The book all your favorite authors
are raving about is finally here!**

**The 1999 Harlequin and Silhouette
coupon book.**

Each page is alive with savings that can't be beat!

**Getting this incredible coupon book is
as easy as 1, 2, 3.**

1. During the months of November and December 1999 buy
any 2 Harlequin or Silhouette books.

2. Send us your name, address and 2 proofs of purchase (cash
receipt) to the address below.

3. Harlequin will send you a coupon book worth $10.00 off
future purchases of Harlequin or Silhouette books in 2000.

Send us 3 cash register receipts as proofs of purchase and
we will send you 2 coupon books worth a total saving of
$20.00 (limit of 2 coupon books per customer).

Saving money has never been this easy.

Please allow 4-6 weeks for delivery. Offer expires December 31, 1999.

I accept your offer! Please send me (a) coupon booklet(s):

Name: _____

Address: _____ City: _____

State/Prov.: _____ Zip/Postal Code: _____

Send your name and address, along with your cash register receipts as
proofs of purchase, to:

In the U.S.: Harlequin Books, P.O. Box 9057, Buffalo, N.Y. 14269
In Canada: Harlequin Books, P.O. Box 622, Fort Erie, Ontario L2A 5X3

Order your books and accept this coupon offer through our web site
http://www.romance.net
Valid in U.S. and Canada only.

PHQ4994R